SPECIAL THANKS

Fight choreography by Lexi Alexander

Marie Brennan
Tara Cardinal
Diana Pho
Steven Stack
Erin Thiessen
Brandon Tracy

and, as always,
Valette, Jacob, Charlie, and Amelia

CHAPEL OF EASE

1

No matter how fast I ran, or how many times I zigged and zagged, I heard the dog getting closer. First his paws, then his growling, then his *breathing*.

Finally, I gave up. I stopped, groped around until I found a fallen branch, and backed up against the biggest tree I could find. I held the stick like a baseball bat and waited to see my pursuer.

He—I assume it was a he—padded out of the shadows into a thin patch of moonlight. In my terrified state he looked as big as a horse, and the first thing I thought of was *The Hound of the Baskervilles*. Reading that story as a child, I always wondered how anyone could be so scared of a mere *dog*. Now I knew.

He had short hair that shone where the moonlight hit it and rippled over his muscles. I couldn't see any teeth when he growled, but I was pretty sure they'd be huge, too. The stick in my hand could not have felt more inadequate. I remembered Rick Moranis in *Ghostbusters*, facing down a hellhound, and thought, *Who ya gonna call?* Nobody came to mind.

He was less than ten feet away now, and his masters drew close as well, although with far less speed and grace. Apparently they trusted the dog to do most of the dirty work of catching me. Which, of course, he had.

And now he was about to finish the job.

Then, for no obvious reason, he took a step backwards and growled in a completely new way. Suddenly he was *frightened*.

Something moved in the corner of my eye. Had the Durants flanked me, or had I just run straight into their clutches? I turned.

A man emerged from the forest and stood beside the same tree I cowered against.

Although I couldn't see his face, his body shape told me it wasn't C.C., or his friend Doyle. All the Durants I'd seen had been larger as well. He was shorter, and slighter, than any of them. He had an unruly shock of dark hair silhouetted by the moonlight, and wore overalls. He carried no weapon, yet the dog continued to back away, his growl now becoming a low, keening whine.

I glanced from the dog to the man, not sure what exactly was happening. Why did this guy frighten the dog so much?

And then I saw the obvious. I mean that literally: faintly but distinctly, I saw the moonlit trees *through* the man's form. He was a ghost.

A *haint*.

I suppose, though, this needs some background.

"His name's Ray Parrish," Emily Valance said over her cup, her pink bangs falling to her Asian eyes. We sat at one of the tables in the tiny Podunk Tea Room on East Fifth Street between Second and Bowery, sipping tea that cost more than some meals I'd had back in my hometown. Neither of us were natives—I was from Oneonta, and Emily was from California— but we both felt like we belonged nowhere else than this city.

"Ray Parrish," I repeated. "No, I don't know him."

"No reason you would. He hasn't had anything produced yet. Well, unless you count a one-man show he did, *Dick from Hicksville*."

"*Dick from Hicksville?*" I repeated rather archly.

"I know how it sounds, it's a terrible title. But it was great. It was all about the difficulties he'd had in making a dent in the theater scene. And, oh my God, was it funny."

"So it was good?"

"It was brilliant. I couldn't stop humming one of the songs for two weeks."

That got my attention. Whenever a professional theater person got an earworm from a new song instead of a Broadway classic, it meant the new piece really *was* pretty good. And even though Emily was a terrible dancer, she knew good music. "And what's this new show about, then?" I asked.

"He's being all hush-hush about it. I know it's got something to do with mountain people. You know, like from down South?"

"What, like *Li'l Abner?*"

"I seriously doubt that. He's from there, so I don't think he'd be making fun of it. And he let me hear the big ballad he's written for the female lead." She paused for effect; actors know just how to do that. "And I want to be the one to sing it, Matt. I do. It's a career-maker, and I'm not just saying that. If the rest of the score is as good as what I've heard, it can't miss. It's like it reaches inside you and brings up all these emotions you haven't felt since you were a teenager, except it's not like a kid would feel it, you know?"

I shook my head. "Emily, I have no idea what you're trying to tell me."

She laughed at her own words. "Good God, I do sound insane, don't I? It's so hard to describe it, you just have to hear it. You just *have* to."

I sipped my own cappuccino. I'd known Emily for a couple of years now, and enthusiasm wasn't something she came by naturally. She was a great singer, an okay actress, and a lousy dancer, all facts she knew very well. But she had nursed a mental image of herself in a Broadway musical since girlhood, and she wasn't about to let a minor detail like lack of appropriate talent stand in her way. Others found her overbearing and bitchy, but I actually admired her. And anything that had a single-minded performer like her this fired up was something I probably needed to pay attention to.

"So when are the auditions?" I asked.

She shook her head. "No auditions. He's just calling up people he knows and asking them to come to a rehearsal studio. If he can get along with them, they're in."

"He's personally doing it? Is he directing it?"

"No. Neil Callow is."

"*Neil Callow?* No shit?"

"No shit. He's apparently been quietly in on this from the beginning. I heard Ray even slept on his couch for a couple of months when he couldn't afford his own place."

Neil Callow had done some huge shows; in fact, I'd danced in one of them, *Sly Mongoose,* three years ago. He was a mercurial guy, to be sure, but his talent was undeniable, and anyone who'd worked for him once would jump at the chance to do it again.

"You keep calling him 'Ray,' like you know him," I pointed out.

"I . . . might," she said, and looked away for a moment.

"'Might' as in 'might have been out with him'?"

"Maybe."

"'Maybe' as in 'more than once'?"

She nodded sheepishly. "But, Matt, he's so old-fashioned and nice, you know? Like I always imagined a real Southern gentleman would be."

"So you can't bring yourself to fuck him just to get a part?"

She stuck out her tongue. "No. I don't do that anyway, you slut."

I knew she didn't, but it was still fun to tease her. "So has he called you? In a professional sense?"

"No," she said, unable to disguise her bitterness. "He hasn't. And I can't ask about it. Mainly because if he said, 'because you're Asian,' then I'd have to punch him in the face."

I nodded. Theater wasn't as bad as Hollywood at race-blind casting, but it was still hard sometimes for actors of an undeniable race to get roles in shows where the characters weren't race-specific.

"Well . . . there's still time, right? They haven't started rehearsing."

"I suppose." She peered into her cup. A guy looked her over blatantly as he left and said, "I sure could do with some Chinese takeout." She ignored it. After a moment she said, "I have to sing those songs, Matt. I don't know how to describe it to you, but it's like he was writing them for me. I know, I know, every singer wants to think that, and he wrote most of these long before I met him. It's just . . . they're *me.* They're my hopes and dreams and nightmares." When she looked up, there were tears in her eyes. "If I don't get that call, I don't know what I'll do. I really don't."

At that moment my own phone rang. The number didn't come up as one I recognized, and I was about to let it go to voice mail, when Emily said, "Go ahead and answer it, I need to freshen up." She scurried to the restroom before anyone else in the place saw her crying.

I answered. "Hello?"

"Is this-here Matt Johansson?" the voice on the other end said in a distinctive and heavy Southern drawl.

"It is."

"This is Ray Parrish. I don't reckon you know me, but I saw you in *Regency Way* and thought you were great."

My heart pounded, and I quickly went outside. I glanced at the restroom door through the front window and willed it to stay shut. "Thank you. What can I do for you?"

"Well, I've got a new show that I've written, and I'd like to talk to you about playing one of the leads. I think you'd be terrific, and really, I just want to see if you, me, and the director get along."

"Who's the director?" I asked as casually as I could.

"Neil Callow."

Oh my God, oh my God, oh my God! my brain screamed at this confirmation. *This is really happening, right here, right now.* My voice said, "Oh, I've worked with Neil before. Sounds interesting."

"All right. I'll text you the address and the time. Great talking to you."

"Great talking to you, too," I said, hoping I didn't sound as numb as I felt. That could come across as blasé, and I was anything but that.

The call ended, and Emily emerged from the tearoom. "What's wrong?"

"Wrong? Nothing. Why?"

"You look like you've seen a ghost. Who was on the phone? Did you get bad news?"

"That? No. It was . . ." Her concern was so genuine, and I'm such a terrible liar, that my brain refused to cough up a reasonable deception. "Some scam call trying to tell me I had a bunch of money coming because some rich uncle died. Heh-heh."

Emily stared at me. I couldn't blame her. I felt myself turn red.

"They called you," she said at last. It was a whisper, but the jealousy and accusation in it were so loud, I was sure they heard it in Queens.

I lowered my head and nodded. "Yes. I'm sorry. I danced in one of Neil's shows, so they thought . . ." I wasn't about to tell her they'd offered me one of the leads.

Fresh tears filled her recently re-mascaraed eyes. Without another word she ran off down the street. I knew better than to follow; the last thing she wanted right now was my presence reminding her that she'd been passed over yet again. I wondered if she'd mention this to Ray, or if this spelled the end of that relationship. Or perhaps her friendship with me.

I went back inside, drank the rest of my tea, and Emily's, in a kind of blank daze. It was just another Off-Off-Broadway show, an original musical at that. The run would probably be two weeks at the most, and the money barely enough to exist on. But I felt a surge of excitement building in me far out of proportion to the reality. Was this how those first performers in *A Chorus Line* or *Rent* felt just before going in to audition for those shows? Did they, at some subconscious, instinctive, primal level, just *know*? Because looking back, it was clear I did.

I stayed in that daze as I headed home to Bushwick. Ray hadn't described it as an audition, and Emily said they were just calling people they already knew could perform. But I didn't want to be caught off guard. I mentally ran through a list of songs I knew I sang really well, and then tried to remember if I had sheet music for them. If not, at least I had time to download it.

And while I was downloading, I could find out a little more about Ray Parrish.

I knew *nothing* about this show yet, I kept reminding myself. But I already knew I wanted it.

2

The entrance to the rehearsal studio where I was supposed to meet Ray Parrish and Neil Callow was at the top of a steep narrow staircase that ran along the outside of the building, ending at a covered stairwell. The lightbulb was out, so as you looked up the stairs, it was easy to imagine going into that blackness and never coming out.

I checked the address again. Yep, this was it, above a fortune-teller's storefront that advertised, in neon, PSYCHIC CRYSTAL AND TAROT READINGS. Perhaps I should stop in with Star Aurora and see if she had any insight. Then I saw that "tarot" was misspelled TOROT, and decided that was a sign.

In college, we'd studied old hero myths and I seemed to recall something about the hero having to pass through the underworld at some point. It was ironic that the underworld might be located at the top of the stairs, but as I slowly took the steps, it certainly felt like I was embarking on something epic.

It hadn't taken long to learn all the Internet had to tell about Ray Parrish. He was from a small town in Tennessee, and he'd come to New York as a session musician, working with some of the biggest names in the business. But he always wrote his own songs, too, and after discovering the fringe theater scene, he decided to put his energies toward writing for the stage. At first he worked with established writers, putting songs to their stories, but now he was ready to do it all himself.

I found only two pictures of him: one was a rehearsal shot, and he was far in the background, while the other was an actor's backstage photo posted on Facebook. In it, Ray sat at an upright piano, hunched over the keys with the kind of serious intent I'd seen on classical performers. Yet he wore a baseball cap with the silhouette of a tractor on it. Ray himself had no social media presence, and I wondered just how weird he was likely to be.

Fortunately, in real life Ray Parrish had a grin that lit up the room. When I tentatively opened the door to the studio, Ray sat in a folding chair beside the piano, engrossed in texting someone. He turned suddenly, and smiled. "Matt Johansson!" he said, and jumped to his feet.

He approached me with his hand out. "I'm really glad you could make it, Matt. I've been telling Neil here all about you. I saw you in *Regency Way,* and you were phenomenal. That song at the end, where you had to break down . . . you had the audience riveted."

"Having a good song helped," I said.

"I reckon so. But I saw it three times, and once with your understudy, so I know how much of it was just *you.*"

"Thank you." *Wow,* I thought. I'd missed one afternoon show after the train broke down and stranded me, and my understudy had gone on in my place. By all accounts he'd done fine, but I was lucky that hadn't been the only show Ray saw.

"Neil!" Ray called. "Come meet Matt Johansson."

Neil Callow strode over to us. He was short, bulky, and wore his hair the same way he must have in the '90s. "Yes, no matter how many times I tell him that I know you, he just can't seem to retain it. Good to see you again, Matt. Are you still dating Chance Burwell?"

Chance had been a featured dancer in *Sly Mongoose,* and we'd been a couple for a few months. It hadn't worked out, but the parting had been genial. "No, he and I broke up."

"That's too bad. I heard he was working on a cruise ship."

"We haven't kept in touch."

"Well, that's all in the past. Let's get started on the future. Take a seat."

Even though I'd been told this wasn't an audition, it was hard not to think of it that way. That was okay, though; auditions were nerve-racking for some, but I always found them exciting. Even when I didn't get the part, which was most of the time, I tried to always leave a good impression, since you never knew what might happen someday. My presence here right now was a perfect sign of that.

"I think we have a mutual friend," I said to Ray. "Emily Valance."

He smiled, and I swear he blushed a little, too. "Oh yeah, I know Emily. She's amazing."

"She says very nice things about you."

"Really? Like what?"

"You can talk about that in study hall, boys," Neil teased good-naturedly. "Right now, Ray, why don't you tell Matt about the show?"

"Sure!" Ray said, brimming with excitement. "It's set back in my home place, Needsville, Tennessee. Ever heard of it?"

I shook my head.

"Well, it's little-bitty, so I'm not surprised. It's way up in the Appalachian Mountains." He pronounced it *Apple-Atcha,* not *Apple-LAYcha,* the way I'd always heard it. "It's about a place called a chapel of ease. Know what that is?"

Again I shook my head, but volunteered, "A whorehouse?"

He laughed. "Naw, but that might make a good story, too. No, it's like a branch church; when the real church is too far away for a lot of people to get to, they set up a small one to kind of fill in the gaps. The preacher comes around every so often to do weddings, baptisms, and so forth. It gives the distant faithful a place to gather."

I had not been raised in any religion; in fact, I'd only set foot in churches for weddings and funerals. So this was as foreign to me as the Russian peasantry in *Fiddler on the Roof.* "Okay," I said. "Sounds interesting."

"It's about two trios of characters, one from the Civil War, one modern. In both, two of the people are in love and about to get married, and the third one is secretly in love with one of the others. So it'll have ghosts, and murder, and all the things that make theater great." He grinned with unabashed delight. "The thing that pulls the two stories together is the mystery of what's buried in the floor of the ruined old chapel."

"Which is?" I asked.

Ray grinned in a way I would soon hear him characterize as "like a possum." "I can't tell you that. See, in the show, we never find out."

"Really?"

"Really," Neil said with a weariness that implied he and Ray had discussed this issue a *lot*. "I know how it sounds, but in the context of the show, it really does work."

"But do you know?" I asked Ray.

"Yeah, of course I know."

"You should also tell him," Neil said more calmly, "that this is based on a true story."

"It is," Ray agreed. "It's something I grew up hearing about, and I used to sneak over to the old chapel just because they told me I couldn't. I always knew someday I'd use it as the basis for something, so I kept turning it over in my mind until I came up with this show." He did a drumroll with his hands on the table. "So you want to try some singing? We'll do something you already know to warm up, then we'll try some stuff from the show."

"Ray's not just the writer and composer," Neil said. "He's also the musical director."

"And I intend to be playing piano in the orchestra, too. Well, it'll be more of a band. But I want to be there."

While Neil went to sit by the wall so he could watch and listen objectively, I followed Ray to the piano. I couldn't help myself checking him out: he was lean, lanky, and walked with his head hunched down the way some tall guys do. His long jet-black hair was tied back in a loose ponytail, as if he'd done it just to get the hair out of his way. He had high cheekbones, and at the time, I thought he must have some Native American in him.

He settled down at the piano bench and I handed him the music of one of my favorite songs, which also happened to totally show off my voice: "Synchronicity II," by the Police. He looked at it, smiled knowingly, and said, "Oh, man, I love this one." Then he imitated Sting's voice: "Dark Scottish loch." He hit a note for me, then said, "Ready?""

I tore through the song, which he played slightly faster than I was used to. He added little fills and at one point during the cacophonous guitar solo part, hit the keys with his elbows. We both laughed. He finished with a glissando.

Because we went so fast, I didn't have time to worry and second-guess myself, but just plowed ahead with as much full-throated enthusiasm as I could muster. I almost wished I had a microphone on a stand in front of me, to grab and use as a prop.

Neil politely applauded when we finished. He'd done this long enough to expertly hide any response other than basic appreciation for effort. "Matt, I can't remember: Can you sight-read?"

I nodded. Ray flipped through some music and said, "Here, let's try this one."

The song he handed me was called "A Sad Song for a Lonely Place." I read through it quickly, getting a sense of the rhythm. It was comfortably in my range. "Okay," I said.

"I'll go through it once, and then you can come in," he said, and began to play.

Except that "play" doesn't do it justice. I knew he could *play* from our first number. And I knew a lot of great musicians, especially pianists, but I'd never seen or heard anyone like him. His fingers worked the keys with the fluidity of a mountain stream, and his body rocked with the grace of a willow bending in the wind. And the music itself was so touching, so affecting that I totally missed my cue. He looked up at me with a grin and, still playing, said, "Wait till I come around again."

I did, and then at his nod, I began:

> *The stones were set to last forever*
> *But the mortar crumbles away*
> *The trees may stand for centuries*
> *But eventually fall to decay*
> *And me, I'm a blink of the great oak's eye*
> *My time so pitiful and short*
> *So why does this pain cut me so to the quick*
> *And leave a hole in my chest for my heart?*

I sang as simply and directly as I could. I understood the audition process: this part wasn't about anything other than making sure I could hit the required notes with as little effort as possible. And I could. It was like it was written for me.

That made me think back on Emily, who'd felt so certain when she heard the songs from this show that they were meant for her. I wondered how many other actors were wandering around New York thinking the same thing.

When we finished, Ray glanced back at Neil, who nodded very slightly.

"That was great, Matt," the director said. "But I wonder if you could try it a little differently? Emphasize the weariness. Try to bring out the weight of time that the singer is feeling. Does that make sense?"

"You bet." Neil was seeing if he and I really understood each other, and if I could take direction. So I sang it again, the way he requested, and damn if the song wasn't even easier this way. My first attempt missed a crucial element, and now I'd found it.

When I finished, I wasn't even out of breath. If anything, the song had energized me.

Ray flipped through the sheets on the piano's music stand. "Let's try another one," he said eagerly. "Your character doesn't sing all these, naturally, but I've heard myself sing 'em so much, it's just a treat to hear a different voice. Okay with you, Neil?"

Neil mock-shrugged. "Sure. But just so you know, Matt, it's not going to be a one-man show."

I laughed, and Ray turned eagerly to me. "You up for it?"

"You bet," I said. I tried not to get excited and read any subtext into his "your character" comment. I knew from experience that I didn't actually *have* the role until my agent got that all-important offer from the producers. But if the rest of the songs were as beautiful as the one we'd just done, then I wanted to sing them just for the pleasure of it.

And they were.

The next song was clearly meant for a woman, and was almost out of my range. Was this one running around Emily's head even as I sang?

> *Too many sorrows*
> *Too many lies*
> *Too many failures*

Too few tries
His love left me hopeless
His touch left me cold
And I, I run to him
Whenever he calls.

We sang the whole score. A few of the other songs intended for female characters really strained my voice, but I never cracked and we all laughed when I couldn't quite hit the high notes. The story that emerged from the score was simple yet moving, a symphony of emotion rather than plot. If it could be effectively translated to the stage, it would be incredible, of that I was absolutely sure.

When we finished the last song, Neil said, "That was great, Matt. Except for that one high note." He teased.

"I think I have the wrong anatomy for that one."

Ray stood, shook my hand, then impulsively hugged me. "Thank you, Matt. Sorry for taking up so much of your time. This was supposed to be a quick meet and greet."

He glanced at Neil. If they had a predetermined signal, I didn't catch it. "We'll be in touch," Neil said.

Ah, the old "we'll be in touch" line. Well, it had been a fun couple of hours. "Thanks."

"I know what you're thinking," Neil said as he walked me to the door. "But we *will* be in touch. This was extraordinary."

I still didn't get my hopes up. "Thank you, Neil. Great to see you again. Ray, nice to meet you."

Ray looked up from straightening his sheet music. "Hey, you got any plans for right now?"

That caught me off guard. "Well . . . no."

"I'm starving. If I don't eat, I get cranky. Want to go grab a sandwich?"

"Uh . . . sure."

I looked at Neil, wondering if he'd invite himself along,

wishing like hell that he wouldn't. He shook his head. "I have at least one agent to call," he said with a knowing little smile. He handed Ray some money. "Can you bring me back a pastrami on wheat?"

"Sure." Ray put his hand on my shoulder. "Come on."

We left the theater and walked three blocks down to Yancy's, a sandwich shop I'd never been to. It smelled great, though, and it wasn't crowded. We ordered at the counter and waited for our sandwiches at a table in the front window.

I watched Ray for any clues that this was meant as a date. Sure, he'd dated Emily, but this was New York, and lines were so blurry here that you had to be in New Jersey to see them, and then only if you squinted. I didn't know what their couple status was, or even if they had one. But I did know that it probably wasn't a good idea to get into even a flirting relationship with the composer of the show my agent might, at this very moment, be making the deal for. Yet he was so cute, in an irresistible floppy-dog sort of way. I wanted to fix his ponytail and turn down his askew collar, using it as an excuse to touch him.

He straightened (no pun intended) me out right away. "Just to be clear, man, I'm not gay, so I'm not hitting on you. I was just really, really impressed with your singing. You have the voice I've always heard in my head for Colton."

"Wow, thanks," I said, and swallowed my disappointment. This was work, after all.

"Neil better be signing you up right now. You mind dyeing your hair black like mine?"

"No. So Colton is based on you?"

"No, not at all. But all the Tufa have the same black hair."

"What's a 'Tufa'? Is that your tribe?"

He laughed. "Yeah, sort of. We're not Indians, though. We're—"

The server arrived with our sandwiches, and since the shop's delicious smell had made me just as ravenous, we tore into them before he could tell me more. When we came up for air, I said, "You were telling me about your people?"

"Oh yeah. Well, according to legend, the Tufa were already in Appalachia before the ancestors of the Native Americans came over from Asia. Nobody knows where we came from, or what race we descended from. And with this hair and skin"— his skin was a dusky olive, like a swarthy Mediterranean—"a lot of people thought we were part black, which you definitely didn't want to be in Tennessee back in the day. So we just kept to ourselves up in the mountains, and still pretty much do."

I'd never heard of them before. "Interesting."

"So most of the characters in the story will have this same black hair." He grabbed a stray strand and held it out as an example.

I briefly wondered if that would make it hard to tell us apart onstage, but then remembered that would be Neil's problem, not mine. And only if I got the job.

"So I gotta ask," he inquired between sloppy bites. "What did you think of the songs?"

"They were great. Seriously."

"I've been working on them a long time. A really long time," he added with personal irony that I didn't get.

"So was Neil serious? That this was a true story?"

He wiped his chin as he thought. "Some parts are true, some are made up. The stuff set in the Civil War is all true, or at least it was told to me as true. But there are rules about . . . Well, a lot of the Tufa back home don't believe any of us should ever do anything to draw attention to ourselves. Sure shouldn't tell our own stories out of school, if you know that expression."

I didn't, but the context made it clear. "Will you get in trouble?"

"Naw. It's not like anyone in Needsville follows the New York theater scene. Besides, the songs are all mine, and ultimately so is the story. Ain't nobody's business who I tell it to, right?"

"Right," I agreed, wishing his Southern accent wasn't so damn hot.

When I got home, I got online and looked up the people he'd mentioned. At first I tried spelling the word in overly complicated ways: "Toupha," "Tewpha," and so forth. It wasn't until I tried the simple *T-U-F-A* that I got a ton of relevant hits.

Well, as "relevant" as this sort of thing could be. At the time, I was more amused than anything else. As he said, they weren't a Native American tribe. They also weren't Scotch-Irish, like most of the other original white settlers of Appalachia. If you believed the Web sites, the Tufa *did* predate both of those.

But the anthropological mystery paled beside the paranormal ones. Supposedly the Tufa had secret magical powers, could seduce anyone, and used their musical skills to get their way. They lived in a tiny, isolated community and had very little to do with the outside world, even today. Their most notable citizen was Bronwyn Hyatt, a soldier who'd been captured and then rescued on live TV during the Iraq War.

I poured a glass of wine and settled in to read these stories in detail. After all, if I got the part, I'd be tasked with bringing a member of this subculture to life. I glanced in the mirror and wondered what I'd look like with black hair; my own was light brown, almost blond if I spent any time in the sun.

As the wine took hold, I realized two important things: I *really* wanted to sing those songs again, for an audience. It had very little to do with being the star, or even being onstage. I just wanted to share them with other people, to watch them have the same effect on strangers that they had on me. They were that good, and that original.

And second . . . I had a totally hopeless crush on Ray Parrish.

3

"Yeah, I know him," Thad Kilby said. "I was in a show he did a couple of years ago. The songs were great. The rest of the show, not so much. But he only wrote the music."

Thad was an old boyfriend of mine, one I was still on speaking terms with. I didn't consider myself high maintenance, but for whatever reason, almost every relationship ended in screaming and burned bridges. Thad, though, was different; we'd realized we worked better as friends, and although we occasionally hooked up again when we were both free, we knew it for what it was.

Now we sat at the counter, eating over-easy eggs and drinking coffee at Cafe Edison while I pried him for information about Ray.

He saw right through me, too. "You do realize he's straight, right?"

"Yes, of course, I could tell that in the first five minutes."

"Uh-huh. Sure you could. You weren't even sure *I* was gay until our second kiss."

Earlier that morning, I'd dug even harder online,

trying to find out more about Ray, checking the social media accounts of the actors, singers, and dancers in his earlier shows. He was mentioned a few times, and there were pictures of him in various people's Instagrams, but he had nothing on his own. It was almost like he was a ghost, popping up and then vanishing. A big, adorable, always-grinning ghost.

And that brought me back to the stories of his people, the Tufa. Talk about some full-bore insanity. The same sort of people who believed in Bigfoot, UFOs, and conspiracy theories put forth elaborate claims about the Tufa, none of which matched up with the photographs of normal people that illustrated their claims. How could you believe a tale of an ancient tribe of Israel when the pictures showed people sitting around drinking beer or driving old pickups? Even the Google Maps photos of Needsville, which Ray said was his home, just showed a typically fading small town.

The only photo that actually supported any of these wilder claims was on a site called *Fred, White and Blue*, which was mostly a right-wing political hub run by one of those overweight white men who writes as if he's screaming at you. He had a zoomed satellite photo that seemed to show the night-vision outline of several flying people soaring over a forest. But the image was as blurry as any Sasquatch photo, and someone with even basic skills could've easily Photoshopped it. It didn't help his credibility that the author went to great rhetorical lengths to tie them into the liberal agenda.

"I hear he's got a new show, one he wrote all himself," Thad said.

"Yeah. I had an audition yesterday. That's when I met him. We went out for lunch afterwards."

Thad reached over and took my hand. "Straight," he said seriously.

"I know," I said with identical emphasis. "But he's just so fascinating. Did you know about his background?"

"I know he was a session musician for a while. Lenny Kravitz came by our rehearsal to talk to him about something once."

"No, I mean, his ethnic background. He's a Tufa."

Thad looked blank. "I don't know what that is."

I gave him the quick rundown. He sat back in surprise. "Wow. I've never even heard of them before."

"Me, neither."

"And he told you all that?"

I nodded, not wanting to admit I'd spent half the night reading up on it. "That's what his new play's about, too."

"Really? Mysterious people, mountains, star-crossed lovers . . . sounds really good. Put in a word for me?"

"Sure," I said.

As I headed into the station to take the subway home, my phone rang, and it was the call I'd hoped for: my agent saying I'd gotten the job. I let out a huge whoop, which no one around me even noticed. Then I danced down the steps to the L train.

The first rehearsal was the following Monday morning. I'd gotten some calls from other people I knew who'd been cast, so I wouldn't be totally alone. Still, I'd be one of the three leads, with the supremely butch name "Colton," and although I'd sung the score, I hadn't even read the script yet. So I wasn't totally sure what I was getting into.

The Armitage Theater—nicknamed "the Armpit"—did not inspire confidence, even if its reputation was better than its structure. Its most notorious quirk was that its only bathrooms were located at the front of the house, near the box office. If you needed to go during a show, you had to slip out the back door, brave the alley at night, and run around the building to the front. I'd heard that the cast of the last show to open here had, as a sort of initiation, made its members strip down to their underwear before making the run, like Michael Keaton in *Birdman*.

Many classic shows had started here before moving to Broadway, and I'm sure every one that opened here had that same dream: certainly I did about *Chapel of Ease*. But it took a special mix of talent, luck, and hitting the public right in the gestalt for that to happen, and truthfully, a Southern Gothic ghost story set to what could only be called folk music didn't sound anything like a sure thing. Then again, neither did a raunchy show with puppets, and look at *Avenue Q*.

As I started to open the door, a young woman touched my arm. She had dreadlocks and a dusky complexion, and dressed very Bohemian. "Excuse me, are you working on Neil Callow's new show?"

I was instantly on my guard. "And you are . . . ?"

"I just wondered. I saw him walk in earlier. He hasn't done anything since *Festival Days and Nights*. Is this his new show?"

I didn't know if she was a stalker or a reporter, and either way, I didn't want to get involved. "I really can't say. Excuse me."

"Who are you?"

"Terry Crewson." Terry was an old asshole roommate who still owed me seven hundred dollars in back rent. I used his name whenever I found myself in situations where I needed a quick alias. Terry had had some interesting adventures over the years, thanks to me.

"Are you a dancer?"

"I'm a janitor. Excuse me."

When I entered the lobby, its concrete floor bare in between bouts of carpeting, the first face I saw was a friendly one: Ellie Bayrens, who had been the stage manager of *Satin Highway*, the first show I'd done after moving to New York. She was bubbly and incredibly outgoing, but when it was showtime, a switch got thrown deep in her psyche and she became a martinet. Which, I now knew, is exactly what every show needs in a stage manager.

"Hey, so you're working on this show, too?" I said after we hugged.

"Yeah, Neil invited me, and it's so hard to tell him no. And I hear you got the big lead role of Crawford."

"I thought it was Colton."

"I think Neil convinced Ray that it sounded too much like a soap opera character."

"He's got a point. Are they inside?"

"Yeah, they're getting ready for the read-through. You're the first one here. Knock 'em dead, cowboy."

I went through the wooden double doors edged with elaborate carvings of Comedy and Tragedy masks. The aisle led past the two hundred or so seats down to the stage, where a long table with a dozen folding chairs around it sat under the harsh work lights. Neil paced and looked at his phone, while Ray sat, his feet on the table.

"Matt!" Ray called out, and jumped to his feet. "Congratulations. Great to be working with you."

We hugged, but before we could speak, two young women entered. They both had black hair, one long and one short, with the sheen of fresh dye jobs still on them. Neil introduced them as Cassandra and Julie.

"I think I'm playing a ghost," Julie said.

"And I'm playing Jennifer," Cassandra said. She tossed her hair, a gesture that would go from endearing to annoying to infuriating before this show was done. "When I was a kid, I always wanted a nice, normal name like Jennifer."

"You think it's normal?" Ray asked seriously. "Is it *too* normal? Will people forget it?"

His intensity startled her. "I was just making a joke."

Ray looked at me sheepishly. "Names are hard."

Cassandra gave me a wide-eyed, uncertain look as Ray wandered off. I shrugged.

"There's coffee and doughnuts over there," Neil said. "No smoking in the auditorium, I'm afraid, but there's a spot out back if you just can't stand it. Although I try not to hire dancers who smoke. It proves right off the bat that they make bad decisions."

"What about actors who smoke?" Julie asked.

"I just want *them* sober," Neil deadpanned.

I shook hands with the girls. "Where'd you get your hair done? I have to do that, too."

"Arrojo Studio," Julie said. "I thought they did a great job."

"Are you a natural brunette?" I asked.

"I'm as blond as Gwen Stefani."

"Then they *did* do a nice job."

Soon the other cast members arrived. One of the men, Jason, I'd known from a couple of other shows, and we cordially embraced. He was black, but as I'd learn later, he'd been cast color-blind because he so suited the character. He was followed in by two strangers: tall, slender Ryan and older, squatter Mark.

This would be the first time we'd all get a sense of the whole show and where we fit into it. We'd also start to understand the interpersonal dynamics that would either weld us into a temporary family or confirm us as inmates of the same asylum.

When we'd settled down, Neil said, "We'll just read through, no acting. And for those of you who know the songs, no singing. I just want us all to get a sense of the show as a whole. Then we'll do some songs, and after that, I want to talk with you one-on-one to see what you think about your part."

That last comment was a bid to short-circuit any ego battles before they started. No doubt everyone would offer suggestions to make their own parts larger; I would, if I saw any places where it might help. Even if none of our suggestions were taken, we'd at least feel like we were heard.

"Oh, and the whole bit about everyone having the same black hair?" Neil continued. "We're not going with it. Ray agrees with me that it would just make people too hard to identify in the crowd scenes."

"Except me," Jason said with a big smile. We all laughed.

Cassandra and Julie looked at each other, then said in deadpan unison, "Thanks."

"Oh, and Matt? Your character's name is changed from Colton to Crawford."

"Because Colton sounds like a soap opera character?" I asked, hoping that it would make Neil think he and I were on the same wavelength.

"That's one reason," Neil said, and looked at Ray.

"Crawford was the guy's real name," he said. "I made up 'Colton,' and it just never seemed to fit. So we went back to reality." He shook his head and said again, "Names are hard."

"Any questions?" Neil asked. "Good. Let's get started."

We opened our scripts and started to read *Chapel of Ease*. I had the first line: "Sometimes the best mysteries are never solved, because the mystery is too important to lose. This is the story about one of those mysteries. Most of it's true, and the parts that ain't, well, they still sound true."

Then I read the lyrics of the first song, an overture that told the whole story, and set up the central mystery: Who or what is buried in the dirt floor of the ruined chapel of ease?

Well, I *tried* to read the lyrics. Despite my best efforts, I caught myself drifting into the melody, a minor-key procession that had evidently stuck in my head since the audition. When I finished and looked up, everyone was staring at me.

When Cassandra failed to pick up her cue, Neil reminded us gently, "No singing, okay? We'll get to that."

"My fault," I said. "Sorry."

I caught Ray grinning at me before he covered his smile with his hands and turned away.

So we went on, reading and absorbing this story. Jennifer, a would-be country music star, is wandering through the woods when she stumbles onto the ruined chapel of ease. She sings a song about her dreams, and then sees another young woman crying over a spot in the center of the dirt floor. When Jennifer calls out to the girl, she disappears. Frightened, Jennifer runs away.

I'd never been in a show that involved a disappearance on-stage, although when I'd seen *The Phantom of the Opera* as a child, the Phantom had vanished from a chair. I wondered what mechanism they had in mind to achieve that.

In the next scene, she returns with her boyfriend, the simple and steadfast Lucas, and his best friend, Colton, now Crawford. Lucas sings a love ballad, in which Jennifer counterpoints that she loves Lucas, but staying behind with him would be the worst thing ever. She's got stars in her eyes.

How would the dynamic of Jason being black play out in the show? I wondered. Especially since we were all supposed to be white good ol' boys and, I assume, Jason's character was originally conceived that way. Would it jar? Would it draw so much attention that the rest of us became, ". . . and the white people?" Or would it add poignancy to his tragedy?

Yet even as he merely read the song lyrics, having no idea what the melody might sound like, Jason's voice grew unexpectedly ragged with the character's emotion. When he finished, I swear it looked like he might be about to cry.

Once again, Neil spoke up. "Great job not singing, Jason," he said dryly. "Now, can we stick with not acting, too? We've got a long way to go, I don't want to burn you guys out at the first rehearsal."

"Sorry," Jason said. "It just crept up on me."

Again Ray tried to hide his delighted grin.

Then Crawford sang about Lucas and Jennifer, who'd been sweethearts since they were little kids. He also admitted that he loved Jennifer, and that unlike Lucas, he'd follow her anywhere she wanted to go, but that she'd never seen him as more than a friend.

We had a dialogue scene where we looked unsuccessfully for any sign of the ghost Jennifer had seen.

JENNIFER: I swear, she was right here. I mean, ghosts have to haunt the same place over and over, right? So she's got to still be here.

CRAWFORD: Maybe she's as scared of us as we are of her?

LUCAS: Hey, y'all know how a ghost keeps from getting fat? He exorcises!

JENNIFER: You're not taking this seriously.

LUCAS: Oh, come on, honey. You was either seeing things, or you saw some girl who lives around here. Might be that little Scarberry girl, she's always been kinda weird.

JENNIFER: Can she go poof right while you're looking at her?

CRAWFORD: I believe you, Jennifer.

JENNIFER: Thank you, Crawford. I reckon my fiancé thinks he's marrying some dumb ol' box of rocks with nice boobs.

Our characters exited, and the ghost girl from the first scene returned. She sings about the world beyond the valley, which she knows she'll never see, and her beloved who is fighting somewhere in the Civil War. At the end of the song, she describes a secret that she must keep hidden, so she's put it in the safest place she knows. She ends the song crying over a spot on the dirt floor. Jennifer, who has returned alone, sees her. Crawford has also returned, following Jennifer, and sees the ghost as well. When the ghost leaves, Jennifer places a rock over the spot where she was crying.

And that was the end of act 1.

We took a break then, all of us wound up from the unexpected intensity of emotion in this simple story. Instead of the usual chatting and gossip as we got coffee or snuck out for cigarettes, we were quiet and introspective. I sat on a stool by the electrical switch box, sipping my drink, when Ray came over and said softly, "What do you think so far?"

"Fucking brilliant," I said honestly.

He looked down as he actually blushed. "Thanks. This is the first time anyone but me and my friends have read the whole thing out loud. I was as nervous as a cat in a room full of rocking chairs."

I almost spit coffee as I tried not to laugh at his folksy humor. Luckily he laughed, too.

"I hope the rest of it goes as well," he continued. "The first act is always easy: it's the setup. It's making it pay off that's the trick."

"I can't imagine it won't."

"Well, we'll see, won't we?" Then he winked. "See you back at the table."

I watched him go, reminding myself that Crawford had the unrequited crush, not me.

We all returned to the table and began reading act 2. Jennifer returns to the chapel that evening with a shovel, determined to dig up whatever the ghost was mourning, and finds an elderly woman arranging flowers at one of the graves outside the chapel. She was played by Estella, an older actress who would, I assume, be aged even more for the actual show.

This newcomer sings a song about Shad and Byrda, two lovers separated by the Civil War. He went off to fight for the Union and never returned; she wasted away from nursing an awful secret. The old woman says her name is Byrda, too, after her great-great-grandmother.

I wondered then how Neil planned to stage all this. I couldn't imagine dance numbers working with this haunting, melancholy music, but I'd seen stranger things. I couldn't wait for us to get on our feet and start blocking, just to see what he had in mind.

First, though, we had to finish this read-through. After Old Byrda's song, Jennifer tells her what she saw. Old Byrda says that she, too, has seen the ghost of her namesake crying over something inside the ruined chapel. She says it's a common sight, and yet no one knows who or what's buried there.

JENNIFER: You mean no one's ever dug it up?
OLD BYRDA: Not to my knowing. You need to be careful,
    little girl. If you ain't, you might find that the troubles of
    someone else's past just might become your own.

Jennifer goes into the chapel and starts to dig. Her phone rings; it's Lucas, wondering where she is. She makes an excuse about driving around listening to music, and says she'll call him later. While she talks, ghost-Byrda appears, along with ghost-Shad. They sing a love song about how their families don't want them to get together. Then he takes his leave, saying he has to join the fight against slavery. Byrda sings about the secret she hasn't told him, one that would destroy their love, and possibly their lives.

Before Jennifer has dug very far, Crawford arrives. He admits he was following her, and when she demands to know why, he finally confesses his feelings for her—in song, of course. She is totally startled, and doesn't know what to say. As they talk, another ghost, of a different young man, appears and watches silently. Then he kneels beside the hole and reverently fills it back in. Jennifer tells Crawford she can't respond to this right now, but gasps when she sees that the hole she's just dug has been filled. They exit in different directions, and the ghost remains kneeling, head bowed, over the hole. He then sings a reprise of the same song Crawford just sang, but with different lyrics explaining that he and Byrda were once happy until Shad came along.

I had another song then, a monologue of sorts explaining all the twists that had just happened. It ended with a line that gave me chills:

> And sometimes, when the story ends
> Only the teller's left to make amends.

Wow. Was my character, Crawford, going to be the only one left alive at the end? And would I be Puck, seeking the audience's approval, or Horatio, left amid a stage full of corpses?

And that ended act 2.

"Anyone need a break?" Neil asked, and we all shook our heads, enraptured by this story of two generations of love triangles. We wanted to see what happened.

Act 3 began sometime later, at the wedding of Jennifer and Lucas, held at the chapel of ease. The entire act consisted of one long scene, and it was here that most of the other actors first appeared, creating the community that Jennifer so desperately wanted to escape. There were gossipy asides, snide comments, and, of course, the insinuation that Jennifer and Lucas *had* to get married. Crawford moped about, followed unseen by the unnamed ghost of the other young man from the chapel.

Most interesting in this act was the character of Sawyer, the only explicitly non-Tufa in the show, played by Mark. He was the drunken husband of a Tufa woman, and he spewed forth an unexpected and vicious stream of racist comments, equating the Tufa with African Americans and referring to them as "high yellows," a term I'd never heard before.

SAWYER: Hey, y'all know why it's so hard to solve a Tufa murder? All their DNA matches!

His long-suffering wife, played by a big, busty actress named Diana, loses it, screaming at him to either leave or shut up. He goes to a corner and continues to drink and mutter asides, a Greek chorus figure for the rest of the act.

When Jennifer and Lucas appear, they are followed by the ghosts of Byrda and Shad. Lucas is delighted to be marrying Jennifer, and sings as much, but in counterpoint, Shad sings about the doubts and uncertainties of loving a woman he couldn't protect from the horrors he'd seen in the war. Jennifer's song was about lost dreams and disappointment, while Byrda recited the list of things she planned for her new home, including lots of children. (She already had names picked out.) Then we reveal that Crawford brought a gun, although it was unclear whom he planned to shoot. The act ended with the first words of the marriage ceremony.

That made me think. Did the ghosts influence the living? Were our characters merely repeating the acts, and therefore the mistakes, of Byrda, Shad, and the nameless ghost? It wasn't explicit in the text, but a good playwright wouldn't need it to be.

Act 4 was set later the same day. Jennifer and Lucas return to the chapel on their way out of town for their honeymoon. Jennifer is insistent that she has to know what's buried there, and begins to dig again. The ghosts of Byrda and Shad reappear, unseen to the other characters, singing a duet about how secrets destroy happiness. Crawford comes onstage followed by his own nameless ghost. Crawford is drunk and still carries his gun, and threatens to kill all three of them. He proclaims his love for Jennifer, while the ghost sings and proclaims his love . . . for *Shad*.

This unexpected homoerotic twist got our attention; we'd assumed the earlier song, when he sang about how happy he and Byrda were until Shad came along, referred to Shad stealing Byrda's affections. This cast it in a whole new light. Neil watched us carefully, cataloging our reactions, interested to see if they gave him anything with which to work. He was a master at pulling emotions from actors, often ones they didn't know they felt. Ray's expression remained neutral, but he watched as closely as Neil.

We picked the story back up. Crawford shot Lucas when he tried to grab the gun to protect Jennifer. Then Jennifer shot Crawford after angrily denouncing him and saying she'd only put up with him out of pity. Then, standing between the bodies of the two men who'd loved her, she put the gun to her own head.

Oh. Well, I guess I wasn't Puck, or Horatio. I was Romeo . . . sort of.

Our three bodies lay onstage as the three ghosts began their climactic number. Byrda sang of her love for Shad; the nameless ghost sang of his love, as well. He also sang that he had killed Shad during a battle, when no one would know, after Shad had rejected him. The two male ghosts departed in opposite directions, while Byrda was left onstage, singing about the love she'd lost and buried in the chapel. Then she disappeared. Old Byrda came back onstage; she looked over the bodies, saddened but not surprised. She sang:

> *Time is not a line, or a river that flows to the sea*
> *It's a circle, bringing the past back to you and me*
> *These old bones, they've seen it again and again*
> *It ain't never a matter of what, only a matter of when.*

She knelt over the place in the floor where something—we'd never discovered what—was buried. She finished her song with:

> *Cover it, bury it, hide it away*
> *A secret will always find its own way*
> *No matter how long, no matter how far*
> *When the time is right, it'll always rise*
> *And carry its truth to all men's eyes.*

We sat in silence after we closed our scripts. No one really looked at anyone else. The work was simply too powerful, too overwhelming for an immediate response. What would audiences think of this, when the songs were performed instead of spoken, when the actors expressed the emotions instead of reciting them in a non-acting monotone?

At last Neil broke the silence. "And that, ladies and gentlemen, is our show."

"But—," Julie began.

"What's buried?" Ryan blurted out. "In the chapel? What is it?"

All eyes turned to Ray.

Ray laughed. "Look, guys, it's a *metaphor,* you know? The audience can imagine whatever they want."

"This is based on a true story, right?" Estella said. "So you must know what was really there."

"I do."

"Well?"

He grinned even more. "Tell you what: I'll tell y'all exactly what it is after our first show. It'll give you something to look forward to."

"Oh, come *on,*" I said, and everyone pretty much echoed that sentiment.

"Take a break, everyone," Neil said. "Come back in half an hour to start singing. And let's remember that it's just a story, okay? It's not history."

I don't know how he'd put his finger on exactly how we all felt, but that was it, all right: we felt like we'd just participated in some kind of reenactment, not just a play read-through. If we could re-create this for an audience, we'd have it made.

As I stood and stretched, I caught Ray's mischievous eye, and he winked. It made me smile in return. And at the same time, I recalled the fates of the nameless ghost and Shad.

4

And so rehearsals went on for the rest of the day. The songs took everyone by surprise; some of the ballads brought those of us listening to tears. I relished the ones I got to sing, and envied those of the others, although truthfully, I couldn't really complain. I definitely had my share of showstoppers.

After we took a short break, Neil returned with someone new. "Everyone, gather around if you would." He indicated the scowling, whip-bodied middle-aged woman beside him. "This is Stella Aragon, the choreographer. You'll start working with her tomorrow."

She put her hands on her hips and said, "That's right, my name is Stella. Ms. Aragon if you're nasty. And the first one of you that quotes Stanley Kowalski at me gets fired."

There was a moment of total silence. Then all of us at once dropped to our knees and did our best Brando-style *"Stel-LA!"* This went on for several moments before we all got back in line, our expressions once again completely deadpan.

The actor who played the nameless ghost said, "To be fair, my name really is Stanley."

"Nice," Stella said with a half smile. "I hope your feet are as smart as your asses. See you tomorrow, wise guys."

We had time at the end of the day to begin blocking, and we used chairs to represent the corners of the chapel itself. I wondered what the final set would look like: Would it be stylized, or realistic? Would the audience immediately know what they were seeing, or would they have to be clued in by the cast? I'd never heard of a "chapel of ease" before; perhaps there would be a note in the program book.

We were all exhausted by the time Neil said, "All right, union rules say we have to wrap it up now. Everyone take your scripts; I want us off-book by next Monday. We have only six weeks to whip this monster into shape."

"Monster?" Ray said in mock offense.

"A beautiful monster," Neil corrected. "Like Lady Gaga."

We laughed, then gathered our things to go. As I headed toward the door, Ray said, "Hey, Matt. You got time for a cup of coffee?"

I wasn't about to tell the genius behind this show I couldn't hang out with him, so I said, "Sure."

We went to a shop around the block, got our drinks, and sat in a corner. Ray sagged gratefully into his chair. "Y'all did great today. Better than I imagined. It was fucking magic."

I grinned, both at the compliment and his use of "y'all." I'd always assumed that was a Southern stereotype that wasn't actually true. "Thanks. Hard not to with this stuff."

"Well, I just wanted you to know how happy I was. Please pass it on to everyone else." He paused to sip his coffee, and I could tell he was working up to whatever he really wanted to say.

At last he added, "So—you know Emily Valance."

"I do. We've been friends for a couple of years."

"So she said." He sipped more coffee. "Do you, ah . . . Is she dating anyone?"

Oh, for fuck's sake, I thought. Here I'd imagined he was

going to ask me about putting her in the show. I wanted to laugh, but I knew better. "No, she broke up with her last boyfriend over a month ago."

He nodded. "I read about that."

Emily's last boyfriend had been Blake Welladay, scion of a prominent business family and once voted Manhattan's Sexiest Bachelor. He'd been a nice enough guy, Emily said, but the bubble of his life was too much for her. They'd parted amicably, and she had been in no hurry to get into another relationship. Apparently that's just when Cupid loves to strike. "How did you meet her?"

"She came to my last show and said some very nice things. At first I thought she was just hinting that I should keep her in mind for the next one, but I think she genuinely likes me. The only thing is, I mean . . . I'm pretty poor. Compared to Blake Welladay, for sure. I can't jet her off to the Hamptons on the spur of the moment, or anything like that."

"I don't think that was all that important to her," I said honestly.

"I hope not. So . . . do you talk to her a lot?"

Holy shit, Neil was right, we were back in high school. "I see her every so often."

"Does she ever mention me?"

"We mainly talk shop."

He nodded, clearly disappointed. He was adorable in his discomfort, and I realized my crush was only getting worse. Still, it had no future, and I didn't want either him or Emily to get hurt, certainly not because of me. I said, "Look, Ray, if she wanted to be in Blake Welladay's world, she still would be. *She* broke it off with *him*. She probably likes you because you're funny, outgoing, enthusiastic, and talented. Money can't buy any of those, you know."

He nodded, and I swear he blushed again. It was the first time I'd ever been jealous of Emily.

"I might bring her to the opening," he said. "Do you think that'll be all right?"

"Why are you asking me?"

"Well . . . I mean, she didn't get asked to audition for the show. There wasn't a part she was right for. She didn't say anything, but I could tell it hurt her feelings. I don't want to rub her face in it or anything."

The intensity of Emily's reaction to my own invitation now made sense. "I can't answer that, Ray. You'll have to ask her. Although I imagine she'll want to be there for you on opening night."

"I hope so. I really want her there." He tucked a strand of black hair behind his ear. "It feels like everything I've ever done has led up to this show, to opening night. You know? You ever felt like that?"

I was sure starting to. "It's going to be amazing. Everyone's going to love it."

"If they do, it's because of the way you guys bring it to life. I mean, I've seen this story in my head for forever, but watching even the read-through today, hearing y'all speak the words, then sing—" He shook his head. "—I can't even begin to tell you what it felt like."

He was so open and honest about his enthusiasm that I didn't know how to respond. I settled for just grinning and drinking my own coffee.

Just as we finished, his phone rang. It was too loud to hear in the coffee shop, so he excused himself and went outside. Through the front window I watched him pace, his black hair swaying with each turn. When he returned, he said, "You in a hurry tonight?"

"I'm kinda tired. It's been a long day."

"I know, but I've got a musician friend recording at a studio near here, and he needs some help. Shouldn't take too long. Want to come along?"

"Who's your friend?"

"I'd rather not say. Let it be a surprise. But I'm pretty sure you've heard of him."

I shrugged and stood. "Sure. Sounds like fun."

"That it will be," he promised.

Cornflake Studios was located in the basement of a nondescript building with signage that said most of the structure was devoted to some sort of financial shenanigans. The separate studio entrance was guarded by an immense black man in a suit, with a visible gun bulge under his arm. He stepped aside for us and said, "Evening, Ray," with such a bass rumble that I wondered what he sounded like when he was trying to be intimidating. We went down a narrow hallway carpeted floor to ceiling with '70s-style shag. Ray stopped at the first open door we came to and said, "Hey, y'all."

Five people filled the control room, and another half dozen milled about in the studio beyond it. The scent of weed and wine was heavy in the air. One of the men at the panel stood up and said, "The genius has arrived."

"Yeah, and I'm here, too," Ray said, and they hugged like old friends.

The door to the studio opened, and Lance Abercrombie stepped out. He was as famous for his cologne ads as he was for his hard-driving music, and if I was a little disappointed to be taller than him, I was still pretty thoroughly starstruck. He looked at me, said, "Hi," then turned to Ray. "Glad you could make it, man. Sorry for the short notice."

"Naw, no problem, I was right down the street. So what do you need?"

"Johnny can't get the drum solo right. We've been trying since noon, and we're all about ready to strangle each other. Can you help us out?"

"Where is Johnny?"

"We sent him back to the hotel, man. He was so high, he was useless. All he wanted to do was play *Minecraft*."

"Tell me what you need. Oh, Lance, this is my friend Matt."

I shook hands with the megastar. "A pleasure."

"Likewise," he said. Then he pulled Ray into the studio. I was left with the production staff, two older men, one black and one white, who looked exhausted. A pair of girls lounged nearby, and barely gave me a glance.

"Hey," the black producer said to me. "Stand behind me and you can see and hear the best."

"Yeah, he always makes sure he gets the sweet spot," the white producer said.

"That's 'cause I'm the sweetest mofo in this room," the black producer shot back.

He was right: I had a view of the whole studio from there. Lance and his band took their positions, and Ray sat down behind the drum set. He adjusted a few things, then experimentally tapped the snare and cymbal. Lance counted four, and the band exploded into a rollicking old-school rock-and-roll number about a girl with a car coveted by the singer, although it was hard to tell which he wanted more. For some reason, I imagined this music being used to sell underwear.

Lance Abercrombie was certainly a hottie, but it was Ray who really held my attention. He played with a certainty and mastery that implied he'd been rehearsing with this band forever. His rhythms propelled the song, and when the guitarist started his solo, he expertly left space for the screeching tones. Then he took his own solo, an insane swirl of pounding that went right to the edge of chaos before snapping back into the pocket for the last verse.

The song ended with a mighty crash, and Lance jumped so high, I worried he'd smack his head on the low ceiling. There was a moment of dead silence, except for a faint buzz from one of the monitors. Then the band whooped and cheered, crowding around the drums.

"That boy can play a pair of tennis shoes and make 'em sound like Jimi Hendrix," the white producer said.

"That's the only black musician he knows," the black producer asided to me with a wink.

"Name one white musician," the white producer shot back.

"Lance Abercrombie," the black producer said.

"Name one who's not in this room."

"Taylor Swift. It don't get no whiter."

Then the rest of the band squeezed into the control room with us, and Ray recorded the drums solo, listening to the track through headphones. I couldn't tell if it was absolutely identical to what he'd played with the band, but it was close, and the band was equally as happy. He went through it three times, and when he finished, the band swarmed him again. Lance picked him up in a bear hug and actually kissed him on the mouth, but it was a playful smack, and not anything truly amorous.

"God *damn*, Ray, is there anything you can't play? *Please* come on tour with us!" The rest of the band chorused their agreement.

"Ah, you don't need me. Johnny can learn that."

"In a year," the guitarist said.

"Well, I can't right now, I have a show opening in six weeks. Matt here is the star." He grabbed my arm and dragged me into the group. "Tell 'em about it, Matt."

On the spot like that, all I could think to say was, "It's great."

"You won't get as many girls playing Broadway as you will on the road with us," the bass player pointed out.

"This ain't Broadway. This is what they call *Off*-Broadway. It's where they put the weird stuff."

Lance took him by the shoulders and said, with total sincerity, "Please, Ray. *Please*. Write your own ticket. We need you."

Considering what a raging egomaniac Lance was reputed to be, this begging was extraordinary. Ray patted the musician's arm and said, "Lance, I wish I could, but I can't be in two places at once. And this show is my baby."

Lance looked down, disappointed. "I understand. Thanks for helping us out tonight. Same deal as always?"

"Same deal. I'll catch your show if you'll catch mine."

"I'll do my best."

Ten minutes later we were walking down the dark street as if we hadn't just spent an hour with one of the biggest stars in the world. I asked Ray, "Just how many instruments do you play?"

"I can find my way around most of 'em."

"'Most of 'em'? You mean you can play *any* instrument?"

He shrugged, as if the truth embarrassed him. "Pretty much. Although I ain't never got to try the cimbalom."

"What's that?"

"It's like a big ol' hammered dulcimer."

I had no idea what that was. "I'm still back at my last question."

Ray laughed. "It's like an inside-out piano, and you hit the strings with little batons."

"Ah. And how do you know Lance Abercrombie?"

"Oh, I do session work when I have to make ends meet. Did some stuff on Lance's big debut album, so I'm always glad to help out."

"What did he mean by 'same deal'?"

"I get union scale but no credit."

"Union scale? For playing like *that*?"

"Hey, it ain't for the money. It's for the jam. Lance may be a pretty boy tabloid star, but he's also dead serious about his music. You notice *he* wasn't drunk or high."

We walked in silence after that, and split up when I headed to the subway. But on the whole ride home, I thought about nothing but him, and the way his play and music mirrored the soul I now knew lived behind those dark, mischievous eyes.

I also remembered some of the wilder rumors about the Tufa that I'd read on the Internet. When I really thought about Ray and his music, somehow they no longer seemed so outlandish.

5

Still, work was work, and putting on an original show in six weeks was *hard*. For my part, learning the songs and words was a breeze; the trick was not getting wrapped up in everyone else's songs, during those long stretches when I was onstage listening. The music was so compelling that I lost myself in it just as we hoped the audience would.

And we guessed. We all had our thoughts about what was buried in the chapel of ease, and it was a source of constant discussion. We combed through the text, looking for clues, and with each revision Ray brought to us, we sought a new piece of the puzzle. After a week, someone hung a bulletin board, and Post-it notes with guesses quickly peppered it. Ray, damn him, said nothing, only smiled when he passed it and ignored our entreaties. (I know one actress offered him a blatant sexual favor if he'd tell her, but he turned her down.)

My crush on Ray, meanwhile, cooled a bit as I started dating Joaquim, a second-generation Puerto Rican dancer who worked in another show about to open. We met on the subway, and hit it off almost at once. I had no delusions that this was love at first sight or anything; I'd yet to meet anyone who inspired that sort of depth of feeling. But he was the kind of guy I could tell anything to, and had to stop myself more than once from sharing secrets never divulged to another soul. Experience had taught me that it was best to wait for such things until you'd been dating longer than two weeks.

At the beginning of our second week of rehearsal, the orchestra showed up.

Up until then, Ray had been playing piano for us. But now four other strange-looking players tromped down the aisle toward the stage, carrying instrument cases and looking around at the Armitage as if it were the Gershwin. When they got to the orchestra pit and began setting up, I saw that two were men, two were women.

One of the men whistled long and high. In a drawl every bit as heavy as Ray's, he said, "Ain't this place purty."

"Looks like that whorehouse in Abilene your daddy's always talking about," the other man said. "You know, where he met your mama."

"Will y'all please act like you've been to town before?" one of the women said.

Ray looked up at us from his piano and gestured to the newcomers. "Y'all, this-here's the band. They're all good ol' boys like me. One's from Texas, one from Alabama, and the two sisters are from Kentucky."

I saw the resemblance between the two women now. One of them said, "Y'all must be tickled to death to be doing a bunch of Ray's songs."

"We are," Jason said. Then he raised his eyebrows and said softly to me, "Can you actually *be* tickled to death?"

"Actually," the other woman said, "tickling was the torture reserved for the aristocracy in ancient Asia."

"Good ears on these ladies," Jason said even more softly.

"Musicians got to have good ears," Ray said. By now the others had set up their instruments: an upright bass and banjo played by the two sisters, and an electric guitar and small drum kit for the men. They tuned up quickly, then began a song I didn't recognize, sung by one of the women and the guitarist. The chorus mentioned something about dust and rattling bones. When they finished, they all expressed their satisfaction in a series of whistles and long calls I knew from our script were known as "rebel yells."

"That one of yours?" I called down to Ray.

"Ha! I wish. That was Kasey Chambers. Australian, if you can believe that." He looked at the rest of us. "So what'd y'all think?"

"Very nice," Neil said. "How long do you need to warm up?"

"Any warmer, we'd burn through the floor," the drummer said.

"Yep, we're ready to go," Ray agreed.

"Perfect. Let's start with act one, then, and see what we've got."

What we had, I realized later, was the soul of the show. We all had to sing harder and louder to be heard over the band, but we responded with our best performances so far. It was as if each added layer of production brought out things we'd missed or simply hadn't been able to create. With a full roots-rock band, the score came to stomping, aching life.

At the end of the second week, Ray invited all of us to his apartment for a potluck dinner. He called it a "y'all-come," and said it was a common occurrence back in his hometown. I found out later that it was also a common occurrence among his extended circle of friends, as he threw one every six months or so.

I almost invited Joaquim, but at the last moment decided to go solo. Joaquim, as much as I liked him, was a gossip, and enjoyed snarking about people. I did, too, up to a point, but not about these people. They were more than coworkers now.

I took along some potato salad, and was surprised by how many people he'd crammed into his tiny apartment on the fifth floor of a prewar walkup in Washington Heights, right around the corner from the 168th Street stop. Not just the cast, but assorted friends and partners as well, all talking and drinking while a long folding table laden with food took up the center of the room. I squeezed my salad onto a corner and felt a small, slender hand on my arm.

"Matt," Emily Valance said. She looked adorable, dressed up but not formal, with tasteful makeup. "I'm really glad you're here."

I looked around, but didn't see Ray. "Are you the host's date?"

"No, I'm the cohost," she said with a smile I'd never seen on her before. It was quiet, content, calm, and happy. Her brittle, harsh edge that I'd always encountered before was nowhere in sight.

"Are you drunk?" I asked.

She laughed. "No, I'm happy. And I'm happy for you, too. Ray won't shut up about how good you are in the show."

"It's hard not to be good with his music." I winced slightly at my momentary obliviousness, wondering if she was still sore about not being cast.

She read my mind. "I know. I've heard it many times. And there wasn't really a part for me in it. Now I'm just looking forward to opening night."

Ray appeared from the crowd, slipped an arm around Emily's waist, and kissed her on the cheek. "Hey-there, honey-bear." To me he said, "Hey, Matt, glad you could make it. Not sick of hanging out with us?"

"This is the most fun I've ever had doing a show," I said sincerely.

"I'm glad to hear that. Hey, sweet pea, do you think we need to steer people toward the table?"

Emily checked the time on her phone. "I think so."

Ray let out a loud whistle, and everyone turned toward him. "Hey, y'all, we better scootch up to the trough."

There were murmurs of confusion at this.

"What he means," Emily said, "is that it's time to eat."

"I reckon that's what I said, isn't it?" Ray deadpanned, and we all laughed.

Emily looked at me. "I'm learning to speak hillbilly, can you believe it?"

"You still look at me funny when I ask for the clicker, though," Ray said.

To my puzzled look, she said, "The remote for the TV."

We found seats in the eclectic collection of chairs around the table. I ended up in a folding one with duct-taped padding and a tendency to squeak embarrassingly if I shifted my weight. Ray, at the head of the table, stood up and tapped his beer bottle with his knife. "Y'all, I want to say something 'fore we start. Is that okay?"

We murmured assent. The way Emily looked up at Ray reminded me of how Nancy Reagan used to beam at Ronnie, as if he generated the light she needed to survive. If you'd told me two weeks ago I'd ever see her acting like that, I would've said you were crazy, and to tell you the truth, it *was* a little unsettling.

"I invited you here because, where I come from, family is super-important," Ray continued. "I have a sister, a dozen uncles and aunts"—he pronounced the word *ants*—"and more cousins than you could fit in this room. But as I'm pretty sure most of you can understand, none of them 'get' me. They didn't understand what I wanted out of life, or why I thought it was important. I mean, not a one of 'em has been to a play that wasn't put on at the high school."

I understood that, for sure. Although my father was surprisingly supportive, both when I came out and when I said I wanted to be a dancer and then an actor, my mother still thought it was phase I'd grow out of. And my grandparents simply stopped acknowledging that I was part of the family. I became "the weird one," which was their code for "the gay one."

"So I sort of gave up that family when I came to New York," he went on, "and I've been okay with that. But sometimes, you just need someone to look when you point at something, you know? You need someone to laugh at your jokes, or cry with you when you're sad. That's what family does, right? And I haven't really had anything to fill that hole since. But those of you working on the show, and the ones who come around here to pick-and-grin, and the ones who just go out of your way to say hi and let me know I'm your friend . . . I ain't exaggerating when I say you've become my family."

We all tapped on our drinks or plates with our silverware in response.

"And I'd like to say something special to the cast and crew of *Chapel of Ease*. Without y'all . . . I mean, people that have lived nowhere but in my head now walk and talk and sing and dance right in front of me. And some of you are no doubt tired of me talking when you want to be eating," he added with a chuckle. "But before we dig into the goodies, I just wanted to thank all of you for bringing my people to life."

We all raised our glasses in response, a few said, "Hear, hear," and I even heard sniffles around me. When he sat down, Emily leaned over and gave Ray a quick kiss.

Ray caught my eye and winked. And in that moment, it really did feel like family.

About eleven, I decided to call it an evening. The wine had made me loose, and I knew from experience that bad decisions lay in my immediate future if I didn't stop now. I had just found Emily to tell her good-bye when the power went out.

We all stood or sat immobile, waiting to see if it would come back on. "Somebody didn't pay their electric bill," came a sing-song taunt. Through the window we saw that the apartments across the way still had electricity, but a quick check of the hall-way outside showed it was the whole building, not just Ray's apartment.

When it was clear that the power wouldn't come back on right away, the room filled with the glow of cell phones as people began to text and post about it. A few people fumbled around as they gathered their stuff and prepared to leave.

"Hey, whoa, y'all," Ray said loudly. "Emily, there's some candles in back of the silverware drawer. We ain't letting a little thing like no power shut us down, are we?" The strum of an acoustic guitar filled the air.

Ray, the instrument strapped across his shoulder, walked into the center of the room. He pointed to the closet and said, "There's another couple of guitars in there, and some drums, too. Help yourselves." He picked away, noodling little minor chords as Emily placed candles on the windowsills.

As the drums, mostly djembes and a couple of bongos, got passed around and the candles grew brighter, Ray said, "We got a roomful of singers here, I reckon we can amuse our-selves. Anybody else know 'I'm Nine Hundred Miles from My Home'?"

No one spoke up. Even by candlelight, Ray's grin was huge.

"What, y'all Yankees ain't never heard of Fiddlin' John Carson? Well, then, let me introduce you to Pickin' Ray Parrish."

Something happened then, something that bound us all together in a way even two weeks' worth of intense rehearsal had not been able to do. The air in the room grew still, and even the candles stopped flickering. Drummers found the rhythm and accompanied him. As my eyes adjusted, I watched people lean slowly forward, wanting to be closer to the music even though Ray was near enough for most of them to touch. And no one used their phone to make a video, preserving the sanctity of the moment.

There was something in Ray's voice, too, an ache that I'd never heard there before. Or for that matter, anywhere else. As he sang about the distance between himself and his home, I felt the distance in my own heart. And, as I looked around, I saw that everyone else did, too.

When he finished, we all applauded. "All right, I ain't the Bon Jovi, now," he said, his drawl growing stronger. "Somebody else pick something, and we'll sing it."

So for the next two hours, that's what we did. We jammed. Ray passed the guitar around, and I took a turn on one of the drums. A neighbor from the floor above stopped by with his saxophone and things got a little jazzy. We sang Broadway tunes, popular songs from the '90s and '00s, and songs from our show. No one came by to complain about the noise. By the time the lights came back on at 3 A.M., we were exhausted, and elated, and never wanted the night to end. But of course, it had to.

Emily kissed my cheek as I left. "Thank you," she said.

"For what?"

"Ray told me he asked you about me. You could've told him all the shitty stories about how I behaved, but you didn't. So thank you."

"If you really want to thank me, you can get him to tell you what's buried in the chapel."

She rolled her eyes. "Like I haven't tried. He said he'd tell me after opening night."

"That's what he told us, too." I waved at Ray, who'd been cornered by two slightly tipsy cast members explaining in great detail why he was so awesome. "Good night, Emily. Thank Ray for a lovely evening, will you?"

On the walk to the subway, I whistled and danced, not worrying or caring that someone might come out of the shadows and decide to beat the shit out of me for it. I felt invincible.

The next Monday found Jason, Cassandra, and me in a nearby dance studio with Stella the choreographer. The too-small room smelled of disinfectant, and the mirrors on the wall were stained and cloudy with age. Stella had a three-foot-square piece of wood propped against her thigh, and as we watched, she let it topple over to the floor. The bang as it struck was like a shot. "Everybody awake now? Good. This is what you'll be dancing on."

"There's only that much of the stage open?" Jason asked. We still hadn't seen the set, only cardboard cutouts representing the chapel, but I thought we had more room than that.

"No, you misunderstand me," Stella said, stepping onto the board. "You'll be dancing on this exact board, or one very much like it. It's a kind of clog dancing they have in the mountains. They bring these boards along, throw them down wherever they happen to be, and dance on them."

The three of us exchanged looks. This was new.

Stella, in tap shoes, began to move. "It's called flatfooting. The idea is to raise your feet as little as possible off the board. It's quieter than real clogging, and you don't flop your legs around like you do in buck dancing."

She wasn't kidding: her feet barely moved. Yet we could tell from the tapping that she was dancing. I'd never seen, or attempted anything like this, and Jason voiced the same immediate concern I had.

"Will anybody be able to tell we're dancing? Because it doesn't look like much."

Before she could answer, Ray came in, carrying an instrument case. "Sorry I'm late, Stella. Have I missed anything?"

"Just showing them what we're doing."

"Great," he said with a big grin. He dragged a folding chair away from the wall and put the case on it. He took out a banjo, put the strap over his shoulder, and said, "Ready, Stella?"

"When you are, Ray."

Ray plucked and turned a tuning peg. "Hey, Stella, know why a banjo is better than a guitar?"

"They burn longer," Stella deadpanned.

Ray let out a cackle of a laugh, then played a lively tune I didn't recognize. Stella started to dance. It reminded me at first of Irish dancing, the way her upper body stayed mostly immobile while her legs from the knees down did all the work. But it was also very different: she actually watched her feet, something I was taught at an early age to never, ever do.

"Can you read music?" she asked Ray.

"Not enough to hurt my playing," he said back.

After a few moments, Ray said, "Hey, what's the difference between a frog and a banjo player?"

"Beats me, Ray."

"A frog might get a gig." He looked at us. "Y'all got no idea what a frog gig is, do you?"

We shook our heads, having no idea how we should respond to all this.

Stella continued to dance as she said, "Hey, Ray, what do you call a guy who hangs out with a bunch of musicians?"

"I don't know, Stella. What?"

"A banjo player."

Jason barked out a laugh, then caught himself. Cassandra tossed her hair and giggled.

"Hey, Stella, you know why all these banjo jokes are so dumb?"

"Why's that, Ray?"

"So dancers can understand 'em." He grinned at us, and winked.

He finished with a flourish, and so did she, leaping up and landing on the floor beside the board. We applauded and whistled. Ray said, "Hoo-*ee*! That was great!"

"Did you just use a hog call on me?" Stella said, and wiped sweat from her eyes.

"That's *soo*-ee," Ray said. We realized that they'd worked up this whole schtick for our benefit.

Ray took off the banjo. "So what do y'all think?"

We exchanged looks; then Cassandra said, "It looks easy enough. I mean, not easy, but like something we can learn."

"Do we have to do the jokes, too?" Jason asked.

"We'll see if they work in the show," Stella said. "The main thing is to learn to do this the way the real dancers do. I'll send you links to videos to watch. But for now, let's get to practicing."

"Wait," Ray interjected. "Can I show you something first?"

The tension in the room immediately ratcheted up: composers didn't upstage choreographers. None of us had ever seen anything even remotely like this before, and braced for the expected explosion of defended territories and union demarcations. But Stella magnanimously said, "Sure," and stepped off the board.

Ray took her place. "The thing is, when I've seen the best dancers in my hometown do this, it's looked like water dropping into a puddle. It's graceful, but it has *impact*. Now, I know Stella probably told you you ain't supposed to move your feet off the board much, and that's true. But what you *do* move, you make it count. Like this."

He let out a deep breath and then sang the old rockabilly standard "Tutti Frutti." And as he sang, he danced.

What he did wasn't hard; it certainly posed no challenge for me, after nearly fifteen years of regular dancing. But it felt exactly the way he described it, like water falling into a puddle. His boots—it was the first time I noticed he wore black cowboy boots—tapped and slid, barely rising an inch from the board, and created a noise like the flowing of a river. And it *looked* like water, because even though his upper body stayed essentially still, and he looked down at his feet just as Stella had done, everything *flowed*. He finished with a flourish on the final, "A-wop-bom-a-loo-mop-a-lomp-bam-boom!"

We clapped. Even Stella smiled her approval. Ray stepped off the board and said, "Okay, who wants to try now?"

"Everyone," Stella said. She indicated two more identical boards propped against the wall. "Get those out here and get up on there. Ray, you got some more music for us?"

"You bet," he said as he picked up his banjo.

6

"Well, that was . . . lacking," Neil said to us the following week, after our first complete off-book run-through with full band and choreography. We all knew it, too. Ray sat on the piano bench with his arms folded, not looking at us.

"Anyone want to hazard a guess as to what went wrong?" Neil continued. "Because I don't really have a clue. Yes, there were some missed cues, but this isn't exactly a complex show, staging-wise. What happened?"

He looked to the side of the stage. "Stella?"

The choreographer also had her arms tightly folded. "They know their steps," she said, defending her dancers while still agreeing with Neil.

"So that's not it. Ray, any trouble with the orchestra?"

Ray shook his head. We all knew that, too. The musicians gazed at their instruments, their sheet music, or the floor.

Neil cupped his hands and shouted to the back of the theater. "Ellie! How's the tech crew?"

"Sharp as a laser," she called back.

"Well," Neil said, pretending to be perplexed. "What could it be, then?"

The pieces had all been polished, but when they were linked together, there was no life to it, no spark. Even the songs, those gorgeous and beautiful songs, didn't properly work. We all looked anywhere but at Neil, whose searching gaze fell on each of us like a prison spotlight.

Finally he said, "Okay, then. Perhaps we're just all tired. We'll run it again, and see what happens. Pick up your cues, put some energy into it, and give it a little heart, okay?"

"It's not about 'heart,'" Julie said suddenly.

We all turned to look at her. She seemed both angry and scared.

"What, then?" Neil asked.

"We're supposed to be telling a mystery story," she said, her voice shaking with the immensity of confronting Neil. "Who or what is buried in the chapel of ease? That's the hook, right? And none of us knows the answer. It's like doing *Ten Little Indians* without knowing who the killer is. We *need* to know so we know how to play it."

Several of the other cast nodded or made little gestures of agreement. I was careful not to respond, but I did watch Ray. He scowled.

Neil turned to him. "Ray? Any comment?"

He got up and without a word stomped from the orchestra pit into the lobby. When the door closed behind him, the drummer added a rimshot.

Neil rolled his eyes, said, "Everyone, take a break," then followed.

We milled about, except the ones who made a beeline for the backstage window and the alley smoking area. I sat on the edge of the stage and, when Julie sat down beside me, I wished *I* smoked.

"Do you think that was too much?" she asked me softly.

"It was kind of blunt," I agreed.

"I yelled at Neil Callow."

"That wasn't yelling. That was . . . emphasis."

"But isn't it how you feel, too?"

"Ray said he'd tell us on opening night," I said. "I can wait."

"But what if it changes everything about what we're doing? Maybe we've all been approaching our characters the wrong way?"

"I think, if that were the case, Neil or Ray would've said something."

"But they're not *actors,*" she said passionately. "They might not *know* how it would affect our performances."

"That doesn't give Neil very much credit."

"Oh my God. Do you think that's what he thought?"

"I think he was probably more worried that we were all looking at him and expecting an answer."

She sighed and nodded. "You're right, I suppose. But I'm up there playing a woman with a secret, and damn it, I want to know what the secret is. And so does everyone else."

I said nothing. Through the open lobby doors, I watched Ray and Neil in animated conversation. Was Neil trying to pry the secret out of Ray for the good of the show? Or was Ray decrying the immaturity of the performers he'd trusted with his masterpiece? Both had valid points.

At last Neil returned. Word reached those outside, and they joined us on the stage. Neil looked up at us from the audience as if we were a misbehaving preschool class.

"I spoke to Ray," he said. "I explained, as I understood it, the situation."

"Did he tell you what was buried?" Ryan asked.

Neil fixed him with a look that, were it a bit stronger, might've frozen off Ryan's face on the spot. "No, Ryan, he did not."

The response was a wave of exasperation and annoyance.

"Stop that!" Neil barked. "This is not some community theater in Wisconsin or someplace. You have a perfectly acceptable—no, a goddamned *brilliant* show in front of you, and you need to suck it up and appreciate that. I tell you, I'm close to canceling this whole thing if we get another rehearsal like that last one. I'd rather the backers take a loss up front than be humiliated when we open."

I glanced at my fellow performers, and saw a fair share of blushes.

"Now, I don't want to hear anything about the goddamn 'mystery' again," Neil continued. "Ray said he'd tell us on opening night, and that's good enough for me. So let's take another half-hour break, then come back and run this fucker like we're getting paid for it." With that, he turned and strode out of the theater.

I had a half hour to kill, so I went for a walk, not wanting to hang around with my fellow chagrined actors. Shame, unlike misery, doesn't love company. The streets were crowded, and I decided I needed a latte to perk up for the next run-through. I stopped in at Think Coffee; the place was crowded but there was no line at the counter. Just as I was about to order, I spotted Ray at a table, all alone, speaking on his cell phone. I intended to look away and pretend not to notice, but he spotted me and waved me over.

There was no graceful way to get out of it, so I got my drink and joined him, ready to take my medicine. He finished his conversation with, "Yeah, I'll see you tonight. Thanks, sweetie. Bye." Then he looked up at me, smiled sadly, and said, "Is the mutiny averted?"

"There was never a mutiny. Just pressure that needed to be let off."

"You know, I had no idea that people felt so strongly about this. I thought it was all just some kind of extended joke."

"Some people fixate on things," I said diplomatically.

"I guess the bulletin board should've told me that. What about you?"

"Well, sure, I'd like to know, but you'd already promised to tell us, right? I was willing to wait for that."

Ray chewed his lip thoughtfully. I'd never seen him this serious. "Matt, do you know the song 'Ode to Billie Joe'?"

"No."

"It was a big hit back in the '60s. About these two teenagers. The boy kills himself. People had seen him and his girlfriend throwing something off the Tallahatchie Bridge. The song never tells you what. Was it flowers, a ring, a baby, what? You never find out."

"Is that what you were going for?"

"Not at first. I mean, when I first started writing this, I figured I'd reveal what it was, and that would be it. But no one remembers a mystery once it's solved, and I wanted people to remember this."

"I'm sorry it's become such an issue."

"Ah, don't worry about it. I'm just a temperamental *artiste*." He smiled wearily. "But I promise, I will tell you guys. Then you'll see that it doesn't really matter." He looked around wistfully at the coffee shop. "I used to work here, did you know that?"

"No."

"Yeah, I only quit a month ago, when Neil got me on the payroll."

"He must be really sure about you."

"He seems to be. Hope it all ends up being worth it."

At that moment a beautiful blond woman did a double take as she walked past our table with her takeout. "Ray?" she said with a dazzling smile. "I haven't seen you here in a while. Are you on break?"

"Honey, I don't work here anymore," Ray said with a grin. "I am a gainfully employed com-pose-er."

"Are you really?" she said with delight. "That is so awesome! Where are you working?"

"Right now at the Armpit around the corner. Oh, Delilah Ross, this is Matt Johansson. He's starring in my show."

I stood politely, and hoped I didn't turn too red when he described me as his "star." "Nice to meet you," I said to her.

She turned her formidable beauty on me. "Likewise." Then she went back to Ray. "Well, be sure and send me tickets to the opening. I wouldn't miss anything you were involved in."

"I'll do it."

When she left, I said, "And who was that again?"

"She's a model. Lingerie, mostly. We went out a few times."

I made no effort to hide my surprise. "You dated an underwear model?"

"Lingerie, son, lingerie," he said in an exaggerated hick accent. "Underwear is what men wear."

"Why aren't you still dating her?"

"Are you kidding? Guys with yachts want to date her. Men who wear tailored socks. She thought the whole starving-artist bit was romantic, but that wouldn't last. So we broke up while we were still friends."

His skittishness about dating Emily now made sense. And somehow it made me like him even more.

He turned sharply away and whispered urgently, "Don't look!"

"At what?" I whispered back.

"There's a girl by the door. She's got dreads. I keep seeing her."

I turned just enough to see the girl standing in the doorway.

I recognized her from the first day of rehearsal. "Yeah, I've seen her lurking around outside the theater before, too."

"Do you know her?"

"No, I figure she's either a theater groupie or a reporter. Why?"

"She's creeping me out. She followed me home last week. I ended up riding the subway for two hours just trying to get rid of her."

"Well, let's ask her what the hell's going on," I said, and stood up to confront her. But as soon as she saw me, she turned and dashed out the door. I thought about chasing her, but decided against it. Too many people might read the situation wrong and decide to intervene.

"Naw, don't worry about it," Ray said. "You're right, it's probably just somebody trying to work up the courage to ask for a part, or a recommendation or something."

We finished our drinks, then walked back to the theater together.

When we got back to the Armpit, though, Ray motioned for me to follow him into the stairwell just off the lobby. We climbed all five stories up to the last exit, where the door had been propped open by a copy of the tenor edition of *Musical Theatre for Classical Singers*. The door squeaked as he pushed it aside, and we stepped out onto the tarry roof.

Most of the surrounding buildings still towered over us, but we were high enough to see the streets stretching off between them, and feel a little of the isolation you get when you're far from the ground. We traversed the sticky roof on a series of boards and pieces of old metal, and I followed Ray over to the edge. He got right up to it and peered down; I stayed a bit back. I wasn't afraid of heights, but I *was* afraid of deaths.

"You like being up high?" Ray asked.

"I don't mind it," I said.

"Do you ever get right on the edge and think about jumping? Not because you're suicidal or anything, but just to see if you can fly?"

"Er . . . no."

"You reckon I could?"

"No," I said more firmly.

He laughed. "That means you're sensible, I reckon." He looked back at me, and the wind tousled his hair. "You remember that speech I gave at dinner the other night? About family?"

"Yeah."

"I wasn't kidding. I do think of the cast, particularly you, as my new family. The problem is, I don't think I'm entirely shed of my old one. I mean, if they knew the story I was telling with this play, they might be pretty mad. No, I take that back; it wouldn't be my family that was mad. It'd be . . ."

He trailed off and fell silent, so I prompted, "Who?"

"Well, there's people . . . The Tufa have sort of an 'elder' system. We have people who set the rules, and then make sure they're followed. They don't like it when we sing songs out of school." He looked back at me. "You know that expression?"

"But you're not home. Surely they can't bother you here."

He chuckled. "It does seem unlikely. But you never know. They can fly a long way if the reason's good enough."

"You really think you're, like . . . in danger?"

His grin grew wider. "Not now that I've told someone about it. You know how things percolate in your head when you keep it to yourself, and then sound silly when you say 'em out loud."

"Is it because you saw that girl who's been following you?"

He shrugged a little. "Maybe. She ain't a Tufa, that's for sure. We can always tell each other, no matter where we are."

I tried to sound as reassuring as possible. "Then maybe you're being a little paranoid."

"You're probably right. Manhattan is a hell of a long way from Needsville."

He stepped back from the edge, and I let out a breath I hadn't realized I was holding. I didn't truly think Ray was su-icidal, but it would be mighty easy for him to fall accidentally, and then I'd have a lot of explaining to do. We went back into the building and down to the theater.

Our second run-through was much, much better. Humiliation is a great motivator, and none of us wanted to continue to be pointed out as a slacker. We put some ferocity into it, to the point that by the time we were done, I was totally worn out. Or, to borrow one of Ray's lines from the show, I was "rode hard and put up wet."

So, of course, Neil pulled me aside and said, "Listen, don't say anything to the others, but will you meet me for a drink in about an hour?"

I stared at him. We were both gay, but there had never been a spark between us.

He sighed. "No, not *that* kind of drink. I just want to talk to you privately, all right? About the show."

"Sure. Where?"

"At the KGB."

I went to clean up. In the dressing room, Ryan and Jason were both as tired as I was, yawning as they changed into street clothes.

Jason's transformation was especially marked. As himself, he had a loose, rangy way about him, the epitome of a hip urban dude from this era or any other. But as soon as he put on the jeans and flannel shirt of his character, Lucas, he seemed to grow straighter, and stiffer, his natural friendliness replaced with the character's reserve. Lucas wasn't stupid, but neither was he tuned in to those around him; it was one reason Crawford, my character, felt he wasn't right for Jennifer. At least, that was how I played it.

I waited until they left, then went onto the stage to look out at the empty theater. It really was a small room, but I had faith in this show: I never got tired of both singing my songs and hearing the others'. When the cast doesn't get bored, it's a good sign. I couldn't help but think bigger venues, on nearby bigger streets, were in our future.

From the stage, I could see through to the street when the inner theater doors were open at the back of the house. As I glanced up, I saw a slender figure standing immobile outside them. Although the distance was too great, something told me it was that same dreadlocked girl. When she saw me looking, she quickly scurried away.

I met Neil at the appointed time. The KGB Bar had appropriately red walls and curtains, with stained glass windows behind the bar. It was crowded and poorly air-conditioned, so the dried sweat from rehearsal quickly returned. It was also dimly lit, so it took a few moments for me to spot Neil.

When I joined him, he said at once, "I saw you and Ray come back to the theater together today."

"We ran into each other at the coffee shop."

"Did you talk about the show? Go get yourself a drink, and we'll talk."

He didn't offer to buy, which annoyed me. When I returned with my gin and tonic, I said, "What's the agenda here, Neil?"

"Look, I know Ray has some problems, and if they're getting worse—"

"What problems?"

Neil tapped his forehead.

"Mental problems?"

"No. Health problems. With his brain."

"He didn't mention anything to me."

"He didn't?"

"No. We talked about the show, like you said." Then I wondered if Neil had just manipulated me into confirming his suspicions. But what was he suspicious *about*?

Neil sipped his martini, then said, "Ray's been having headaches. Worse than migraines. I had to take him to the emergency clinic twice because he couldn't stop throwing up. They want to send him for tests, but he doesn't have insurance, so that's out."

"What do they think it is?"

"They mentioned a tumor as the worst-case scenario."

Fuck, I thought. "He didn't say a thing about it."

Neil nodded. In the dim light, I couldn't really read his expression. "Okay, then. Did he mention anything else? Or did you notice anything . . . unusual?"

I thought instantly of the dreadlocked girl, but it seemed far too insubstantial to add to a list that included possible brain tumors. I shook my head.

"Keep this to yourself, Matt. This show is going to be terrific. It *is* terrific. I don't want gossip getting in the way."

"You're asking musical theater performers not to gossip?" I said, trying to lighten the mood.

He looked at me dead serious. "No, I'm asking *you* not to gossip about *this*."

"All right, sure. Mum's the word. But—"

"No 'buts.' You just keep it to yourself, and tell me if you see any signs he's having trouble."

We left it at that, finished our drinks in silence, and then Neil departed. I finished my drink, trying to process all he'd said.

———

As I left the station to walk to my building that night, I got a text from Joaquim asking if he could come over. I said yes, and found him seated with his back against my apartment door, reading a book about ancient astronauts. He got up and kissed me when I came up the stairwell. He was also tired and sweaty from his rehearsal, but the kiss reinvigorated us both.

"Why don't you ever take the elevator?" he asked.

"I do sometimes. But I'm a dancer, and I'm closing in on thirty. I need all the exercise I can get."

"I thought you were an actor," he teased, accenting the final syllable in the word.

"I am. But an actor who can't sing and dance gets a lot fewer jobs."

We kissed in the hall some more, until the distinctive chihuahua barking told me my neighbor, Mr. Shipp, was about to bring his pocket dog out for its evening constitutional. Mr. Shipp was gay, too, but he had old-fashioned ideas about PDAs, so we stopped before his door opened. He waved to us as he shuffled toward the elevator, and Joaquim and I went inside my apartment.

I dropped my backpack on the couch and went to make a drink. Joaquim said, "You kissed like a man with a lot on his mind."

"No, I promise you, I was thoroughly in the moment."

"You were *acting* like you were in the moment. I've dated enough actors, I can tell. It's something about Ray, isn't it?"

Before I could stop myself, I said, "Yeah. He's not well."

"Cancer? AIDS?"

"I can't really say. I shouldn't have said anything at all."

"Wow."

"Yeah. We're so close to opening, and the show is really, really good."

"I know. That night I saw the run-through of act one, it was great. Has he seen a doctor?"

"I really can't talk about it. Keep it to yourself, okay?"

"Sure. I hope it's nothing serious." We sipped our drinks and stared out at the night, listening to the noises, until Joaquim put down his drink and drew me close. Then, for a while, I forgot about Ray, and the show, and the mystery of the chapel of ease.

7

So of course, I spent the next weeks, as we honed the show to a crystal clarity and level of emotional honesty few of us had ever experienced onstage, watching Ray for any sign of imminent collapse. There was nothing. He sat in his usual place at the piano, occasionally taking notes and whispering something to Neil. He joked with the band. He smiled a lot, always said hello when he saw me, and generally acted like a guy whose show was about to premiere.

As the press preview approached, we all grew more excited. Julie and Ryan, who played Byrda and Shad, had begun dating, which lent serious poignancy to their songs. A fiddler and a bodhran drummer joined the core of the band and added discreet fullness, somehow making them sound both ancient and timeless. The few people lucky enough to see the show all the way through, mostly friends of Neil and Ray, couldn't say enough good things about it.

Ray and Emily continued to date, and she occasionally sat in on rehearsals. I noticed that she often brought along a book or her iPad, but inevitably ended up watching the show.

The dreadlocked girl either got better at stalking, or abandoned her quest. I never spotted her again, and Ray didn't mention her.

All the omens were good. Great, even. What could go wrong?

The press preview, held on the Tuesday before our Friday opening, went as well as we could possibly have hoped. Word had gotten out, thanks mainly to Neil's reputation, and we'd invited all our spouses, partners, and families. The little theater was packed, and the energy, even before the curtain rose, made the air buzz with excitement.

My hand shook as I applied my makeup, this being too low-budget a production to afford makeup people. I closed my eyes and tried to ground and center, using techniques my first acting teacher in high school had taught me. Beside me, Jason hummed his first song to himself, and on the opposite side of the room, his back to us, Ryan actually dozed off, his makeup done. I envied his total lack of nerves.

After a soft knock on the door, Ray peeked in. "Hey, guys. Fired up?"

"All except Ryan," Jason said.

"No, I'm awake," Ryan said woozily. "Look, I'm blinking and everything."

"Well, I just wanted to tell y'all, no matter what happens tonight, no matter whether it goes good or bad, y'all have been great. I've been involved in my share of shows, and I ain't never enjoyed getting one ready as much as I have this one. I know you guys will do your best, and can't nobody ask any more than that."

We expressed our thanks, and he slipped back out. In the mirror, I looked at my face and saw myself, just for an instant, with Tufa-black hair and a soul-deep sadness. The instant passed, but I wondered if that meant I'd truly, fully connected with Crawford at last. If so, it wasn't a moment too soon.

I adjusted the microphone against my cheek for the final time. The houselights went out, the recorded music ended, and Ellie's voice crackled through the earpiece, "Places for act one, everyone. Places for act one." I rushed to my spot for the show's first number, which was also *my* first number.

We took our places in the wings, waiting for Ellie's announcement to go on. The instrumental bluegrass music that played over the house PA only energized me more. I looked at Cassandra and winked for luck; she tossed her hair and blew me a kiss. The noise of the crowd shuffling itself was louder than I expected, no doubt due to the theater's small space.

And then we were on.

We were so nervous, our collective sweat threatened to make the floor too slick to dance, but somehow that funneled into our enthusiasm, and we fucking tore the place down. Everything worked, *everything,* and when Julie did her climactic song, we heard sniffles from this professionally blasé crowd, and we knew we'd aced it. Whatever the reviews, whether anyone came to see it or not, we knew we'd done ourselves, and Ray, proud. We got a standing ovation.

Backstage it was all hugs and tears, with the kind of relieved camaraderie the movies showed only after the team has won the big game. We took lots of selfies and peppered social media with them. Then we cleaned up and went to meet the new fans.

Critics surrounded Ray and Neil, looking for quotes and expressing their appreciation. Emily stood beaming beside Ray, their arms linked. I watched Delilah the lingerie model pay her respects, and the look Emily gave her could've melted concrete.

Some of the critics approached me and the rest of the cast as well, and we were careful to give only positive, general statements. None of us wanted our misstep to be the source of scandal in press that promised to be stellar.

Even snarky Joaquim had tears in his eyes when he hugged me and said, "I knew it would be good, but not *good* good. Holy shit, Matt. Holy shit."

"So you liked it?"

"If you'd told me even a week ago that songs with fiddle music would have me in tears, I would've laughed so hard. But I swear it did." He kissed me, then said, "I have to go. I have an early call tomorrow. Want to come over after this finishes up?"

"I'll text you when we're done. If you're still awake, definitely."

He kissed me again, then disappeared into the crowd.

I continued to accept congratulations until a young woman with the same jet-black hair and perfect teeth as Ray came up and shook my hand. The instant we touched, it was like a bubble of silence came down around us. She said, almost too quietly to hear, "I was very impressed. You did a wonderful job."

She even had Ray's Southern lilt. I said, "Thank you. Are you from where your accent is from?"

"I beg your pardon?"

"I'm guessing you must be a friend of Ray's."

"Why do you say that?"

"You kind of look like him, and he told us that his people all resembled each other."

She did not smile. She was a little younger than me, maybe twenty-five or -six, and carried herself with easy, straight-backed confidence. Not the confidence of the beautiful, although she was that; instead, it was the cool assurance of someone who knew that, in any situation, she could probably kick ass and take names. She said, "So he told you about us?"

I suddenly felt the way I did when talking to reporters: like

I was navigating a verbal minefield, and had to be careful not to give away the wrong crucial bit of information. "He explained his background and how it influenced the show."

"Well. You certainly captured what it's like to live in the mountains," she said, and at last managed a little smile. "Except for the hair. It should be black."

"The director thought it would be confusing if we all had the same color."

"He's right. It is, sometimes. So you'll keep going with the show?"

"Me, personally?"

"The theater. Everyone."

"Depends on the reviews and ticket sales, I suppose. But as long as they're both good, then yeah, we'll keep going."

"What if Ray asks you to stop?"

"Asks us to stop? I don't understand."

"Just thinking out loud. Well, I'd better go congratulate Mr. Parrish. It's his big night, after all."

She faded back into the crowd, and I was immediately accosted by more well-wishers. I tried to watch for her, but it was like she'd vanished, until I saw her across the room, talking to Ray.

I posed for a couple of selfies with some dancer friends, got hugged far too hard by someone I knew had a crush on me (everything about this show seemed to involve crushes), and accepted a dozen more handshakes before I could slip away. I eased over near Ray and the black-haired girl, close enough to hear their conversation. Just as she had with me, she seemed to project a bubble that held people back while she spoke to him. But as I said, theater people love gossip, and if eavesdropping were an Olympic sport, we'd all have medals.

"You can't tell this story," the girl said. "That's a secret that's supposed to *stay* secret."

"I didn't tell the secret," Ray said defensively.

"No, but you drew attention to it. Now people will come looking."

"That's silly. No one can find it, anyway." As he spoke, his Southern accent, never entirely absent, grew stronger. It would've been funny if I hadn't gotten the sense that this whole conversation was potentially earthshaking.

"Someone will. Remember that flatlander that sung Rockhouse's dying dirge? He wasn't supposed to be able to find that, either, but he did."

"He had help."

"And somebody contrary might help anyone who comes looking for this."

"Well, anyway, it's done. The show'll get great reviews, it'll open, and that's that."

She put her hand on his face, and the sadness grew. "I surely did hope that you wouldn't do this. I surely did. Now . . ."

"Now, nothing. It's *done*. And that's that. You saw it, and heard it, right?"

"I did."

"Wasn't it great?"

"Of course it's great, Ray, but it's not about that. Look, I agree with you, things have to change. We have to engage with the world now, we can't keep hiding from it. But I also agree with"—and here she said a name I didn't quite catch, which started with an *M*—"that it needs to be on our terms."

"How is this not on our terms? I created this. It's one of our stories, told by one of us."

"This is not the place to have this conversation, Rayford."

Rayford? I thought. I'd assumed "Ray" was short for Raymond.

"There's no point to this conversation at any time," Ray said. "What's done is done."

She smiled like she'd just heard the worst news ever, but it was news she'd expected. "Yes, it is. That is purely that. Good-bye, Rayford." With that she turned and once again vanished into the crowd.

Ray continued to stare after her, ignoring the people who instantly re-swarmed him. I pushed my way through and said in his ear, "You need a break?"

He turned and I saw tears in his eyes. They hadn't been there before, despite the emotions of the evening. He nodded, so I took his elbow and guided him to the door that led to the roof. We ran up the stairs like children sneaking out of school, and when we emerged into the open, it was like bursting out of some prison. The city lights seemed to twinkle in celebration of our triumph, and the traffic noise was like a comforting lullaby.

Ray dug out a joint and lit it. He offered me a drag, and I took one to be polite. He inhaled deeply, as if doing it for both himself and Bill Clinton. He kept glancing up at the buildings around us, almost as if he expected something to come swooping out of the night sky. It was hot and humid, and he sighed as he leaned against the brick wall of the stairwell exit.

"Hell of a press night," I said. "They loved it."

"They did," he agreed.

"Well, everyone except your friend."

He smiled, in that same sad way the girl had done earlier. "She's not my friend. She's from back home."

"In Tennessee?"

"Yep. Apparently it's not so long a flight as I thought."

"You didn't know she was coming?"

"No." He rubbed his temple and frowned, and I immediately remembered Neil's warning. But it seemed to pass. "She was the last person I expected to see, honestly."

"Kind of flattering that she came all this way."

He inhaled deeply again, and let the smoke settle in his lungs for a long time before letting it out. His voice tight, he said, "Distance isn't so big a barrier as it used to be."

"What were you two talking about?"

He chuckled, but with the cool, calm fatalism of a man before the firing squad. "How much trouble I was in for telling the story of Byrda and Shad to people like you."

"Gay actors?" I deadpanned.

"No, anyone who's not a Tufa."

"But didn't this happen a long time ago? Like, *centuries* ago?"

"Yeah. But time doesn't work the same for everybody."

The way the night breeze blew his hair, and the light played across his face, restoked the fire of my unrequited love. I wanted to hold him, to give him someone strong to hang on to so he didn't have to be. But instead I just said, "I'm sorry. That must be disappointing."

He shrugged. "You ever disappoint your family?"

"Some of them. When I came out, especially."

"Yeah." He took another long hit off the joint. "Well, the problem with my family is that it's probably a lot bigger than yours. Everybody from my hometown is related if you go back far enough. That means everybody thinks they have a say in what you do. Sometimes so much of a say that they come all this way just to tell you."

"Is she gone, then?"

Again he looked up. "I think so." Then he rubbed his temples hard and closed his eyes. "Well, I better get back in there. Neil will get mad at me if I don't filter off some of the glad-handers."

"The reviews should be great. I bet we sell out the run."

"Maybe. Guess we'll see." Then he took my arm. "Hey, can I ask you a favor?"

"Sure."

"If anything happens to me, make sure you're there for Emily."

"What's going to happen?" I said, trying to sound jaunty.

"I don't know, it's just . . . women who fall in love with Tufa men have a very hard time if we go away. It's my fault, I should've been more careful. And I know how that sounds, believe me, but if something does happen to me, Emily will be . . . very distraught. And lost. And she'll say some crazy things. Just be kind to her and don't make fun of her."

"Yeah, I will," I agreed, taken a bit by surprise.

He ground out the roach against the board we stood on and strode back toward the entrance, with sagging shoulders as if he'd gotten the worst news in the world. I caught myself looking up as well, but saw only the night sky, a muddy haze of light reflected by the heavy humidity.

8

I opened my eyes, and the first thing I saw was my phone on the nightstand. The screen was lit up, which meant I had messages.

The exertions of the show, the celebratory well-wishing afterwards, the tokes off Ray's joint, and the half a bottle of wine I'd consumed all conspired to knock me out. Joaquim had surprised me by waiting for me outside my door, although he was asleep when I got there. He'd pinned a note to his chest that said in big letters, NOT HOMELESS. WAITING FOR MATT. DON'T CALL THE COPS. We were both so wiped out that we went to sleep without fooling around. By the time I noticed my phone, it was nearly eleven o'clock in the morning.

I reached across Joaquim and picked it up. There were dozens of messages and tweets. The most recent one, still displayed, said, "I'm so sorry."

My heart sank; were the reviews *that* bad?

I turned on the ringer, and almost immediately "The Man Who Shot Liberty Valance" by Gene Pitney—Emily Valance's ringtone—blared out at me. Joaquim moaned and pulled my pillow over his head. I got out of bed as I answered. "Hey, Emily."

"Where have you been?" she said, her voice both angry and distraught, with the emphasis on the latter.

"Sleeping. I turned my ringer off. I'm exhausted. Why, what's wrong?" My first thought was that, if the reviews had been hatchet jobs, we were all out of work.

"You don't know?"

"No, I don't know. What is it?"

"Ray's dead."

If this were a movie, it would be one of those shots like in *Jaws* or *Vertigo,* when the camera zoomed in as it dollied back, conveying the protagonist's sudden disorientation. "What? Ray's *what*?"

"He's dead." She drew out the word, giving it greater weight and meaning. It wasn't simply an announcement; it was a shifting of the world, her world, *my* world.

All I could think to say was, "What happened?"

"He went to sleep and just . . . died. I couldn't wake him up. He was cold, and stiff. I called 911, and they said he'd been dead for a couple of hours." She dissolved into sobs, and all I could do was stare at the phone in my hand while it cried at me.

I promised Emily I'd go there as soon as I got showered and dressed; then I checked the other messages. Most were from the cast, a couple from theater reporters I knew casually, and a half dozen from Neil. He was the only one I called back.

"Matt," he said with such evident relief that I wondered what exactly he thought I could do. "I've been trying to reach you all morning."

"I turned off my ringer. I wanted to sleep in."

"Are you sitting down?"

"Ray's girlfriend called me already."

"It's awful. He went home, lay down, and died. Just like that."

"Was it a tumor?"

"Fuck if I know, although that seems like a pretty good bet, doesn't it?"

"Yeah." I remembered the way he'd rubbed his temples on the roof. My God, had I missed a crucial sign? If I'd called 911 then, would he still be alive? Was this all *my* fault? "I guess they'll do an autopsy, and we'll know."

"It doesn't really matter, does it?"

"No, I guess it doesn't."

"Listen, we're calling the cast together this afternoon for some announcements. Three o'clock."

My stomach dropped even further. "Are we closing?"

"Have you read the reviews?"

"No. Are they terrible?"

He laughed, with real amusement. "Matt, we're the best thing since sunshine. Marion Davies didn't get reviews like this when Hearst owned the papers. No way we're closing down. But we can't just act like nothing's happened, either."

"No, I guess not."

"And would you mind asking Ray's girlfriend, Erica—"

"Emily."

"Oh, that's right, Emily. Would you mind calling her and inviting her to come, too? I plan to let everyone say a little about what Ray meant to them, and it might do her good to hear it."

"Sure."

"And don't talk to the press; we'll take care of that. Everyone else in the show is already tweeting about it, so there's no point in asking you not to, but just try not to say anything about the future of the show."

"Okay."

"And, Matt? I know you and Ray had gotten close. I'm really sorry."

"I'm sorry, too."

I continued to stare at my phone after he hung up, as if it might spit out details that I craved but didn't dare ask. When it rang again I jumped, then turned it off and opened my laptop. I searched for reviews of the show.

A MAGICAL MOUNTAIN EVENING was both the headline and the overall theme. "Like being right there in the Smokies," one critic gushed, as if he'd ever been south of Baltimore. "Songs that will pierce your heart while they make your feet tap," said another, a quote I hoped ended up on the CD cover.

Damn, Rayford, I thought. *Your timing is exquisite.*

I took a quick shower, then called Emily and told her about Neil's offer. She sounded numb, but she agreed to go with me.

As I rode the elevator down, it hit me all at once: Ray was *dead.* That smile, that goofy, stooped walk, that amazing musicianship, all were *gone.* Alone in that tiny metal box, I cried.

And I hated myself for my next thought, but there was no holding it back: *Now we'll never know what's buried in the chapel of ease.*

I pushed the buzzer outside Emily's building in Hell's Kitchen and said, "Hey, it's me." She let me in without a word.

When I got to her floor, the door was already open. Emily stood in the kitchen in a black dress that would've been sexy in almost any other context. As it was, she looked gaunt and willowy, like a twig in the winter.

She hugged me as soon as she saw me. "I'm not crying," she said, as much to herself as to me. "I'm not."

"It's okay if you need to."

"No. I've got to make it through this without collapsing. Neil might want to hire me someday, and I don't want his most vivid memory of me to be sobbing with snot running down my face."

I remembered my pledge to Ray to look after Emily; whatever his reason for making me promise it, I was now bound to my word. At least he seemed to be wrong about her, because she wasn't falling apart. "Do you have anything you can take?"

She shook her head. "I'll manage it, thanks."

I looked around her slightly rumpled apartment. An overnight bag was open on the couch. "So you were at Ray's place last night?"

She nodded. "We were waiting for the reviews to show up online, and he went to lie down. I came to bed about an hour later, after reading the first couple. They were raves, I couldn't wait to share it with him." She hiccuped a little, but maintained control. "Do you think he knows? I mean, wherever he is?"

I wanted to be comforting, but I didn't have it in me. "I don't know, Emily."

"Well, I'm going to assume he does. And that he's proud. He's got a right to be, doesn't he?"

"He does. Are you ready?"

"No, but I've never let that stop me."

Emily turned heads the whole way to the theater. I kept looking for the black-haired woman I'd spoken to after the show, but I don't know what I would've done if I'd seen her; my nagging, unshakable sense that she had something to do with Ray's death wouldn't go away. But that was crazy, right? Ray had been sick, and with Emily the whole time.

When we were about a block from the Armitage, a voice behind us said, "Excuse me. Muh-Mister Johansson?"

We stopped and turned. The dreadlocked girl stood demurely there, head down, her shoulders shaking. "I j-just wanted to say . . . how sorry I am to hear about . . . Ray Parrish. I know he was your friend, and—"

"Who the hell *are* you?" I asked, my temper going from zero to sixty almost at once. "Why the fuck have you been following Ray around?"

She burst into tears. "I'm so sorry, I am, I didn't mean any harm, I wasn't doing anything, I never spoke to him, just like she told me—"

"Like *who* told you?"

People stopped around us to watch the scene.

"I'm so sorry," she said again, almost a wail. Then she turned and ran off. In moments she was lost in the crowd.

"Who was that?" Emily asked, eyes wide with surprise.

"Ray's stalker," I said.

"Ray had a stalker?"

"Yeah." The urge to chase her down was overwhelming, but my main duty at the moment was to Emily, and to the cast of the show.

"He never told me about it," she said numbly. "Never mentioned a word."

"He probably didn't want to worry you." Then I took her hand and we resumed our walk.

Some of the cast waited outside, smoking and looking despondent. We nodded and muttered hellos as we entered. The lobby was empty, and I heard murmuring inside the auditorium.

Emily stopped. "Oh my God. There's a lot of people here."

"Yeah."

"I don't know why, but I didn't think of that. I'm the girlfriend, they'll all be watching me, to see if their stories make me cry. Won't they?"

That was Emily: the center of the universe even when it wasn't her funeral. If she'd been malicious about it, I would've hated her, but I knew there was a fair bet she was right. We were a bunch of actors, after all.

"We can leave if you want," I said.

She stood up straight, put her shoulders back, and said, "No. Ray deserves this to be about him, not me. Right?"

"Right," I agreed as wholeheartedly as I dared. She took my arm and we went into the auditorium.

Neil stood on the edge of the stage, talking to a few people in the orchestra pit. He looked up when we entered, then waved us down front. There were probably forty people there, cast and crew and friends whom we'd all gotten to know to various degrees. Everyone looked solemn and preoccupied, and a few people had the red, bleary signs of recent tears. I helped Emily settle into a seat on the front row, sat beside her, and waited for whatever would come.

Neil said, "Ellie, would you let everyone know we're going to get started?"

Ellie went backstage, and a moment later her voice came over the house PA. "Please come and take your seats. We're ready to begin."

The people outside filed in at an appropriately funereal pace, and Neil waited patiently for them to get settled. We were clustered at the front of the seats, except for those few who sat far in the back for their own reasons.

"This is an unexpected and sad occasion," Neil said. "This has never happened to me before, and I'm not at all sure what to say here, so if I ramble, please excuse me. First, for those of you in the cast and crew, the show is *not* closing. You've all seen the reviews; we've got a hit here, and truthfully, we all knew it anyway. But we *are* shutting down for a week out of respect for Ray, and to get our own heads together. When we do open, I don't want any of us thinking of anything but how great it is to be doing this play."

That seemed an unrealistic goal, but I knew it was just to give us something to focus on other than the tragedy. Neil, as were most great directors, was a master manipulator, and knew how to get people to do what he wanted. And right now he wanted us to focus on the future, not the past.

"This is a major loss, not just to theater in general, not just to the show, but to each of us personally. And that includes me, I assure you. I'd been working with Ray for a year on this, and in that time I'd gotten to know him very well. He was a man who loved the theater and its music with a passion that reminded me of why I'd chosen this career in the first place. His eyes would light up as he talked about his favorite plays or numbers. And . . ."

He paused, and seemed to legitimately choke up. That was one of the problems with theater people: you could never *really* be sure they weren't acting. But I'd known Neil long enough that I was pretty sure this was genuine. And to share this moment with us was especially powerful.

After a deep breath, he continued. "Some of you were lucky enough to hear Ray sing. But most of you had no idea he could dance as well. A lot of the choreography came from steps and moves he showed me and Stella, from his hometown. If the people in the show seem like a community, it's because Ray showed me how a community dances and sings."

That brought the dark-haired woman back to the front of my brain. I discreetly glanced behind me, pretending to look at the other mourners but actually checking to see if the woman was there. I didn't spot her.

Neil then opened the floor to the rest of us. We told stories about how we'd met Ray, what we felt about his work, and how much his enthusiasm had rubbed off on us. Emily took it all in, only once letting a single tear escape when someone mentioned the way Ray would listen as if the other person were the entire world.

The most surprising testimonial came from Lance Abercrombie, whom I hadn't even seen arrive. He walked down to the orchestra pit and stood, with his leather jacket and perfect hair, looking up at all of us.

"You probably know who I am," he said. "I only heard about Ray an hour ago, and I came here out of . . . respect, or homage, or something. I had no idea you were having this service. But I'm glad you are, because there's things about Ray you may not know, and you should.

"Ray Parrish was the best musician I ever met. Certainly better than me. If he'd gone into performance instead of composing, he would've been the biggest star in the world by now. You may think I'm exaggerating, but I promise you, I'm not."

His eyes filled with tears, but his voice remained strong.

"The thing is, he never tried to show up me, or anyone else. When he played with us, he supported whatever we were doing. If he was adding rhythm guitar, he didn't try to convince us he should play lead. If he harmonized on a vocal track, he blended in perfectly. In a world filled with fucking egos, he only cared about the song at hand."

He wiped his eyes. "Thank you for letting me crash your party today. I'm looking forward to seeing this show when it opens."

And with that, one of the biggest rock stars in the world walked out alone.

More people from the company spoke, all reiterating sweet or funny things Ray had done. The mood grew lighter. But then Mark said something we all were thinking, but only someone as egotistical and clueless as him would ever utter aloud:

"Well, I guess we'll never find out what's buried in the chapel of ease, will we? Unless he told somebody here—?"

"Oh, come on, Mark," someone said.

"Hey, I'm just saying what I know we're all thinking," he said. "Is there anyone here who isn't dying to know?"

Whether his word choice was deliberate or not, a wave of

groans went through us. He sighed and crossed his arms petulantly. "All right, you people don't want to be honest with yourselves, fine."

"Thank you, Mark," Neil said sternly. "But let's keep this about Ray. There's plenty of time for gossip and whining later."

His words had their effect: no one else mentioned the secret, or Ray's promise to reveal it. Instead, people spoke of their memories of Ray, little vignettes that illustrated his warmth and tenderness. Yet for me, that damn secret stayed right at the edge of my consciousness, gnawing away like a patient and particularly determined rat. Was I no better than Mark?

Emily's moment came at last, when Neil said, "We also have here with us Emily Valance, Ray's girlfriend. Would you like to say anything, Emily?"

At least he got her name right. She glanced at me, and I nodded encouragingly. She stood and turned to face the crowd.

"I'm an actress," she said, her voice trembling, "and a dancer. I met Ray just before Neil didn't cast me in this show."

There was some uncomfortable laughter.

"I was, and probably will be again, a bitter, cynical bitch who is only out for herself. I started dating Ray because I thought, even if I didn't get into this show, I might have a better shot at his next one. But . . ."

She looked down and took a deep breath.

"Once I got to know him, the show didn't matter. Acting and dancing didn't matter. I wanted to be with him because of *him*. If you spent any time with him, you know what I mean: he was just simply *good*, without any agendas or ulterior motives. He laughed when he was happy, cried when he was sad, listened when you spoke—do you know how rare it is to have someone not interrupt you, to listen to your stories without trying to trump it with one of theirs?—and just generally made you a priority when you were together. I never told Ray that I loved him, but . . ."

And then she lost it. Not in some dramatic look-at-me way, but she just lowered her head and began to cry, softly and simply. As I stood to help her sit back down, I heard many, many others join her.

Even Neil looked like he might, but he kept it under control. He said, "Ray's ashes will be sent home to his family. They're not able to make the trip up to get him, apparently. So unless someone volunteers to take them, I guess I'll be doing it."

I leaned close to Emily. "Do you want to do it?" I whispered.

"God, no," she said. "I've never been south of D.C."

"I'll do it," I announced suddenly. "I'll take his ashes home."

Neil looked at me oddly. It wouldn't affect the show, since we were already planning to be closed anyway. "Are you sure?"

"Yeah," I said. "We don't want to just FedEx him home, do we?"

"Okay, we'll talk about it afterwards," he said, still giving me a sideways look. I sat back, patted Emily's hand, and listened to more tales of Ray's awesomeness. But inside, damn my shallow soul, I was excited at the prospect of meeting people who might know the secret of the chapel of ease.

Later that afternoon I sat in Neil's office as he asked me, "Are you sure you want to do this?"

"Yes. You don't need me here, and it'll take, what, four days at the most? Fly down, drop off the urn, attend whatever funeral service they have, fly back. No problem."

"That's not what I meant. Ray told me a lot about his hometown. It didn't sound like the most progressive place." He gave me a steady, significant look.

"I'm not flaming," I said, unable to keep the defensiveness from my voice.

"No, you're not. But you don't exactly radiate butch, either."

"So you think I'll get beaten up?"

"I think that's a distinct possibility."

"I'm a black belt in muay Thai, you know."

"No," he said, surprised. "I did not know that. How did that happen?"

"Hard work and dedication." There weren't really belt ranks in muay Thai, but sometimes it was simpler to just say there were than to explain how it really did work.

"No, I mean . . . I assume you were also taking dance classes as a kid."

"Yes."

"So didn't they . . . conflict?"

"Well, I never accidentally used a flying knee on a dance partner, or did a grand plié in a sparring match, if that's what you mean."

"Why did you take . . . what did you call it?"

"Muay Thai. It's from Thailand. Well, when I came out to my family, my dad said, 'Okay, but you're gonna get picked on, and I don't want to read about it on the news. So you're going to learn to defend yourself.' And I did."

"That's a hell of a thing."

"My dad is very practical."

He looked down at his desk for a moment. "Matt, I appreciate you doing this. I really wasn't looking forward to it. But I have to ask why you want to."

That caught me off guard. "Well . . . Ray was my friend."

"Ray was my friend, too, but I'm in no hurry to run around Tennessee with his hick family."

"But you were *going* to go," I said, hoping it didn't sound like an adolescent whine.

"Sure, because I felt like it was my responsibility."

"Well, now it's not your problem."

"Don't get smug. Maybe you're the toughest fag in Manhattan, but it won't stop a bullet. And everybody down there carries a gun, remember?"

"You really think someone will try to shoot me just because I'm gay?"

"I know what Ray told me. I'd prefer not to send you in the same way, and for the same reasons, that I'd never send Jason." Jason, of course, was black.

"Well, I'm not worried. I'll get a hotel room, keep to myself, and only show up for the funeral. It's not like I'll be out barhopping."

"No," Neil said knowingly, "you'll be out chapel-searching."

I said nothing, but felt my cheeks burn.

"I'm as curious as any of you," Neil continued. "Maybe more, since I've been working with Ray on the story for so long. But whatever's buried in the chapel of ease is not worth risking your life for. Knowing it won't change the show: Ray was adamant about that."

"I know," I agreed sheepishly. Ray had stressed that enough throughout rehearsals, but none of us believed it. It was the central secret of the story, and Cassandra was right: knowing it *had* to change how we behaved and related to each other as characters.

"All right. I'll let the funeral home and Ray's family know you're coming. You'll be flying into Nashville, and either someone will pick you up, or you'll rent a car."

"The company paying for this?"

"Yes, yes, just keep your receipts and don't buy dinner and drinks for everyone. I'll call Ray's parents tonight. And remember, they've lost a child, so behave accordingly."

"What sort of person do you think I am, Neil?"

He let out a long breath. "You're right, I'm sorry. Just . . .

be careful, Matt. We need you for the show. Yes, Steve has understudied the part and could go on in your place, but Ray picked you because you brought something special to the part that he felt was essential. And he was right. I want you there when we open."

I tried not to let my reaction show, but I left feeling unaccountably buoyant. It wouldn't be a fun trip, exactly, but I knew I'd be bringing back knowledge that would no doubt improve my (apparently already pretty darn good) performance. If nothing else, my Southern accent would be note-perfect.

9

Joaquim, surprisingly, was totally against it.

"Are you crazy?" he said as we walked through Chinatown, sipping our milk tea. His had bubbles of tapioca in it; mine was free of what I called "phlegm balls."

"No," I said patiently. "It's something that needs to be done for a friend, and I'm going to do it. I'll be gone four days at the most. I have to be back for opening night, after all."

"But why you? I mean, my friend Titus died last year, his body was cremated, and his ashes were just mailed home."

"Really?" I said dubiously. "In one of those 'whatever fits' boxes?"

"I don't know, but it's the truth. Send them UPS if you don't trust the post office."

"Look, Joaquim, I *want* to go, okay? I liked Ray, and I want to be sure his family understands how talented and creative he really was."

"Then send them a video along with the ashes. I'll help you put it together. We can talk to people who knew him—"

"Look, what is wrong with you? Why does this bother you so much?"

We found a space against a wall to lean, and after a sip of his tea, he said, "I think I'm just jealous, Matt."

"Of what?"

"Of Ray. Of the way you talk about him. Did he know how you felt about him?"

"He's *dead*, Joaquim, in case you didn't notice."

"I noticed. That makes it perfect, doesn't it? He can't disappoint or reject you."

The urge to ask Joaquim to come with me was strong, and I knew that's what he was maneuvering me to do. His passive-aggressive tendencies were really starting to bug me; I hated being manipulated. But I didn't want him to come with me, for a couple of reasons. I knew I could play straight, and handle any rough trouble that came along. Joaquim, bless him, could not. He wasn't a flaming cliché or anything, but he also had never tried to hide his sexuality, and I doubted he could if he wanted to. Plus, as a Puerto Rican, he'd be going into a hotbed of racism as well as homophobia.

And . . . there was some truth in what he said. I just wanted this trip to be about Ray's memory and me. Plus if I *did* decide to track down the mystery of the chapel of ease, I didn't want Joaquim constantly trying to talk me out of it. He didn't understand my fixation on the chapel mystery. I doubted anyone not in the show *could* understand it. Hell, *I* didn't entirely understand it.

"Look," I said, hoping I sounded reasonable, "I know it seems weird. You're not an actor, so you've never experienced what it's like to bring a character to life like this. That's why I'm so attached to Ray: he treated me like one of his creations."

He looked at me. "Bullshit."

He was right, and I knew it, and he knew I knew it. I sighed and said, "Whatever, Joaquim."

"Just be careful, will you?"

"I will."

"And come back."

"I will. I have the lead in a great show, why wouldn't I?"

"And a great boyfriend."

"Oh yeah, that, too," I teased, and we kissed.

I was packing for my trip that evening when Emily called me. "Matt," she said with exaggerated calm, "I need your help with something."

"What's that?"

"Will you go to Ray's apartment with me tonight?"

"Why?"

"I need to get some of my stuff that's there. He gave me a key, don't worry."

"I'm leaving for Tennessee tomorrow, Emily. I have to pack."

"Oh, come on. It won't take an hour. Please, Matt, I don't want to go by myself."

"Can't you ask somebody else?"

"Sure, I *can,* but I'd rather it be you. You knew him, Matt. I don't have to explain things to you. Please?"

No polite way to get out of *that,* not with my promise to Ray to look after her. At least he'd been wrong about her collapsing or freaking out. If anything, she was a model of calm in a crisis. It might be an act (hell, given her profession, it probably *was* an act), but it was a good one. I told her I'd meet her at his building in an hour, which would give my laundry time to finish.

Emily was pacing outside the building, smoking and watching for me. Her eyes were red-rimmed and her face splotchy. As she hugged me, she said, "Thank you for coming, Matt. Thank you so much."

"No problem," I said into her hair. She wasn't just hugging

me out of politeness, either. She had her arms locked tight around my neck. "I can't breathe, Em."

"Oh! Sorry." She released me and laughed a little. "I spoke to a reporter about Ray this afternoon. He wanted to know if Ray was on drugs, or had HIV, or even Ebola. They weren't interested at all in what kind of person he was."

"And that surprised you?"

"I just . . . I thought when I told them . . . Ah, never mind, I'll just start crying again. Come on."

The last time I climbed these particular stairs had been the night of the y'all-come. The atmosphere couldn't have been more different, and as we approached his closed door, it was in stark contrast to that evening, when the door had been open and the sound of happy people had filled the hallway. Now it was silent—*dead* silent, I thought with cold irony.

Emily put her key in the lock, then paused. She stood very still for a long time, until I said, "Emily, we don't have to do this."

"Yes, we do," she said, and turned the key with such force, I worried it might snap.

The apartment was much smaller than it had seemed the night of the party. The long table was gone, and light came through the streaked windows with a funereal grayness. Ray had a futon for both a couch and bed, a coffee table, and a closet full of clothes. The walls were plastered with posters, an eclectic mix of music figures and musical shows. I hadn't really paid attention to them the night of the party, but most of the musicians looked to be old-timers, whose black-and-white images I didn't recognize. The shows, though, were all recent ones, many within the last ten years.

Emily gazed down at the futon. I had to nudge her aside a little to close the door behind us. I realized she was breathing heavily, and thought at first she was about to cry.

Then she walked over and put a hand on the back of the

futon. Her other hand clenched into a fist, and a shudder ran through her. I had the uncomfortable feeling that she was, in fact, turned on; as in, *really* turned on.

"Emily?" I said quietly.

"Just g-give me a minute," she said. She slowly sat down on the futon and leaned her head back, eyes closed. She put her hands flat on her thighs and slid them slowly up and down her jeans.

I felt very uncomfortable. I looked around at anything other than Emily's aroused face, until finally she let out a shuddering sigh. Then she curled up and sobbed.

I sat down on the futon beside her. "Emily, honey," I said gently. "Let's get your stuff and get out of here, okay? You don't need this, not today."

"He'll never touch me again, Matt," she said into the futon mattress. "I can't tell you what knowing that feels like. I've never been with anyone like him, and knowing it'll never happen again . . ."

Well, this was awkward. Apparently Ray, in addition to his musical skills, was quite the cocksmith, too. I grew a little irritated, which I tried very hard to keep to myself. "I understand, Em. We can talk about it later if you want, after I get back."

She crawled away, then turned to glare at me. "Talk about it? He's dead, what's there to talk about?"

"Emily—"

"He took part of me with him, Matt!" she yelled. Her voice echoed in the still, empty air. "Something I didn't even know I had! It's gone, gone with him, and I'll never feel it again!"

If she was acting, or exaggerating for effect, she was a better performer than I ever thought. I got to my feet and tried to go to her. "Emily—"

"Stay back! Don't touch me! Nobody can ever touch me again!" She ran into the bathroom and slammed the door. Her sobs were just as loud through the thin wood.

I sat down at Ray's desk. His computer, hooked up to keyboards and a drum machine, was still on, humming contentedly. I nudged the mouse, curious to see what the last thing he looked at might have been. It was the show's review from the *Post*.

No, I reminded myself. Ray never saw this. Emily had left it up for him, but less than six feet away, he'd already taken his last bow.

The bathroom door opened, and Emily emerged. She was still shaking, but seemed more in control. "I'm sorry, Matt. Maybe it just hasn't really sunk in yet."

"No worries," I said, keeping very still. It felt like one of those moments where any move could set off chaos.

"I'm fine now," she said. "I've got my stuff from the bathroom."

"Who gets the rest of this?"

"I don't know. Family, I guess, if they make arrangements. Thrift stores if they don't."

"What about his manuscripts and stuff? That could be valuable."

"He didn't do much work on paper. It's all in his laptop."

"Where is that?"

"At my place."

"Shouldn't that go to his family, too?"

"It will when I finish copying everything."

"Why are you doing that?" I said suspiciously. It wasn't out of the realm of possibility that she intended to sell the stuff later, if the show took off as we all hoped it might.

"So I can print it out and roll around on it naked," she said. Just when I thought she might be serious, she smiled a little. "Because it's too good to lose. You ever read about what happened when Stieg Larsson died? His girlfriend has his laptop locked up in a safe deposit box because she doesn't trust his family with it."

"You don't trust his family?"

"I don't know them. He hardly ever talked about them. But this way if they *do* try to lock away everything he worked on, out of some weird Southern religious thing, there will at least be one copy."

"Do you think—?" I started, then thought better of it.

"That the secret of what's buried in the chapel of ease is in there somewhere? I don't know. But if I find it, I promise I'll tell you."

"Thanks," I said. Of course, Ray had promised, too, and that hadn't worked out at all.

She went to the dresser and began removing clothes. When she finished, she also took a long look around. There was a poster of *Hedwig and the Angry Inch* next to one advertising the '50s rockabilly star Byron Harley. "Look at these pictures. Old music, new shows."

"Did he ever tell you what they had in common?"

"Sort of. He said, 'The only music I care about is the real kind.'"

"So he didn't like older musicals?"

"He thought they were fake. They were written by people who'd lived phony showbiz lives. They didn't have any mystery to them, no . . . hidden depths." She laughed. "And good God, did he hate *Wicked,* and that whole thing of rewriting old fairy tales."

"He never mentioned that to me," I said. Then again, that sounded about right. A man with so many secrets would naturally write a final show with a secret at its heart.

The front door opened, and a lean Hispanic guy poked in his head. "Hey, what are you two doing? Oh," he added when he saw Emily. "It's you. Sorry."

"Ramón is the super," Emily said. "He used to come play guitar with Ray."

"Yeah, I'm very sorry to hear he's gone," Ramón said. He

had very little accent, and wore a Slipknot concert T-shirt. "Did the paramedics mess anything up?"

"I don't think so," Emily said. "They were very conscientious."

"Hmph." He looked around. "Rent's paid up until the end of the month. So take your time about getting this stuff out."

"We will," I said quickly, before Emily could tell him just to sell it or junk it. "I'm going to see his family tomorrow. I'll let them know."

Ramón didn't meet my gaze. He was nervous, but I couldn't tell why. He said, "Tell them he was a good man. He helped me to play better. I never used to get *respeto* before he showed me what I was doing wrong."

"He loved playing with you, too, Ramón," Emily said.

Ramón nodded, then crossed himself. *"Adiós, mi hermano,"* he said. Then he left.

Emily resumed pulling clothes from the drawers. I noticed she packed a few things that were unmistakably Ray's, but I figured it was harmless. I spotted his cowboy boots in the corner, and considered taking them, but they were far too big for me.

We turned out the lights and closed the door. Emily locked the apartment, and I accompanied her home. She said nothing else the entire way.

That night I couldn't sleep, so I left Joaquim snoring contentedly and went to a Greek-owned all-night diner a few blocks away. I just ordered coffee, since I wasn't hungry for the fried rice balls that were their specialty. I put in my earbuds and listened to Ray's voice on the original demo for the show that we'd gotten that first day in rehearsal. He was also, I was pretty sure, playing all the instruments. But it was his voice I wanted to hear.

"What are you listening to?" the waitress asked as I got a refill.

"Songs from a new show I'm in. You should come see it."

"Oh, I don't care much for that sort of thing," she said. "My tastes run toward George Clinton. Know who he is?"

I shook my head. "Related to Bill and Hillary?"

That made her laugh, and I turned up the volume to drown it out. Well, she might not care about it, but I bet she'd know the name before long. I just had that sort of feeling, that the title of the show would slip into modern-day parlance, like *Rent,* or *Cats,* or *Oliver!* Then again, those were all one-word titles, so maybe we should cut ours down to *Chapel.* I'd have to run that past Neil when I got back.

But that was all for later. My mind was already in the air and heading south.

10

The flight to Nashville went through Atlanta, which according to my understanding of geography was quite a bit out of the way. Since it was on the show's nickel, I insisted on flying first class, and the flight crew was incredibly kind. The box with the urn inside (prominently featuring the funeral home's logo) probably helped.

When I landed in Nashville and emerged into the baggage claim area, I was surprised to see my name on an iPad, held by a slender young woman with the same black hair as Ray. She smiled when I waved, and said, "Hi, I'm Bliss."

I offered my hand. "Contentment. Nice to meet you."

She laughed. "I assume you're Matt. I'm your ride to Needsville. Bliss Overbay." Then she noticed the box, and her face grew more serious. "And that must be Rayford."

"That's Ray, yeah." I felt the need to assert the name I knew him by over his hick name. I held the box tighter to discourage her from snatching it and running off, which of course, I had no indication that she'd do. On the whole flight down, though, I'd concocted various scenarios, including one in which I never made it out of the airport. Ray was stolen away and I was left shouting for help as a bunch of people in overalls jumped in their waiting flatbed truck and drove merrily away, to the accompaniment of the *Beverly Hillbillies* theme.

"It's a real shame, bless his heart," she said.

"Did you know him well?"

"Grew up with him. We were in the same grade at school. He was something."

"He was that."

"What about you? Did you know him long?"

"We were doing a show together. It's a high-pressure environment. You get to know people pretty well, pretty fast."

She nodded. "Can I help you with your bags?"

I indicated my backpack. "Got everything in here."

"Okay, then. It's about three hours to Needsville, so let's get started."

I followed her into the parking garage. I expected a battered old pickup, or maybe a sedan with rusted wheel wells, so you can imagine my surprise when she stopped at an ambulance marked CLOUD COUNTY FIRE DEPARTMENT. "I'm an EMT," she explained, "and technically this counts as transporting a body, so they let me use it."

I'd never ridden in an ambulance as a patient, let alone as a passenger. I thought of the box under my arm, and how ironic it was that Ray was getting his second ride in less than week, and neither of them did him a bit of good.

As I climbed up into the high seat, I flashed back on an ancient Springsteen song in which he urges a suicidal girl to "climb into my ambulance." I couldn't remember if the girl died at the end or not.

Bliss didn't run the lights or siren as we negotiated the airport traffic and emerged onto the congested interstate. After a while the other cars thinned out and we were able to get up to speed. We spoke of the weather, which was actually not so hot and humid as Manhattan had been, and I told her a little about the show. She was politely interested, but I sensed she held something back; whether information or her own opinion, I couldn't tell.

I texted Joaquim that I was safely on the ground. I wanted to take a selfie to show him how I was being chauffeured, but it seemed rude.

Eventually we left the interstate for a smooth two-lane rural highway, and the scenery grew rounder and more lush, with the heavy green of summer quickly blocking out most signs of civilization. I saw what I assumed were deer standing in an open field. There were homes, and power lines, and lots of churches, but you got the sense that once you left the four-lane, there might be nothing.

"Ever been down South before?" she asked.

"Been to Florida a few times," I said. "Worked in Orlando for a summer. They had cockroaches the size of this ambulance."

"Palmetto bugs," she said. "We don't get them this far north, thankfully. Or fire ants."

"What do you have?"

"Rattlesnakes. Coyotes. Oh, and feral emus."

"Excuse me?"

She laughed. "Do you know what an emu is?"

"It's like an ostrich, right?"

"Right. Well, we had a farmer let a bunch of 'em go, and they've settled in. They're breeding, and doing quite nicely for themselves."

"Are they dangerous?"

"They can be. But they're so skittish, they usually run off before you even catch a glimpse of them."

I looked out at the passing woods, glancing between the

trees for a birdlike shape. But then my attention was drawn to the trees themselves, and from them to the mountains that supported them. I was used to things towering over me, but those were man-made, geometrically regular shapes. Here everything was random, and instead of being strictly vertical, they rolled into the sky, the curves making them seem organic and connected in a way buildings never would be.

It was beautiful, for sure, but there was still an undercurrent of something that wasn't benign. I couldn't quite think of a name for it; "danger" was too blatant, but "caution" didn't capture the urgency. It was like walking home at 2 A.M. with your boyfriend and seeing a lone person approach down an empty street. You should be safe, you outnumbered him and you weren't doing anything wrong, but you could never entirely be sure until he was out of your sight. And the mountains were never out of sight here.

With a start, I realized Ray had written about this very sort of moment, and had captured the emotions I was feeling with his usual vividness. In one of Jennifer's songs, as she contemplated what it would be like to leave, she sang:

> When I was a baby I lay on the bed
> And my mother's hips rose before me
> The mountains are my mother now
> And I can feel the way she adores me
> But like my mama, these mountains can rage
> They can roar and bellow and shake the sky
> I can only cower before her fury and hope she remembers
> How fragile I am. . . .

Bliss turned on the radio to a country station, which wiped Ray's song right out of my head. I knew virtually nothing about modern country music, so the song went right over my head. But Bliss sang along, just loud enough that I could tell she had an achingly pure voice that must leave a lake of tears behind it when she sang something sad. But this particular tune, about the troubles of being a girl in a country song, was jaunty and humorous.

When it ended, Bliss looked at me with a shy smile and said, "Sorry. I tend to sing along. Hope you don't mind."

"Not at all."

"Are you hungry?"

"Actually, I am. I only had pretzels on the plane."

"Do you like waffles?"

"Waffles?"

"Yeah, there's a Waffle House just up here. We can stop if you'd like."

"That'd be great."

The distinctive yellow and black sign rose out of the trees as we neared. Several semis too big for the parking lot idled along the highway. I carefully left Ray's ashes on the floorboard and followed Bliss past old pickups and sedans into the restaurant.

A few people waved at her, all of them with the same jet-black hair. The rest looked quickly away, as if afraid she might notice *them*. I recalled some of the stuff I'd read about the Tufa. Were they afraid of her? Or of the other Tufa in their midst? Should *I* be scared?

We got a seat in a booth and ordered coffee. As I looked over the menu, she said, "So tell me more about Ray's show. What will happen to it?"

"Well, we open next week. We pushed it back out of respect for Ray."

She looked surprised. "I figured with him gone and everything . . ."

"No, the show must go on, as they say." I sensed that this either annoyed or disappointed her. "Why?"

She looked out the window at the trees, which waved in the

summer wind. "I guess it's better that you know, since you'll be around them, but . . . Rayford's family wasn't too keen on him putting his songs out there this way."

"Why not? He was successful. He was about to be *really* successful, if the reviews were any indication."

"It's not about that. To a Tufa, music is . . . well, sacred."

I'd read that, too, but hearing it from an actual person made it sound stranger somehow, like a convert talking about her religion. "We certainly take it seriously," I said, hoping I didn't sound defensive.

"That's not what I mean. Rayford was gifted, even for one of us." She seemed to read my thoughts, because she smiled and said, "I must sound like a crazy person. What I mean is, most of the Tufa are musical. We start learning when we're babies how to sing and play. But only a few of us have the gift of creating great music out of whole cloth. Rayford was one of them."

"And you don't approve of how he used that gift?"

"It's not me. It's . . ."

"His family?"

"Partly. They never approved of him running off to New York."

"Why?" I pressed.

Bliss looked out at the trees again. I could practically see the truth straining to get past her reserve. "Because he was drawing too much attention to himself."

"Too much attention?"

"Had you ever heard of the Tufa before you met Rayford?"

"No."

"Exactly. And a lot of us want to keep it that way. We like being forgotten, and it's getting harder and harder to do."

"Is that why you sent somebody to New York to talk to him?"

"I beg your pardon?"

"A woman came to the press preview and spoke to him. She said some of the same things to him. She had black hair like you, and him. And the same Southern accent."

"I don't know anything about that."

"Maybe your tribal elders did it without telling you."

That made her smile again. "Our what? We're not Native Americans, Matt. We don't have 'elders' who tell us what to do. I don't know who went to see Rayford, or why."

The conversation was getting stranger, as every effort to put the Tufa into a context I could understand failed miserably. "Bliss, I don't mean to be rude, but what exactly *are* the Tufa? I've read some crazy stuff online, and Ray told me a bit, but if you wouldn't mind, please give me the party line on it."

For just an instant she looked afraid, as if being questioned so directly panicked her. I wondered what role she held in the Tufa community; had I inadvertently offended their chief or high priestess? Then it vanished and she was back to being lightly amused.

"The Tufa," she began slowly, "are just a group of families who have always been together, and always will. We don't wish harm on anyone, and we don't steal children or souls, despite what people whisper to their kids to make them behave. We've all heard the same stories you have, the ones that end up on the Internet or the History Channel between Bigfoot and ancient aliens. None of them are true."

I realized she'd denied more than she'd confirmed, and had offered no new information. Smooth. So instead I asked, "Do you know what Ray's play was about?"

"No."

"A chapel of ease somewhere in Cloud County. With a mystery about what's buried in it."

"Ah."

" 'Ah' means . . . ?"

"Well, like I said, we don't generally share our stories with outsiders."

"Why?"

Again she looked panicked, but by God, if these people were going to be all mysterious and wonky about stuff, they really needed better stories to fall back on. "Would you want a bunch of people who'd seen a play or a movie to come traipsing around your backyard, digging up places just to see what's there?"

That was exactly what the black-haired girl had said to Ray. "I suppose not."

"Well, neither would we. The chapel's been left alone for a hundred years; we'd like it to stay that way."

"So you know where it is?" I asked, trying to keep the excitement from my voice.

"No, I've never seen it. But I've heard of it all my life. It's just a bunch of rocks now, barely anything left. Wouldn't take much to tear it down for good."

For someone who's never seen it, I thought, *you sure know a lot about it.* "Is there a graveyard beside it?"

"Is that what Rayford said?"

"It's what he put in his play."

"I don't know. Like I said, I've never been there."

"So you don't know if the story of Byrda and Shad is true?"

Our food arrived before she could answer, delivered by a waitress with the unlikely name of Alsie, and it turned out I was hungrier than I thought. As I devoured my waffles, I realized Bliss wasn't eating. Instead, very softly, she hummed, a tune I almost recognized but couldn't quite catch. It reminded me of Ray's songs from the play, and I wondered if he'd borrowed them from folk melodies all his people would know.

"What's that song?" I asked between bites.

"What song?"

"The one you were humming."

"Was I humming? I'm sorry, that was rude."

Once again she'd answered without answering. I began to resent the woman, and vowed to be more direct with any other Tufa I met.

11

We drove some more after that, and the heavy, gentle motion of the ambulance as we went up and down hills and around curves started to lull me to sleep. I held Ray's ashes safely between my feet and tried to concentrate on the scenery, but it had become monolithic: trees, with trees behind them, and great rounded mountains of trees looming over them. The radio continued to play contemporary country music, and the sheer sameness of it would've been maddening if I'd been fully awake.

"Matt," Bliss said gently. "Are you asleep?"

"No, just dozing off a little," I said, and forced myself fully upright.

"We're almost to Needsville. Ray's folks live about a half hour past that, out in the country."

"Is there any kind of hotel or motel nearby?" I hadn't made reservations; I just figured I'd stay at the cheapest place around.

"There used to be, but it closed down last year. The owner's husband died, and she didn't want to keep it up anymore."

That wasn't good news. "So where can I stay?"

"With Ray's people. They're expecting you."

With Ray's people, a half hour away from town, even. "I don't suppose there's a car rental place on the way, is there?"

"No, I'm afraid not. Needsville is pretty small."

"So how do I get back to the airport?"

"Somebody'll take you," she said diffidently.

At last we topped a particularly steep little hill and passed a sign that said, WELCOME TO CLOUD COUNTY. A few minutes later we entered Needsville itself.

"How many people live here?" I said as I looked around. The post office was new, and the convenience store, and the bank looked relatively recent, but the rest of the abandoned and shuttered buildings looked like they might've last been used in the '80s. The town looked like one of those bushes that's dead except for a few tiny sprigs of green here and there.

"About three hundred," Bliss said. "But not many live in town. Most have farms or houses out in the country."

I looked at the circle of hills that surrounded the town, and the mountains beyond. The sense of isolation hit me anew, and impulsively I pulled out my phone. I got no signal.

"Yeah, sorry," she said when she saw what I was doing. "We had a cell phone tower in town once, but something happened to it, and they haven't replaced it."

"So I'm cut off from all civilization?" I said, trying to sound light and not admit my apprehension.

"We're civilized, Matt. We may be isolated, but we're not backwards. You can get a signal a bit further on."

She didn't say it harshly, but I realized I was accepting the cliché idea of Southern rural life. "Sorry. Didn't mean any insult."

We went through town and turned onto a road bumpy with fresh repairs to its asphalt, and followed it until we reached a small fire station. Bliss parked the ambulance and said, "We have to change cars here. I don't want to take the ambulance down Geeter Road."

"What if somebody gets sick on Geeter Road?"

"Their bill comes with a charge for new ambulance shocks and tire alignment."

We got out and drove on in her pickup. The lighter vehicle meant more bouncing, and I held Ray's ashes tight in my hands. We turned onto a gravel road and, after another fifteen minutes, pulled into the driveway of a small farmhouse. A car and two trucks were parked beside it, and I heard dogs barking from inside after Bliss turned off the engine.

"Those dogs sound big," I said.

"Don't worry. Like I said, they know you're coming."

We got out. I left Ray's box on the seat; I wasn't sure of the etiquette of this situation, but I didn't want to just show up and hand them over like a UPS driver. That was the whole thing we were trying to avoid, after all.

The screen door opened, and two big dogs of indeterminate breed rushed out, practically knocking each other down in their haste to reach me. When they did, they jumped up and licked my hands. Their paws were big and broad, and I felt their nails through my jeans.

"Get off'n him!" a man ordered, and the dogs did, but continued to mill around my feet, thick tails wagging. "Sorry about that, they get all wrought up when they meet somebody new."

The man was about fifty, with white touches at the sides of his otherwise black hair, and his resemblance to Ray was undeniable. He strode out and seriously shook my hand. "Reckon you must be Matt. That fella Neil said you'd be coming."

"I am," I said.

"My name's Gerald. Pleasure to meet you."

"Likewise."

The door opened again, and an older woman emerged onto

the porch. She wore denim cut-offs and an orange T-shirt that said VOLS, which I assumed was a local sports team. "Is this Rayford's friend?" she called.

"It sure is," Gerald said. "Matt, this is Ladonna, Rayford's mother."

She came down and graciously shook my hand as well. "I want to thank you for bringing Rayford home."

"It was the least I could do," I said. "He was a good friend."

A third person came out. He was bigger, with broad shoulders and a narrow waist, and his black hair was tangled with sweat. He looked at me, and I felt a jolt all the way down to my toes. Things suddenly got a whole lot more interesting.

"Who's this?" he said, and his voice was just as deep and full as you'd expect from a rural Adonis.

"Rayford's friend from New York City," Ladonna said.

The man stepped off the porch and sauntered over. "Hi. Cyrus Crow. Folks call me C.C."

"Matt Johansson," I said. His grip was firm, and the muscles on his forearm flexed when we shook. He was, without a doubt, the best-looking guy I'd ever been this close to, and given some of the dancers and actors I'd met, that was saying something. This was a complication I had not foreseen, and would have to do my best to shake off.

"Rayford and I grew up together," C.C. said. "We've been friends since we were knee high to a polecat. It was a real shock to hear about him."

"It was a shock to all of us, too," I agreed.

"Bliss, thanks for hauling him all the way from Nashville," Ladonna said. "Bliss and Rayford used to date, did you know that?"

I could tell by the look on Bliss's face that Ladonna was mischaracterizing the relationship. "No," I said, "we didn't really talk about that."

"It was a while ago," Ladonna said. "I reckon we should get

the formalities over with here. Matt, would you bring us our son?"

I took the box of ashes carefully from the truck and handed it to Gerald. He solemnly took it, bowed his head over it, and instead of praying as I expected, he hummed, similar to the way Bliss had done at the Waffle House. Ladonna put her hand on the box's top and joined him in a kind of soft, harmonized keening. He took the ashes inside.

"That's just our way," C.C. said when he noticed my puzzlement. "Music's a big deal around here."

"So I hear," I agreed.

Bliss handed me my backpack. "Pleasure meeting you, Matt."

I realized I was about to be left alone at a house where I knew no one, and with a dangerously attractive—and probably dangerously straight—man right under my nose. I tried desperately to think of some way to convince Bliss to stay, as she was, at the moment, my only lifeline back to my world.

As if reading my mind, C.C. said, "Why don't you stay for dinner, Bliss?"

"Ain't having dinner," Ladonna said. "We'll eat at the wake."

"And I'll be there," she said.

"Are you sure you can't stick around for a little while?" I said, and tried not to sound desperate.

She smiled, and it was one of those Cheshire–*Mona Lisa* smiles filled with amusement and hidden knowledge. "There's nothing to worry about, Matt. Gerald and Ladonna will take good care of you."

I leaned very close and said softly, "Like the family in *Texas Chainsaw*?"

She laughed and said with equal quiet, "No, like good people with a guest. Don't worry, you're perfectly safe here."

I had no real choice, so I watched her drive off, trying not to panic as my only contact with the outside world disappeared.

I felt the presence before I heard the words, and turned to find C.C. right behind me. This close, he was even more handsome, and the sweat only emphasized his overwhelming, and probably straight, masculinity. I looked up at him, because he was a good four inches taller than me, and the sun backlit his black, wavy hair. He said, "I know what the stories say, but these are nice, good people, and they're very glad to meet one of Rayford's friends from the city. Ever since he left, they haven't heard much about him."

"I'm just not used to this . . . lifestyle," I said weakly.

"What, rural family life?" he said with a laugh.

That made me smile. "Yeah."

"It's just like urban family life, except with less traffic and much lower to the ground."

Oh, great—he was funny, too. I was doomed. "I suppose you're right."

"C.C., why don't you show Matt where he can unpack?" Ladonna said.

I followed him into the house, wondering how many times Ray had walked these same steps. The dogs flanked me, still sniffing at my city odors. "These dogs have names?" I asked.

"The big yellow one is Ace," C.C. said, pronouncing the color as *yeller*. "The blue heeler mix is Tom."

"Ace and Tom," I repeated, and the dogs happily lolled their tongues at me.

Inside the house was a schizophrenic mix of old-fashioned rural life and unmistakable modernity. The fireplace was big and worn, but the flat-screen TV mounted to the wall was practically new. Old work boots sat beside the door along with a pair of recently bought tennis shoes. A rack held three long guns, while a mounted deer head and two fish looked down on us with glassy disdain. On an end table beside the couch rested a black rotary phone, the kind I'd only seen used as props in period plays.

"You can put Rayford on the mantel, Gerald," his mother said.

Gerald opened the box and took out the pearl gray urn. He placed it on the brick shelf, stepped back, and crossed his arms. Neither he nor Ladonna expressed any emotion, but just looked at it with the same blasé evaluation they might show a vase of flowers.

"A little to the left," Ladonna said at last. Gerald did as she asked. Then she turned to me and said, "Matt, bring your bag after me."

I followed her into a back bedroom. It was as small as anything you'd find in New York, and the corners were stacked with boxes and small bits of machinery I didn't recognize.

"This used to be Rayford's room," she said sadly as she looked around. "We were using it as a storeroom, so you'll pardon the mess."

"It's fine, Mrs. Parrish," I said, and dropped my bag on the bed. "Thank you for putting me up. I had every intention of staying in a hotel, but there wasn't one nearby."

"No, the Catamount Corner closed up last year. Shame, too, but I understand why. Ms. Peggy, the owner, lost her husband, and I'm sure the place had too many memories for her."

"Bliss mentioned there would be a wake tonight?"

"Yes, over at the barn dance. You're welcome to come."

"I'd like to. I'd enjoy meeting some of Ray's friends." I just couldn't bring myself to call him "Rayford," the way everyone here did. "Do I need to dress up?"

"Lord A'mighty, son, no. It's nothing formal."

"Well, I brought a suit for the church service."

She looked at me through narrowed eyes, as if I'd suddenly revealed myself to be some sort of spy. Before she could speak, her husband joined us and said, "You're probably pretty tired after your flight. Bathroom's right down the hall on the left. Feel free to freshen up, or take a nap if you want."

I remembered what Ray had said about churches in Cloud County, and wondered if I'd committed some major faux pas. Everything I knew about the South centered around God and guns, and that included hating people like me just for existing. Still, they didn't seem to be aware of my sexuality, and I certainly wasn't going to mention it.

Of course, if C.C. was around much more, I might not be able to hide it.

12

At 5 P.M., there was a soft knock at my door. I'd fallen asleep, and before I could get up, the door opened and a beautiful young woman poked her head in. Black hair peeked out from beneath a baseball cap and framed her small, delicate face. "Hello? You awake?"

"Yeah," I said as I swung my feet over the side of the bed. "Come in."

She was perhaps twenty, with a terrific figure and a coquettish air. She wore overalls and a cropped T-shirt, and in a lot of ways fit the stereotype of the hot hillbilly chick perpetuated by *The Dukes of Hazzard* and *True Blood*. I guessed that she was the sister Ray had mentioned. "Get some sleep?" she asked.

"Yeah. Too much, maybe. Is it time to go?"

"Pretty soon. I wanted to talk to you first. I'm Thorn."

"Matt."

"Short for Matthew?"

"Yeah."

"Mine's short for Thornblossom."

"Really? Why don't they call you Blossom, then?"

She grinned, and the resemblance to Ray was unmistakable. "I suspect after you get to know me, you'll understand."

"You can't be that bad."

"Maybe I'm that *good*?"

Oops. I'd inadvertently been flirting with a straight girl. That happened sometimes, when I was in situations where it wasn't generally known that I was gay. I said quickly, "Well, I need to freshen up a little before we go to the wake. Your parents said it was in a barn?"

"Yeah. It's where we all meet to sing and play. Ray used to love going there. He'd play until doomsday if nobody stopped him."

"Well, I'm looking forward to it." I waited, but she showed no signs of leaving. "If you'll excuse me?" I prompted.

"You don't have to be shy around me," she said.

Oh boy. As softly as I could without actually whispering, I said, "Uhm . . . look, Thorn, I need to tell you something. I'm gay."

Thorn looked skeptical, then surprised, then disappointed. "Really?"

"Really."

"So you and Rayford were . . . ?"

"Ray? No! He wasn't gay. In fact, he dated one of my best friends. A woman friend."

"People around here always figured he was secretly gay."

"Why?"

" 'Cause he liked those musicals. And he always talked about the theater." She pronounced it *THEE-ate-her.* "We all just figured when he got to New York, he stopped pretending."

"No pretending. He was straight."

"Mama and Daddy'll be glad to hear that."

"But I'm not."

"You're not glad he was straight?"

"No, I mean *I'm* not straight." Although she was more right than she knew.

"You got a boyfriend back home?"

"Yes."

"You ever been with a girl?"

"Thorn, I don't think we should pursue this. If you'll excuse me, I'll get ready for the service. Thanks for waking me up."

She nodded, as if still mulling over my presumed gender preferences. Then she left without another word. I wasn't sure what to make of that, except the obvious: I was a fairly good-looking male from the big city, and she was a small-town girl with an itch the local boys could never scratch.

Of course, she hadn't volunteered anything about Cyrus, such as, "Oh, you mean gay like C.C.?" That would've been too easy, I suppose.

I put that out of my mind, changed into some nicer casual clothes, and went into the living room. Gerald stood looking out the front window and turned when he heard me enter.

"All ready?" he said.

"I am." I looked around. "Is, uhm, C.C. around?"

"He'll meet us there." After a moment, Gerald added, "You play anything?"

"I'm sorry?"

"Instrument."

"Oh. A little piano."

"Do you sing?"

"Yes, sir. That's part of my job."

"Well, you might get asked to sing tonight, if that's okay. Seein' as you knew Rayford and all."

"That's fine. I'm glad to do it."

He nodded, almost identical to the way his daughter had, as if this didn't answer things so much as cause him to think even harder. He resumed looking out the window. "Rayford was always writing songs," he said distantly. "Little story songs, not just tunes. They always talked about things that happened."

"He got very good at it, too."

"That's why he left. He said nobody here understood what he was doing."

"Was he right?"

"I sure never did. He wanted to do what he wanted, and that was that. He was always gettin' DVDs of musicals from Netflix, then he'd watch 'em and do nothing but bitch about 'em. Said they just gave up on trying to show the real world, or how people really are." He tapped the windowsill with his fingertips. "Then he started writing his own musicals."

"Was that a bad thing?"

"No. But he sure didn't make things easy for himself. He still kept writing about things that really happened around here. Some people don't like that, especially when it happened to them."

I didn't know what to say to that. Through the open door to the kitchen, I saw several dishes covered with aluminum foil waiting on the table, I assumed to be taken to the wake. I got a rush of nervousness, and pulled out my phone to check the signal. There was one tiny bar.

While I had it, I quickly texted Joaquim, *Getting ready for the wake. Ray's family has been very nice to me.* It took a couple of moments, but at last I got the *whoosh* sound that said it had been sent.

"All ready?" Ladonna said as she entered. She was dressed in jeans and a blouse with appliqué musical notes on it. Her hair, black with bits of gray, was pulled back and up into a bun.

"Yes, ma'am," I said. "Can I help you with anything?"

"You're way too polite to be a Yankee," she said. "You can take a couple of these dishes with you out to the car. Gerald, you about ready to go?"

"Pretty set," he agreed. "Thorn!"

"I'm coming," she called, and then entered in a sundress and cowboy boots that even made me do a double take. She saw it, too, and grinned knowingly.

Gerald said, "Well, let's get going. Thorn, help Matt carry some of that stuff out to the car."

Thorn did not look at me as we picked up the dishes and went to the car. I sat in the back with her, the dishes stacked between us on the old bench seat, and we headed out into the dusk. I tried to keep track of the turns and directions, but quickly realized it was hopeless.

I checked my phone, but Joaquim had not texted back, or at least it hadn't gotten through; once again I got no service at all.

It was, as they said, a barn dance, and it took place in a literal barn. It was at the end of a gravel road, and through the trees I caught glimpses of enormous letters on its roof. When we got close enough, I saw that it urged people to SEE ROCK CITY.

"What's 'Rock City'?" I asked.

"It's a place down in Chattanooga," Gerald said. "Up on a mountain. They say you can see seven states from there."

"Is that close to here?"

"Nope. But somebody a long time ago had the bright idea of buying up roof space on barns all over the place to advertise it."

"You ever been there?"

"Naw. I got no need to see Alabama, and I've seen enough of the rest of 'em to do me for a while."

We parked beside the barn, in a space I realized must have been left empty for us. There were a lot of vehicles already along the road, most of them older, and you never saw so many pickups in one place in New York. People clustered outside the barn, talking in little knots, and as we approached, they offered condolences to Ladonna, Gerald, and Thorn.

At the barn entrance sat an older man with a small wooden box on his lap. He wore a suit with an old-fashioned string tie, like a preacher in a Western movie, and looked sad and tired. But he managed a smile when he saw my hosts.

"Howdy there, Parrishes," he said with forced joviality. "You got quite a crowd inside already. Mmm-*mm,* and smell that food. That your famous stuffing under there, Ladonna?"

"It is, Uncle Node," she said.

I looked at the box he held, for all the world like a cashbox you might see at a place that charged admission. But I'd never heard of paying to get into a wake, although I'm sure someone like the Kardashians would try it someday.

Then the man they called Uncle Node saw me, and his eyes narrowed a little. I put on my best smile. He said, "And who's this gentleman?"

"This is Matt, a friend of Rayford's from New York City."

He continued to scrutinize me. "You really from New York?"

"I am."

"Ain't that something. Don't know that I've ever met anybody from New York City."

"Well, you can't say that anymore, can you?"

He grinned. "Reckon not."

He opened the wooden box he held, and inside I saw, not money, but rocks, of all shapes and sizes. Gerald carefully placed four more in the box, and Uncle Node closed it with a snap and a smile. "Well, you best get on inside before people stampede over me to get to that stuffing. And I'm very sorry for y'all's loss, Gerald."

"Thank you, Uncle Node," Gerald said, and led the way inside.

The barn itself was packed with people, and I was surprised to see that it was arranged as if for a concert: there was a small stage area at one end, an open space for dancing, and then bleacher-style seats made out of hay bales covered with thick blankets. It didn't smell like I'd always imagined a barn would smell, either; the odor of food, laid out on one long table, overwhelmed everything else.

We put down our dishes, then turned to look over the room. Gerald leaned close and said, "Some of these folks are likely to be a little wrought up."

"I don't know what that means."

Just then a large round woman dressed all in black came through the crowd wailing and threw her arms around Ladonna. "Oh Lordy, I'm so sorry! I'm so, *so* sorry for your loss! I'm *so sorry*!"

"It means that," Gerald said.

"Ah," I said. There was a similar moment in *Chapel of Ease*, in the wedding scene, and we'd all laughed about how overblown and exaggerated it was. I couldn't wait to tell everyone that it was, in fact, totally realistic.

I scanned the crowd, all black hair and bright, perfect teeth, wondering how true the stories of hillbilly inbreeding really were, and trying not to think about *Deliverance*. My own family had been so proper and withdrawn, we barely raised our voices even when we were furious; since they also never made me feel weird or wrong about coming out, I really had nothing to complain about. But I was totally unprepared for this great crowd of mourners, all of whom seemed to know Ray, or "Rayford," better than I did.

"Y'all remember that time Rayford and that Jennings girl . . . ?"

"I tell you, that Rayford sure could play the piano. . . ."

"He was on the cable news, even. They mentioned his name, sure enough. . . ."

I turned, and Thorn was right beside me. She said, "He ain't here yet."

"Who?"

"C.C. I can tell you're looking for him."

I hadn't been, but I felt myself blush anyway. I felt extremely vulnerable in a crowd of people who might not approve of my lifestyle, or existence. I said quietly, "Thorn, if you—"

"Oh, calm down, I'm not going to out you. But it would take a blind man with a sack over his head not to notice how you looked at Cyrus back at the house."

I desperately wanted to ask about him, but I could think of no graceful way to do it. And she *knew* that, because she smiled and winked at me, then twirled off into the crowd.

This is about Ray, I told myself again, and pushed thoughts of C.C. to the back of my mind. I looked around to find Ladonna and Gerald still surrounded by sympathetic mourners. Ladonna motioned me over, and I was quickly introduced to a dozen people whose names escaped me the moment I heard them. I was familiar with that from too many cast parties, and hoped that, like those other soirees, I'd never have reason to regret not remembering these names.

Then a voice came over a loudspeaker. I looked up, startled, and saw that the whole place was wired for sound, with speakers nestled in the rafters. The voice said, "If I could have y'all's attention for a moment?"

A serious-looking man stood onstage before a lone microphone. He held his wide-brimmed black hat against his chest. I wondered if he might be the local minister. He said, "Thank all of you for coming out today to honor Rayford's memory. It's a sad time when anyone dies, but especially a young man with so much promise."

A general mutter of assent rose from the crowd.

"And now Miss Mandalay Harris would like to say a few words to you."

He stepped aside, and a girl took his place.

I mean *literally* a girl. She was no more than thirteen or so, with big eyes and long black hair pulled back from her surprisingly severe face. She had to lower the microphone stand so she could speak into it. I wondered who she was: she was far too young to be an old girlfriend, and I'd met his only sister.

"Hello. As Mr. Hathcock said, thank you all for coming out this evening. We're here to celebrate a life, not mourn its passing; Rayford is with the night winds now, and he sure doesn't need our tears. Let's get the music started, what do you say?"

A half-dozen men and women came onstage. Most wore black, as befitting the occasion, or at least sported black armbands. All carried some sort of musical instrument that, six months ago, I might not have recognized. But thanks to my time in the play, I knew the hammered dulcimer and washboard, as well as the more traditional banjo, guitar, and upright bass.

The band whispered among themselves, then exploded—that's the only right word—into sound, a perfectly timed and tuned burst of music that almost knocked me back a step, not with volume but with intensity.

I didn't know the song, but its appropriateness was obvious right off:

> Oh, they tell me of a home far beyond the skies,
> Oh, they tell me of a home far away;
> Oh, they tell me of a home where no storm clouds rise,
> Oh, they tell me of an unclouded day.

The words may have been tinged with sadness, but the music was anything but. People around me started clapping along, and I did, too. Then a group of people, mostly older, moved into the open area and began dancing in a flatfooting style that reminded me of our show's choreography. Ray had definitely made certain we re-created his home, all right.

> *Oh, the land of cloudless day,*
> *Oh, the land of an unclouded day,*
> *Oh, they tell me of a home where no storm clouds rise,*
> *Oh, they tell me of an unclouded day.*

Everyone around me sang along. There was something truly joyous in this communal chorus, something very different from singing along with professionals in a show. These people sang for the fun and joy of it, to mark the passage of their lives. During rehearsals, Ray had said, "For some folks, music is the only way to speak about things that won't go into words," and now I sensed he was right.

I didn't know the song, but I was ready for the chorus when it came back around; one skill I did have was picking up a tune quickly. And there was something so warm and open about singing this song with these people, a feeling completely different from what I got singing onstage. I sang because it was my job; whether rehearsing or performing, it was what I did for a living. These people sang for their lives.

When the band finished, the crowd whooped its approval. Suddenly I imagined Ray in this room, standing exactly where I was, clapping along and cheering whatever musician or band was performing. For a moment I truly thought I might see him if I turned around.

The band performed another pair of tunes, traditional-sounding but unrecognizable to me. They had the air of religion, and I wondered if they were, in fact, hymns that had been secularized.

Then Thorn appeared onstage, twirling in her sundress, and stepped up to the microphone. Someone wolf-whistled in approval. I'd never heard *that* at a funeral before.

"We got a surprise for y'all," she said. "One of Ray's friends from New York City is here. He knows the last songs Ray wrote, and I bet if we ask nice, he'll come up here and sing a couple. What do you say, Matt?"

I was too startled to respond at first. I wasn't worried about singing, but even though Thorn had warned me, I hadn't expected to be asked to take part in the wake. But everyone applauded, and the people near me gently urged me forward.

Well, who was I to turn down a cheering crowd, even at a funeral? I strode to the front and stepped onto the stage, then went to the microphone. "Thanks," I said. "Yes, I've been working with Ray on his latest play, *Chapel of Ease,* which will open Off-Broadway in a week. We had our press preview, and the reviews were all raves. So I'm actually very happy to share this with you."

I paused, letting myself settle into character, or at least as much as I needed to to sing the song. "I'm going to sing my first big number, the one that opens the show. I hope you enjoy it."

I took a breath, closed my eyes to get where I needed to be mentally, then began to sing.

> *Deep in the woods*
> *There's some old stone walls*
> *With no frame, no roof, no floor.*
> *Yet buried inside*
> *The old chapel of ease*
> *Is a truth folks would kill and die for.*

I wasn't watching the crowd at first; my usual trick was staring into the middle distance over their heads, so that their reactions wouldn't throw me out of character. I also usually had stage lights in my eyes. I sang as simply as I could, the way my character Crawford did, although obviously I wasn't also acting the part.

But then something amazing happened. As I began the second verse, a long, low fiddle part accompanied me. I glanced over and saw the fiddler from the earlier band, an older woman with short black hair, watching me closely, as if my body language somehow helped her play. Instantly I felt self-conscious, something I hardly ever did onstage, and had to wrench my focus back to the song.

As I continued, the fiddle was joined first by the upright bass, and then by the guitar and banjo. Before I reached the second chorus, the whole band was with me, and they were spot-on. If our pit band had been this good, the critics' heads would've exploded.

At the bridge, I turned to the band and said, "You take it for a while." They smiled, nodded, and went off on solos, first the fiddler and then the banjo picker. The fiddler nodded that it was time for me to come back in, so I began the third verse.

> Shad was a man
> with a furrowed brow
> He thought long and he thought deep.
> He loved little Byrda
> like the dew loves grass
> And her heart was tender and sweet.

I sang with a drawl now, something I'd failed miserably at in rehearsal. Neil had even said, "Your speaking accent is fine, but your singing accent sounds like you ate Andy Griffith and he's stuck in your throat." But here, I managed it without even trying.

And on the reprise of the first chorus, not only did the band play along, but the crowd sang as well. I found myself leading a choir of a hundred . . . or maybe more? It was hard to tell; the inside of the barn seemed larger than it had been before, and the crowd seemed ridiculously huge.

The song ended, and I applauded along with everyone else, because this wasn't a performance; it was a communal event. I'd only led the ceremony.

I glanced over at Thorn, who jumped up and down in excitement and approval. I guess she wasn't trying to humiliate me after all. But how could she have known it would go over like this?

I stepped offstage and accepted congratulations from dozens of black-haired strangers. I looked around for Ladonna and Gerald, but didn't see them. Uncertain of where to go—surely they hadn't just abandoned me here—I found a spot on the wall and waited.

"Excuse me," said an older man I didn't know. "Have you got a moment?"

"Sure."

"I know this might be bad manners at a wake, but my name's Don Swayback, and I work for the *Daily Horn,* the newspaper over in Unicorn that covers Cloud County. I understand you were friends with Ray Parrish."

"We worked together, and I'd like to think we were friends, yeah."

"You brought his body back home?"

"His ashes."

"Ah. Well, I wondered if I could talk to you on the record about Ray. Not too many people from this area make it to Broadway."

"Technically he only made it to Off-Broadway."

"Well, it's still a long way from Needsville. How long are you in town for?"

"Three more days."

"Do you think you could work me in? The Tufa get a bad

rap for being backwards and weird, so this would be a nice balance for that."

"I guess. I'm staying with Ray's parents. Do you know them?"

"I know his sister, Thorn. Okay if I call you out there to-morrow?"

"Sure."

We said our good-byes, shook hands, and he left. I still saw no sign of anyone I knew, although I got no sense of danger. At least, not yet. Then the music resumed, and I had the almost uncontrollable urge to dance.

13

So I did. Dance, that is. After all, I'd been practicing steps like this for weeks. I watched long enough to get a sense of the basic moves, then slid into one of the lines between an old woman in a big skirt and a little barefoot girl. Instantly I felt like one of the community, and the music seemed to guide me so that I never put a foot wrong. And I couldn't help smiling and laughing at both the ease of it, and the beauty of the music and what we were all creating with it. I'd felt similar things on occasion in shows, but never this strongly and never all the way through.

Exhausted, I stepped off the dance floor and looked around for something to drink. I saw Thorn standing by the door holding two beers, and when we made eye contact, she raised one in my direction. I nodded and started toward her.

Suddenly a firm hand grabbed my arm and turned me. C.C. stood there and said seriously, "Don't drink that."

"Why?"

"It's complicated. If you're thirsty, come out to my truck with me."

"There's beer right over there."

"You drink that beer, you may live to regret it."

I looked back at Thorn, who scowled at C.C. in annoyance. "Did she poison it?" I asked.

"There's things you don't understand about the Tufa. Come on and I'll explain them to you."

"I don't know—"

Now *he* looked annoyed. "Dude, you either trust people or you don't."

"I barely know you."

"Yeah, well, with that attitude, that ain't likely to change."

I thought I heard a hint of . . . something in there, and it was enough to overcome my reticence. As we passed Thorn, C.C. snagged one of the beers from her, leading her to exclaim, "Hey!" But we were already out the door.

It was full dark by now, and the trees hummed with insects that were easily as loud as the traffic in Manhattan. "What makes all that noise?"

"What noise?"

"The insect noise."

"Oh. Crickets. Cicadas. Tree frogs."

"Are they always like this?"

"Like what?"

"So loud."

"Except in the winter. Then they go, 'Brrrrrr.'"

He said this so deadpan that it took a minute for me to re-alize he was joking. By then we'd reached what I assumed was his truck, a much newer and shinier model than most of the others. I didn't know if it meant he was better off financially, or just had a little more pride in his ride.

But wait, I thought. Hours earlier, I'd seen this truck at the Parrishes', and it was just as dusty and worn as their vehicles. That meant he'd gone somewhere and *washed* it. Was it because he knew I'd be here? . . .

No, don't be an idiot. He was coming to a wake. It was no doubt out of respect for the dead.

He opened the passenger door and handed me a beer from a cooler. I couldn't read the label in the light. "What makes this beer different from the one Thorn had?"

He turned his up and drank. I was desperately thirsty and wanted to do the same, but sensed that his answer might be important. Then he belched lightly and said, "Henry Hudson."

"I beg your pardon?"

"You ever read 'Rip Van Winkle'?"

"The kids' story?"

"It's not a kids' story. It's a cautionary tale. Rip drinks some beer from the strange people he meets, who're led by Henry Hudson, and sleeps for twenty years."

"Yeah. And?"

"It just goes to show that accepting drinks from the wrong people can have consequences."

I looked at the beer he handed me. "But you're not the wrong people?"

"Not tonight." He touched the neck of his bottle to mine. "Cheers."

I took a tentative swallow. It tasted fine, and I recognized it: Heineken Dark.

"Is that all right?" C.C. asked.

"It's my favorite," I said truthfully.

"I thought you looked like a Heineken man," and for the first time, he smiled. We tapped bottle necks again.

"You sounded great in there," he continued.

"It's my job."

"Then you're bound to be a star."

"I shouldn't take credit for it. It's mostly Ray's songs. They're so good, anybody would sound great singing them."

"Maybe. I wouldn't."

"You don't sing?"

"Nope. I'm probably the least musical Tufa you'll ever meet. Never really learned to play anything beyond basic chords, can't sing, and sure can't dance." He shook his head. "If I didn't have the hair and the teeth, I'd wonder about my parents."

"Well, I'm sure you have . . . other qualities." Luckily, it was too dark for him to see me blush as I realized I was openly flirting now, regardless of what he was doing. I still couldn't tell: all the usual clues I was used to recognizing in my social milieu didn't seem to apply here.

"I can fix things, and build things, and I'm pretty good in a crisis," he said. "Of course, there has to *be* a crisis for that last bit to apply. Things pretty much just cruise along here."

We stood in the relative silence for a moment, until the music started back in the barn. I said, "I suppose I should go back inside, in case the Parrishes start to think I've wandered off."

He held up another bottle. "Want one for the road?"

"No, I need to keep my head reasonably clear. Wouldn't want anyone to get the wrong idea."

It was an opening the size of an eighteen-wheeler, but he didn't take it. Instead he just said, "Well, I'll see you around, I'm sure. I'm doing some work for Gerald out in their barn."

Impulsively, I asked, "Say, do you know where to find the real chapel of ease that Ray wrote about?"

He stood very still for a long moment. "Maybe."

"I'd love to see it, and take some pictures for the rest of the cast. We all kind of have our own ideas of it."

"Don't you think that's better? What lives in your mind and heart is always better than reality."

Well, *that* wasn't the kind of insight I'd expected. "I don't know if it's 'better,' but I know they'd like to see it."

"I'll see what I can do." Then he closed the truck's door and headed back to the barn. I followed, more unsure now than I'd been before we started talking.

It was well past midnight when I returned to Ray's old bedroom. I'd danced more tonight than I had since I was new to New York, when youth and various substances kept me going at a maniacal pace until dawn. I'd had nothing but beer tonight, and not much of that; it was the music that gave me energy and made sure I continued dancing and singing. Well, that and the fact that everyone around me seemed as good as, if not better than, the professionals I knew back in the city.

I fell on the bed, intending to take off my clothes and check my phone, but fell asleep almost at once. My dreams were strange and disturbing, and consisted mainly of scenes from *Chapel of Ease,* except it wasn't Jason, or Julie, or Ryan. Instead the people in my dream all had the Tufa look, as well as the hard, harsh angles that mountain living seemed to give to the faces around here. They spoke to me, and I responded— but when I opened my eyes all those words went *whoosh.*

I turned my head slightly, momentarily disoriented, and thought I heard the faint trace of someone humming "The Sun on the Ridge" from the play. The dawn was gray and faint, and in the shadows beside the window I saw a shape I recognized immediately.

"Ray?" I said, my voice ragged. Then I blinked, and the shadow was gone.

Well, that got the old adrenaline going. I sat up straight, eyes wide open, and stared into the corner where I thought I'd seen him. There was nothing but a stack of boxes that, if I squinted, looked vaguely human-shaped. I waited for my heart to stop pounding.

I dug out my phone and found a text message from Joaquim: *Tried to call, but it kept going to voice mail. Let me know how you're doing.* Then, below that, another text from him: *I'll pick up Chinese on my way over. Don't get dressed on my account.*

It took me a minute to process that. He knew I was out of town, so . . .

Oh.

Clearly it was meant for someone else. The implications were also unmistakable. I should've been upset, or at least a little sad, but actually, I felt nothing. Whatever I had with Joaquim had not progressed to the point that I now felt its loss, and I had enough other concerns to occupy my time.

I put on some pants and a shirt and went into the kitchen to see if there might be coffee. Sure enough, a big pot had brewed, and Thorn sat at the table, sipping a cup. She wore a man's athletic shirt and, from the evidence of her bare legs, little else.

"Morning, glory," she said when she saw me. "You're up early after all that dancing."

"So are you," I said. A cup was set out by the coffeemaker, so I assumed it was mine. I sat down at the opposite end of the table. "Wherever he is, I'm sure Ray really enjoyed that."

"I'm sure he did, too," she said.

"What time does C.C. come around to start work? He said he'd take me to the chapel of ease today."

"Did he, now?"

"More or less. Why?"

She put down the cup and looked at me seriously. "Matt, you seem like a nice guy. But let me ask you something: Did you see any churches on your way here?"

"I didn't really notice." Church, and religion in general, had not been part of my life since I was a small child. Once my grandmother passed away, no one else stepped in to make sure I felt guilty and damned. "I'm not very religious, and I remember Ray saying there weren't many here."

"He wasn't being quite honest."

"No?"

"No. There's none. Zero. Not a single operating church in

the whole county. Closest one's across the county line in Uni-corn. Doesn't that seem a little strange? We're in the Bible Belt, after all. And while we may not be the actual buckle, we're definitely that little loop that keeps the end from flopping all over the place."

"Is it because the town is so small?"

She barked a laugh. "There's a place called Frog Jump that's got a population of less than fifty and three churches."

"So what are you telling me?"

"Churches don't go here, Matt. Religion doesn't. What we believe . . . well, it goes back long before churches. So not only will you not find any Baptists or Methodists, that chapel of ease is . . . well, it ain't exactly welcome, either."

"How did it get there, then?"

She sipped some more coffee and stared out the window. "There's always been people who think they know better'n everyone else. People who're so smug and certain that they think they can do what they want. Helps if they're rich, too. Well, one a'them decided us heathen Tufa needed some churchin' whether we wanted it or not. So he built that chapel, and started sending his own people over to attend services there. He thought the sight of such good, upstanding Christian folk would shame us Tufa into joining them."

"I take it that didn't work?"

"Not too well," she said with a chuckle. "So then he sent some of his people around with guns, to give us a little more incentive."

"He tried to make you go to church *at gunpoint*?" I said, and made no effort to hide my disbelief.

"You ain't never spent much time around Southern Chris-tians, have you?"

"No, and I'm glad, if they're like that."

"Well, on that day, they couldn't find a single one of us."

"You hid from them?"

"I ain't sayin' that. I'm sayin' they couldn't find us."

That seemed needlessly enigmatic, but I didn't comment. "So what happened?"

"The fella behind all this dropped dead of a heart attack from all the frustration we gave him, and the chapel just kind of fell apart over time. Most people don't even know where it is."

"But you do?"

"Me?" she snorted. "You couldn't get me near that damn thing. I got enough bad luck without courtin' more."

"So it's bad luck to go to the chapel?"

"It's bad luck to even mention it."

"You're mentioning it."

She smiled at me. "No, *you* mentioned it. So I'd be watching my back for a while if I was you."

"I don't believe in that kind of thing."

Her smile grew wider, and darker. "Neither did Rayford."

With that she got up and left me alone in the kitchen. The sun was up enough that it backlit the clouds of tiny flies hovering in the yard between the house and the barn.

I turned at the sound of heavy footsteps. Gerald came in, fully dressed down to his boots, and poured himself some coffee. He grunted, "Morning," then sat down.

"Good morning," I said.

"You have a good time at the dance last night?"

"Well, actually, yes."

"Good. That's what it's for."

Keeping in mind what Thorn had told me, I asked, "Will there be any kind of . . . service for Ray? Other than that, I mean?"

"Service to do what? Like a funeral?"

"Yeah."

"Ain't our way," he said.

"You don't do funerals?"

"Not unless it's somebody we want to make sure stays in the ground."

"So what will you do with Ray's remains?"

He nodded at the mantel. "Reckon they'll stay right there. Can't think of a better place for my son to be, can you?" Then he started putting sugar into his coffee.

Well, that was that. I wished fervently that I was back on West Forty-seventh Street, walking into Joe Allen on Forty-sixth Street for a normal lunch, and not among these strange and slightly frightening hill folk.

Then I remembered the reporter. I said, "Mr. Parrish, I need to ask you something. A newspaperman came up to me at the wake and asked if he could talk to me about Ray. I said yes, but if you and Mrs. Parrish don't want me to, I won't do it. I don't want to be disrespectful."

"At the barn dance? Fella named Swayback?"

"I think so, yeah."

He made a dismissive gesture. "Talk all you want. He's one of us."

And that was it for Gerald's morning conversation. He finished fixing his coffee and took it out the back door. The cloud of gnats parted for him, then re-formed behind him. Ladonna came in whistling to start breakfast, and I went to take a shower.

When I'd cleaned up and returned to the kitchen, C.C. was there, looking out the back window. I stopped before he saw me and just looked at him, appreciating the way the morning sun backlit his tall, strong body. I knew a lot of gym rats—and, of course, a lot of dancers—but there was something unbelievably attractive about simple physical strength that was the result of just living, not narcissistic exercise. Dancers danced; it was basically all they knew. What might C.C. know?

"Good morning," I said.

He glanced back at me. "Howdy. Did you have a good time last night?"

"I did."

"Good." He resumed looking out the window. I tried to guess what he watched so closely, but saw nothing. After a moment, I said, "Do you think you'll have time today to show me the chapel of ease?"

He turned to look at me fully. He was backlit, so I couldn't quite make out his expression, but he mumbled, "Yeah, sure, why not?"

"Great," I said. "When?"

He looked at his watch. "Right now suits me."

"Okay."

And with no more than that, I found myself riding in his truck along bumpy gravel roads, immense thick forests on either side. C.C. drove in silence, his radio playing what seemed to be the same country music station Bliss had put on before. Again, all the songs had a flat similarity to them, which helped them become white noise to my racing thoughts.

"You ever been down South before?" he asked.

"What? No. Not unless you count Orlando."

"Huh. Well, no, I wouldn't count that."

"Why?"

"Because it's a big city, and people from all over—"

"No, I mean, why were you asking?"

He didn't speak for a moment. In profile, he was even more handsome. At last he said, "You met some good people last night. They were friends of Ray's, and his family. But not everybody around here is like that."

I suddenly grew tense. Was he about to tell me that he knew I was gay, and that I liked him? Had I just walked into a redneck homophobe's trap?

"The chapel of ease belongs to the Durant family," he continued. "We call them the Durocs. Do you know what a duroc is?"

"Never heard of it."

"It's a kind of hog. It's known for being bad-tempered, and for having giant balls. The Durants are kind of like that."

"Ah."

"This early in the morning, they should all be sleeping off whatever they got into last night, so it shouldn't be a problem."

"They weren't at the wake?"

"No. They'd never show themselves at our barn dance."

"So . . . they're not Tufa?"

"No, they're Tufa. But they're not our people. I wanted you to know that if we run into them, you might not want to mention that you're gay."

"Okay." So he knew. How? Had he spoken to Thorn? Had she sought him out to tell him? Was it because of how I sang, or danced? He didn't look at me, so I couldn't see if there was any belligerence in his eyes, let alone sympathy or, dare I hope, interest. I forced myself to stay as calm as I could. I began, "Maybe we should—"

"You're here for, what, three more days, counting today? There ain't gonna be a better time. If you want to see it, we need to do it now."

"Okay," I said again.

"If I thought there was a real danger, I wouldn't have suggested it," he added. "I just wanted to be honest with you, and have you know this wasn't entirely risk-free."

"I appreciate that."

The road grew rougher, and I sensed we were ascending higher into the mountains. The nature of the trees changed as well, from the thick forests around the Parrish house to gnarlier, sparser ones that gave glimpses of the mountains around us. We were as high as some of the clouds now, which clung to the treetops like wisps of smoke or steam.

"They built the church way up here?" I asked.

"Oh, no. This is just the back way in."

"Are we sneaking?"

"We're discretin'."

We hit a bare spot of road—well, a pair of ruts with a grass strip between them that I assumed passed for a road around here—and I got a long look at the mountains, their rolling slopes receding into the distance. Those farther away appeared gray, then blue, and finally dissolved into the misty horizon. It was breathtaking, and I either gasped loud enough to be heard over the engine and road noise, or C.C. was used to this response.

"Yeah, it's something, ain't it?" he said. "Probably feel about it the way you do about skyscrapers."

"Skyscrapers don't . . ." I trailed off as I realized I didn't have the words for what I felt. Whatever it was, though, I never got it from looking up at buildings in New York. They just made me feel tired, and small. The mountains, though, they made me feel . . .

C.C. was smiling at me. "Yeah," he said. "I bet they don't."

Then we descended again, into a valley with even thicker woods than the one we'd just left. The trees were huge here, and at ground level, the weeds and vines between them were thicker. Even from inside the truck, there was something spooky about them. They closed around and over the road like the passageway into a dark, enchanted, and dangerous land.

C.C. abruptly slammed on the brakes, and the truck skidded to a stop. The dust behind drifted over us, momentarily obscuring whatever it was that prompted such a reaction.

Then I saw what he'd seen. Two four-wheelers, their bodies painted in a camouflage pattern, were parked right off the road.

"I take it they mean something?" I said after a moment.

"Yep," he said, still looking at them. The only sound was the engine's uneven rumble.

"They belong to those people you mentioned? The Duponts?"

"Durants. Yeah. They must be up in here hunting."

"What do they hunt?"

"Deer. Bear. Pigs. Anything they want. You won't see no game warden up in here telling 'em something's out of season."

"Should we go back?"

"This might be the only chance you get. It's your call."

"Are they seriously dangerous?"

"They are seriously dangerous. But this is a big valley, and chances are we won't be anywhere near 'em."

"Then let's do it."

We drove on, deeper into the valley, and the sky grew more and more narrow above us, until it was merely a bright blue strip between treetops. C.C. turned off this road onto one that was even less traveled, and the passage repeatedly bounced me high off my seat despite the shoulder belt. At last we topped a rise and traveled almost vertically down until we hit bottom. We stopped, he put the truck in park and said, "Well . . . we're here."

14

Through the dirty windshield, past the trunks of intervening trees, I saw the shape of a building in a small clearing directly ahead. I couldn't move. I'd lived with the image of the chapel we constructed on-stage, as well as the one I built in my head, for so long that the thought of seeing the real thing was somehow paralyzing.

After a moment C.C. asked, "You all right?"

"Did you ever bring Ray out here?" I asked softly.

"No. He's the one who showed it to me, back when we were around twelve or so."

I thought about the distance we'd traveled from Ray's house. "That's a long way for a couple of twelve-year-olds."

C.C. chuckled, as if he was in on a joke I didn't catch. "Yeah. Well, come on, let's take your pictures and get out of here."

We got out of the truck and hiked the short distance to the clearing. It felt like the trees conspired to keep me from getting a clear view of the chapel. C.C. kept glancing around us, looking for signs of the Durants, I supposed. His eyes were narrowed, and his lips drawn tight. Was he more worried than he'd admitted?

Then we stepped around the final tree, emerged into the open space around the chapel, and I got my first clear look at it. A bright ray of sunshine shone down onto the building, and a burst of the "Hallelujah Chorus" wouldn't have been out of place.

I had a shock I totally didn't expect: the chapel before me looked almost exactly like the one on our stage. It was larger, but the design was the same down to the lone column outside the entrance, which once supported the porch overhang. The contours of the walls, the places where major sections were missing and huge cracks rent the stone down to the foundation, were identical. Sure, there were differences in the details, but Ray had ensured that the overall outline was the same.

Our chapel was *this* chapel.

I wondered at this amazing similarity, then realized: of course Ray had pictures of it. I mean, he had to, right? Even if he'd described it in excruciating detail in the script (which he didn't), there was no way the designer could've gotten it so right without visual references. But why had we never seen those photos?

Oh, who was I kidding? Actors never saw things like that. We only saw the results.

The walls appeared to be made of stones about the size of cinder blocks, cut into rectangles and held together with some kind of cement or plaster. All the wooden parts were gone: there was no roof, no door, not even any window frames. Grass and weeds grew up all around it, inside the walls as well as outside, and vines climbed the walls at one end.

"Don't touch that," C.C. said when he noticed the vines. "That's poison ivy."

"It is?"

"Yep. Gives you a hell of a rash. You ever had it?"

"No. Never even seen it before."

"Well, you don't want it. I knew a fella who threw a stick into a campfire once. He was a little drunk, so what he thought was tree leaves turned out to be poison ivy wrapped around it. Whatever that chemical is that makes you itch, it got into the smoke, and he breathed it in. Got poison ivy in his *lungs,* man." He shook his head. "They had him sedated in the hospital for a week."

I stared at the innocuous-looking vine. "Thanks for the warning. Anything else here that might kill me?"

"Oh, that won't kill you. It'll just make you wish you were dead."

I took several pictures with my phone as we approached the open, vine-free end. C.C. perused everything *but* the chapel, watching the woods with quick, darting eyes. He looked so hot standing in a shaft of sunlight, his broad shoulders straight and his feet spread defiantly, that I snapped a quick shot of him.

He caught me. "Did you just take my picture?"

"Yeah. Hope that's okay."

"Yeah, well, you can take a picture of me anytime. This is your one chance to see this place."

I belatedly realized that, whatever he'd said earlier, he really *was* worried, perhaps even scared, at the prospect of meeting these Durants. And *that* scared *me*. I went to the chapel entrance and peered inside.

The floor of the real chapel was all dirt, with weeds sprouting wherever they could. Sunlight bathed the whole area, eliminating shadows and making everything pop in high-def clarity. A few big chunks of the wall had fallen off and remained where they landed, and a snake basked across one of them.

Our set was different: we had a platform at the back for the ghosts to stride so they'd be above the other actors onstage.

And yet in the center of the real chapel's floor, where we had our ghosts burying something, there was in fact a clear spot, bare of weeds and stones, where the hard-packed dirt lay naked.

"Watch out for snakes," C.C. said, and threw a rock at the one stretched across the piece of wall. It slithered rapidly away. "Copperheads and rattlesnakes love this sort of place."

"Which one was that?"

"That was just a spreadin' adder. It won't hurt you. But you gotta watch for those others."

"I had no idea the woods were so dangerous."

"Yeah, good thing nothing bad ever happens in the big city."

I crept carefully closer to the empty spot in the center of the chapel floor, watching for snakes as instructed. I saw none. When I reached the spot, I said casually, "Wonder what's buried under here?"

"Where?"

"In the center. This clear spot."

"What makes you think something's buried there?"

"Ray's play says there is. Says a woman named Byrda buried something there."

"What did he say it was?"

"He never told us."

"What, you mean if you see his play, you never find out?"

"No."

C.C. chuckled. "That doesn't sound like a very good play."

"It's about more than that," I said a little defensively, sounding exactly like Ray.

Before I could fully appreciate that irony, C.C. grabbed my arm. I'd never felt a grip so strong. He said, "Shh!" in a way that gave you no choice. I shut up and listened.

Then I heard it, too: voices. Two men, talking.

"Follow me, keep up, and for God's sake, stay quiet," C.C. said. He led us out of the chapel and into the woods. We slid down into a small gully just as the voices grew loud enough to be distinct. We could peer over the edge and see the chapel, and his truck.

Footsteps, the kind people make when they're not trying to be quiet, grew louder as well, and I could at last make out the words.

". . . and that ass of hers, it just don't quit, man, you know what I mean?"

"Do you ever think about what you're saying?"

"What the fuck are you talking about?"

"You're always saying 'that ass won't quit.' Asses only do one thing; you saying she's got the runs?"

"What?"

"I mean, think about it."

They came into the chapel clearing then: two big men in camouflage, each carrying a large gun of some kind. One had a *Duck Dynasty*-style beard, while the other sported a mustache that drooped past his chin. The one with the mustache carried what I eventually realized was a dead turkey.

"Durants?" I whispered.

"Durants," C.C. agreed just as softly.

They stopped dead when they saw his vehicle. The one holding the dead bird put it carefully on the ground. They walked over to the truck, opened the door, and peered inside. One of them looked in the bed. Then they methodically scoped out the woods all around. When their eyes passed over our hiding place, I swear I felt the air grow colder.

"It's that faggot's truck," one of them said.

"Hey, faggot!" the other one yelled. "You better get out here right now! You on Durant land, you know that?"

C.C. didn't move or, obviously, reply.

I looked at him in a mix of wonder and amusement. So he *was* gay, or at least the Durants thought so. That, at least, explained my attraction to him. Subconsciously I must've picked up on something.

"We ain't gonna hurt you, faggot!" Mustache Durant said. "But you best have a good reason for being here."

As silently as I could, I put my hand on top of C.C.'s. He didn't look at me, but he did curl his fingers around mine.

Beard Durant slammed the truck's door and looked around at the woods again. "What the hell could he be doing up in here?"

"Hunting?"

"Ain't got nothing on our land that you can't find on everybody else's."

"Meeting another faggot?"

"Here? That don't make no sense."

Mustache Durant pulled a knife out of his pocket and snapped the blade open. It looked as big as a sword to me. "Want to slice his tires?"

"Naw, we do that, he'll just have to get somebody to tow it out. You want a bunch of other people up in here, getting in our business?"

"Maybe somebody stole it and dumped it here, figuring he'd never find it."

"Maybe," Beard Durant said. "Or maybe he's hiding, listening to us right now."

"Want to try to track him?" Mustache Durant asked as he put away the knife.

"Naw. We need to get this turkey home." Then, louder, he continued, "If you can hear me, cocksucker, you best know we'll catch up with you one day. Don't nobody come up on our land without asking."

They waited for the reply that neither C.C. nor I were ever going to give. Then they collected their turkey and walked away back the way they'd come. After their footsteps faded, I started to rise, but C.C. jerked me back down. "They're not gone," he whispered, icily calm.

I looked at him closely. Our faces were inches away now,

and in his dark eyes I saw little flecks of gold that you had to be very close to see. I wondered if all the Tufa had that, or just him. With a surprisingly steady hand, I brushed his hair from his forehead. He didn't pull away.

Perhaps it was the danger of the situation giving me courage, but I slid closer and kissed him. It was a simple, gentle, tongueless kiss, sweet and as innocent as it could be under the circumstances.

When our lips parted, I whispered, "Okay?"

He smiled wryly. "Okay."

The next kiss was not so innocent.

When it broke, he motioned for me to stay put, then carefully rose up to look around. He stayed absolutely still, listening. I heard only the wind in the trees. He looked back at me and motioned me to follow him.

We had reached the truck when a voice said, "Well, if it ain't the lovebirds."

The two Durants came out of the woods. Mustache Durant still carried the turkey, but the other one held his gun, some type of shotgun, leveled right at us. My breath caught in my throat.

C.C. moved to stand between me and them. "Just sightseeing, Winslow. Not looking for any trouble."

Beard Durant, whose name was evidently Winslow, said, "Then it's your lucky day, 'cause we ain't, neither." He looked at me. "Who are you?"

"He's a friend of Rayford Parrish's from New York," C.C. said.

"And he cain't talk?" Mustache Durant said.

This whole confrontation now felt familiar. I'd been having them since junior high school, and believe it or not, the fear suddenly receded. I knew exactly what I was doing. "I can talk," I said, and stepped past C.C. to stand close to them. They didn't back up, but they looked at me uncertainly. "But you don't really care what I have to say, do you?"

C.C. gasped like I'd lost my mind.

Winslow laughed, a smug-bully chortle. "Well, lookee here, this big-city faggot thinks he's all tough, don't he?"

"No," I said calmly, letting my shoulders relax and my hands hang loose. "I'm not tough. I just don't like wasting my time. C.C. and I would like to leave. Either let us, or stop us." I spread my hands in a shrug, using the gesture to distract from sliding my feet into position.

C.C. whispered, "What are you—?"

I was close enough now, and when I moved, I moved fast. I turned my hips and grabbed the barrel of the gun in my right hand. I pushed it so it pointed toward the empty woods.

Then I kicked backwards with my right foot, directly at Winslow's groin. It wasn't a hard blow, but it didn't need to be. He squeaked, and his hands dropped the gun as they flew to belatedly protect his balls.

I caught the shotgun's stock with my left hand. It was heavier than I expected, but I spun counterclockwise and drove the butt into the side of Mustache Durant's head.

He dropped the turkey and his own gun, then stumbled away from us. By then I had stepped back beside C.C. and had the shotgun leveled at the brothers. I'd never fired a gun in my life, but I was a goddamned actor and I'd seen a lot of movies. I knew how to look intimidating.

The whole thing took less than five seconds.

C.C. picked up the other gun before Mustache Durant's head cleared. Winslow was on his knees, hands between his thighs, eyes scrunched tightly closed. Tears streaked the dirt on his cheeks.

Mustache Durant shook his head, looked around for his gun, and when he saw we held them both, growled like an angry animal.

"I'm sorry," I said, "what was that you said about big-city faggots?"

He continued to growl, and a little spittle collected at the corners of his mouth.

"We'll throw your guns out when we get down the road a ways," C.C. said. "I wouldn't recommend trying to follow us."

We backed up to the truck and got inside. I admit a rush of relief when the doors closed on us. C.C. propped the shotguns stock-first against the floorboard, the barrels wedged against the cab roof. He spun the wheel and slammed the gearshift into first. The vehicle roared back onto the road and we headed, not the way we'd come, but deeper into the Durants' valley. I had to assume he knew what he was doing as he whipped us around sharp turns and near intimidating drop-offs.

"That was something," he said with a rough laugh.

"I didn't really hurt either of them."

"You did worse, you made 'em look stupid. What was that? Karate?"

"Muay Thai."

"Never heard of it."

"It's from Thailand. It means 'the art of eight limbs.'"

"It sure looked like it."

I flexed my fingers, which were numb from the intensity of my grip on the shotgun. I remembered my dad's words the day I came out to the family: "All right, son. But you're learning a martial art."

"Why?" I'd asked him.

"Because lots of people will want to hurt you just because you're gay. It's not right, but it's true. We have to face the world like it is before we can make it like it should be."

I'd said nothing; I already knew that from school. You couldn't be a boy taking dance lessons without getting beat up for it, let alone a gay boy. We tried several forms before we found one that didn't directly contradict what I was also learning in dance class, and muay Thai was perfect.

"So they were Tufa, too, huh?" I asked C.C.

"Oh yes. But they were from the other side."

The other side of what? I wondered, but it didn't seem like the time to ask.

We hit the bottom of the valley, and the road straightened out. I saw a big, ramshackle house ahead, the first sign of civilization I'd seen other than the chapel itself. Two old cars sat up on concrete blocks, and a pair of big dogs moved to the shoulder of the road to bark at the truck as we approached.

C.C. slowed enough to toss the shotguns out the window into the yard. As we passed, I saw a young girl and an old woman on the porch, looking at us with dead, malignant eyes.

"That's the Durant pigsty," C.C. said. "Anyone following us?"

I looked out the back window. It was hard to tell through the dust. "I don't think so."

"Then our luck continues."

The trees closed in around us again, and in the enforced dimness, he reached over and rested his hand on mine. It was only momentary, because he needed both hands to drive, but it was there. He didn't look at me, and neither of us said anything.

15

We got back to the Parrish farm and found only Ladonna at home, hanging laundry on a line in the side
yard. "Well, where have you boys been?" she asked.

"I took Matt to see the chapel of ease," C.C. said.
"Spooked a couple of Durants."

"Oh, good heavens, those Durants are pure white
trash. Worse than the Gwinns, even. Was there any
trouble?"

"No." He looked sideways at me. "Just a few
words exchanged. Sticks and stones, you know?"

"Well, that's good. We don't need no feudin' around
here."

"Mind if we help ourselves to some iced tea?"

"You go right ahead."

I followed C.C. into the kitchen. He got two
glasses, ice, and a big pitcher from the refrigerator.
After he poured, he called, "Thorn? You back there?"
When there was no response, he said, "You can understand why I don't want to talk where someone can
hear."

I took a long swallow, grateful for the drink.
"Yeah."

He didn't look at me when he said, "Not a lot of people know about me."

"Doesn't seem like the easiest place to live out in the open."

"No. Are you . . . ?"

"Out? Yeah."

He still didn't look at me. "Can you keep quiet about me?"

"Sure. I don't want to hurt you."

"I appreciate that." Finally, he looked at me across the table. "It was nice."

"Yeah."

"I wish you were in town for longer."

"Me, too."

I waited to see if he would say, or do, anything else, but he just turned to look out the window. I guessed that was that. I got out my phone and checked the signal, but there was still nothing. My hand still shook a little bit, but the adrenaline from the confrontation was fading at last, leaving me with that numb postcrisis feeling. I almost laughed out loud. I wanted to call my dad and tell him, then thank him for that long-ago decision. It had saved my ass more than once in New York, but never with guns involved. He'd be so proud. And then I had to call my teacher, Master Tracy, and let him know how well it had gone. "Might for right!" was the affirmation he taught us, and this had surely been that.

I said, "Hey, I hate to ask for another favor after the last one, but could you run me into town? Or anywhere I can get a cell phone signal?"

C.C. put down his tea. "Sure. I'll buy you lunch at the Fast Grab."

I laughed at the name. "What's that?"

"It's the convenience store. They have picnic tables outside. It's all we've got since the Catamount Corner closed down. They used to have a nice little café."

We both looked up as music began just outside. I followed C.C. to the living room and we peered out through the screen door.

Someone new sat on the porch with Ladonna and Thorn. He strummed a guitar, Thorn tapped on a bongo-style drum, and Ladonna sang in a pure, high voice that might've been the cleanest mezzo-soprano I'd ever heard.

> *They hadn't been a week from her,*
> *A week but barely three,*
> *When word came to the carlin wife*
> *That her three sons were gone.*
> *I wish the wind may never cease,*
> *Nor worries in the flood,*
> *Till my three sons come hame to me,*
> *In earthly flesh and blood.*

It was impossible to hear this without thinking of Ray, and I wondered if this was part of her mourning process. I'd really never thought about the way a parent would feel if her child died; none of my close friends were parents. But the ache and sadness in Ladonna's voice told me exactly what she was feeling, with a directness I didn't expect. Even the bright summer sun blasting on the yard couldn't overcome it.

Not that Ladonna was breaking down. She held her chin high, her eyes open and clear, her voice full and strong and perfectly controlled. It wasn't in the singing, and it wasn't in the song, but in the ineffable way they all combined to create the immediate experience. The music carried the ache of the missing, and it touched me in a way nothing had at the wake.

When they finished, we clapped and C.C. let out an approving whistle. That seemed awfully casual for what we'd just heard, but when they all turned to look at us, none of them seemed offended.

"How long y'all been standing there?" Ladonna said.

"Long enough," C.C. answered.

"Matt," Ladonna said, indicating the guitarist, "this is Don Swayback, from the newspaper over in Unicorn. He wanted to talk to you a bit about Rayford."

"I met him last night at the wake. How are you, Mr. Swayback?"

"Good, but please, call me Don." He put his guitar in its case. "Ladonna, I hate to break this off, but I have to go on the clock or ol' Sam will have me writing nothing but obituaries again. It's been a pure pleasure, though."

"You know it," Ladonna said. "You come back anytime, Don."

He nodded at Thorn. "And Miss Parrish, always a pleasure."

"Likewise, Mr. Swayback," she said with a smile.

I opened the door and he entered, propping his guitar case against the wall. He said, "C.C., you reckon you could give me and Matt here a little privacy for this?"

"Sure," he said. "I'll go rustle up Gerald, see if he needs any help with anything."

After he left, I said, "Come on, I guess we can use the kitchen."

Don followed me. I took the liberty of pouring him a glass of tea. We sat down across the table, and he took out one of those narrow little reporter's notebooks. "You don't record things?" I asked.

"There's only one thing worse than attending a county board meeting, and that's having to listen to it again later. I use notes; I'm pretty good at getting the quotes accurate. And this is a feature, not a news piece, so I'm not out to rake anyone over the coals."

"That's good," I said, and laughed a little nervously. "So where will this article show up?"

"In the paper, and on the Web site. Web site's just for subscribers, though, so it won't be a big circulation either way. Sorry."

"No, that's fine, I just wanted to know."

His pen poised over the notebook, he asked, "So how did you meet Rayford Parrish?"

"We're starting? Okay. I met Ray"—again I was careful not to use his hick name—"when he called me to come audition for his show, *Chapel of Ease*. He'd seen me in another play, and liked my performance."

"And what was your first impression of him?"

I wanted to be on my guard against manipulation, but really, all I could do was trust: I'd be long gone by the time the story appeared, and reporters could twist facts to suit agendas just like actors could cry on command. I resolved, then, to be honest, so that at least I'd have a clear conscience about what I'd said.

"He was kind of goofy," I said. "Theater encourages people to be enthusiastic, especially about their own work, but Ray was just . . . he was happy about everything. Every aspect of the show: the music, the dancing, the rehearsals. He'd been struggling to get a show that was entirely *his* off the ground for a while. He'd written songs for other people's shows, but this was the first time the music, the lyrics, the book, were all him, and he was determined to make it the absolute best they could be. Still, I only saw him get testy once."

"And when was that?"

"When everyone demanded he tell them something about the script that he didn't want to tell."

"And what was that?"

Oh boy. I wondered if he knew, and had simply maneuvered me into this position, or if I'd been so eager to talk that I'd just run headlong into it myself. "Well . . . can it be off the record?"

He shrugged and put down his pen. "Sure."

"The play is about a ruined church. A chapel of ease. Do you know about it?"

"I know what one is."

"Did you know there's one here?"

He looked dubious. "A church? In Cloud County?"

"It's there. I saw it a couple of hours ago."

"Where?"

"Beats me. C.C. took me there. It was on land owned by the Durant family."

"Ah, that explains it. Most people wouldn't go near their place. You know those old stories about revenuers who went up into the hills and never came out? The Durants may have invented that."

I did know about revenuers, but only from the play. "Well, I saw the actual church Ray wrote the story about."

"What is the story? Oh, and can this be back on the record?"

"Sure. Sometime during the Civil War, a couple named Byrda and Shad were in love, but he went off to fight. His best friend stuck around. When Shad came back, he asked Byrda to marry him, and she agreed, but something had happened while he was gone. She buried something in the floor of the chapel, and then Shad was killed by his best friend, who was actually in love with him."

Swayback's eyebrows rose. "In love with *him*?"

"They had gay people back then, you know."

"Well, yeah, I mean, it's just . . . a surprise."

I could tell what he wanted to ask. "Ray wasn't gay."

"I never thought he was."

"Did you know him?"

"No, but that sort of thing . . . Well, there aren't a lot of secrets around here. Everyone knows everyone else's business."

I wondered how many knew about C.C. "And they don't approve?"

"They don't care either way. It might not look that way from the outside, what with everyone having the same hair and everything, but this is a whole culture of iconoclasts. The rule is, mind your own business and let the other fella do his thing. Even," he said with a wry little smile, "if that thing is other fellas."

"Really?" I said, and made no effort to hide my dubiousness. I'd just that very morning heard the Durants call C.C. and me faggots.

"I know what you're thinking. And of course, there are some people here who have issues with it. But I think you'll find for the most part that the Tufa, certainly the ones that came to Rayford's wake, believe in letting people be who they are."

I remembered C.C.'s "other side" comment, but decided to let it drop; after all, I'd be leaving in two days. I said, "Is there more you wanted to know about Ray?"

"Actually, yes. What do you think Rayford Parrish was trying to say with his play?"

This was the sort of question I might get asked about any show, and I knew just how to respond, since Neil had given us "approved verbiage" for just this sort of thing. "That depends on the playgoer. We all imagine something different buried in the chapel, and what we imagine determines what the play means."

He looked at me with another sly smile. "That's a canned answer, isn't it?"

"Well, you asked a clichéd question."

"Fair enough. How about this one: What's your favorite memory of Rayford?"

That one took me aback. I thought about our coffee dates, our lunches, the times he'd joked, a bit cruelly but never maliciously, about some of the other actors. He'd told me things about Emily that would make her turn so red, we'd see the glow from here. And yet . . .

"I think it was the first time I met him. I came in for an audition, and I already knew the director, but I'd never met Ray before. He played piano while I sang, which is kind of unusual for the composer to do. And when he played, there was just this immediate connection. Like he somehow knew exactly what I was going to do with my voice, and exactly how best to support it. Does that make sense?"

Don smiled, that same damn secretive, knowing little grin I'd started to notice on a lot of Tufa faces. "That makes perfect sense. You know, I'm only part Tufa, and for a long time I didn't acknowledge it. Then one day, I pulled my old guitar out of the closet, and it was like . . . coming home. The music was the only way I could really be myself. I'm sure Rayford felt that way, too, and that he really enjoyed sharing it with you." He paused, then asked, "So do you think the show will be successful?"

"Well, the reviews are spectacular."

"Reviews? I thought it hadn't opened yet."

"We did the press preview the night before Ray died."

"Did he see it?"

"Yes. He died later that night."

He let out a low whistle. "Ain't that some irony."

"Yeah."

"But how do *you* feel about it? Especially now, without Ray there?"

Boy, this guy was good. Carefully, I said, "It really means a lot to me. Singing his songs means a lot, too. Watching how they work on people. Almost like—" I stopped before I said "magic," realizing how lame it would sound.

Don closed his notebook. "Don't be afraid of saying what you know is true," he said. "Especially around here. Nobody'll laugh at you."

"I'll keep that in mind."

"Oh, and C.C.? He's a good guy. Better than most, in fact. Anything he tells you, you can believe."

I glanced at his hand; he wore a wedding band. He also seemed very familiar with Thorn, which I knew wasn't mutually exclusive with the ring. But now he spoke about C.C. as if he was very familiar with him as well. Was it the same kind of familiarity, or just the friendship bred of being from the same isolated little town? Or was my big-city cynicism, so used to seeing sexual indiscretions everywhere, simply imagining things?

He said, "Do you mind if I take your picture for the article?"

"Sure. Where do you want to do it?"

He looked around. "Eh, this'll do." He took out his camera and stepped back, looking for the proper framing. He took three quick shots, then reviewed them. "Huh," he said.

"Did I blink?"

"No, just . . . well, look."

He brought the camera over. On one of the three frames, there was a blur behind me that looked for all the world as if someone standing there had started to move just as the shot was taken.

"Digital," he said, as if that explained everything. "Never had these problems when we shot on film."

I followed him outside. Thorn and Ladonna were gone. C.C. sat on the open tailgate of his truck, casual as a model in a cigarette ad. Gerald stood beside him, and they stopped talking as the reporter and I approached.

"Get all you need?" Gerald asked Swayback.

"Got plenty. It'll make a good story. Thank you, Gerald, and again, I'm sorry for your loss."

"Appreciate it, Don."

"I'll send you some extra copies when the issue runs."

We waved as he drove off. "Nice guy," Gerald said. "Real nice guy."

C.C. climbed down from the tailgate. "Ready to go into town?"

"What you need in town?" Gerald said.

"A cell phone signal," I said.

"You welcome to use our phone."

"I appreciate that, but I have so many minutes paid for, I hate to waste them."

"Well, if you get stuck, feel free."

As we pulled out onto the road, C.C. took my hand again, and this time he didn't let go. I could see him smiling as he drove.

"How'd it go?" he asked at last.

"Fine. I've done enough interviews, I know how to do them pretty painlessly."

"What did he ask about?"

"Mainly Ray in New York. I guess he knows all about Ray here. Lots about the show."

"Did you tell him about the chapel?"

"That we went to it? Yeah. Why? Should I have kept it a secret?"

C.C. thought for a moment, then said, "No, I don't suppose it makes any difference. It's not like the Durants read the paper."

16

I got three bars, the best reception I'd had since we left Nashville.

I stood outside and dialed Neil's number while C.C. went into the Fast Grab convenience store. Neil answered and said, "Hey, Matt. Tried to call you a half a dozen times. How's the trip going?"

"It's been eventful. I don't get any reception at Ray's parents' house, or many other spots up in these hills. How are things there?"

"Our run is entirely sold out, and we're adding two more weeks. And there's already talk about moving to Broadway. Marketing-wise, this was genius. It's just hard not to think of it as some kind of blood money."

"I know what you mean," I said sadly.

"How was the memorial service?"

"It was basically a party. Lots of music. I sang 'The Chapel Song' for them, and they loved it."

"They're not mad because Ray's talking about them? He was always worried about that."

"No, they're not. They're a little perplexed by the fuss, but that's all."

"That makes me feel a little better."

A big truck rattled by, and the woman in the passenger seat looked at me. Her meaty arm blocked the lower half of her face, but her eyes almost gleamed with intensity. Was it because I was so obviously a stranger? Or was she a friend of the Durants, about to call them and tell them I was in town?

I shook my head to get rid of my paranoia. I'd seen way too many movies with dangerous country bumpkins. This wasn't *Wrong Turn;* not every small town in the South was a hotbed of danger, right?

"I just sent you some pictures of the real chapel of ease, too," I told Neil. "It's amazing how close our set is to it."

"Thanks. I'll look at them when we get off the phone. See if there's anything we want to add to our set. So what was buried there?"

"Well, I didn't . . . ," I trailed off, suddenly embarrassed.

"You're kidding me," Neil said in his icy scolding voice. "You went all that way, you were actually *there,* and you didn't dig to see what it was?"

I didn't want to tell him about the Durants, since he'd warned me about that very thing. "It wasn't exactly the right time."

"Uh-huh. After all that shit you and the rest of the cast kicked up about, 'Oh, we have to know the secret, we can't possibly act it if we don't know,' you didn't find out?"

"It's on private property, Neil," I said defensively.

"And that's what stopped you? Look, you dig it up, see what it is, take some pictures, put it back, and fill in the hole. No harm, no foul."

"It wasn't a good time."

"Right. Well, you've got, what, two and a half more days? I expect an answer by then. Seriously, Matt. It was you and the rest of the cast who made this an issue; they'll rip you apart if you come back without it. When they're not moaning about Ray's death, it's all they talk about."

His tone had gotten harsher and was starting to piss me off. I said, "I thought I was here to represent the cast at the funeral."

"You did that. Now you have another job."

"I'll do the best I can, Neil. Tell everyone I said hello."

I hung up before he could say anything else. It was rude, but not as rude as I wanted to be. Then I dialed Joaquim. When I got his voice mail, I said, "Hey. Just checking in. Everything's fine here. I'll try again the next time I'm somewhere I get a signal." I started to mention that he'd sent me the wrong text, but I assumed he knew that by now. I'd have that scene to play out when I got back home, but it was probably for the best.

Through the glass front of the Fast Grab, I watched C.C. talk to the girl behind the counter. Yes, breaking up with Joaquim would definitely be for the best.

Finally, I called Emily. "Hello?" she said. She sounded tired and slurry.

"Hey, Em. It's Matt."

"Oh, hey," she said, and perked up a little. "I didn't look at the phone first. Are you still down with Ray's parents?"

"Yeah, for a couple of more days. How are you?"

"Mostly sober, which is a change. The only way I can sleep is without dreams, and the only way to kill the dreams is to kill a bottle of wine first. But I can't do that forever, can I?"

"You getting out any?"

"A little. I have an audition later that I suppose I'll go to. I don't really care if I get the part or not."

That didn't sound like Emily at all. Ray's death must have hit her even harder than I'd thought. "Then you'll probably get it without a callback," I said, trying to sound light. "Isn't that always the way?"

"I keep hearing his voice, Matt. I'll be about to drift off to sleep, and I'll hear him singing, just softly and right out of range so I can't quite catch the words. But I know the tune, it's songs from the show, he used to sing them all the time when he was working on them." She paused, and I'd never heard her voice sound so vulnerable as when she said, "Do you believe in ghosts, Matt?"

"I don't know, Emily. But if you've been drinking as much as you said—"

"Yeah, I know. I've also been going through his files. I haven't found it."

"Found what?"

"What's buried in the chapel."

So I wasn't the only one nursing this particular compulsion. "Maybe you should stop looking for a while."

"But it's got to be there. He wrote so many songs, Matt, and kept so many notes. Ideas, lines, melodies . . . reading through all of it is like crawling into his head. Except he can't hear me."

I was really concerned now, and tried unsuccessfully to remember the names of any of Emily's other friends, someone who might be physically present and could watch out for her. "Go to the audition. Go out to eat afterwards. Maybe go dancing. See some friends, hear some voices that *aren't* ghosts. When I get back, we'll go down to the Hamptons for the day. Sit on the beach."

"That sounds nice," she said, like a child being promised a reward after the dentist.

"I took some pictures of the actual chapel of ease. Do you want me to send them to you?"

"Please do. It was such a special place to Ray."

"Okay, I'll send them as soon as I hang up. Love you, honey."

"Love you, too. Be safe."

When she hung up, C.C. came out with a bag of chips, some dip, and a couple of sodas. We sat at the picnic table across from each other, the sun behind him so that it cast a thin halo around his unruly black hair.

"Get ahold of your friends?" he asked.

"I did. Ray's girlfriend is having a rough time of it. They hadn't been dating for long, but she's really taking it hard."

He nodded as he chewed. "That happens when a non-Tufa gets involved with one of us."

"Oh?"

"Especially somebody like Ray, who's almost a pureblood. Once a girl gets a taste, it's like she's addicted. I knew one guy who must've driven half a dozen girls to suicide after he dumped them. Happens when Tufa girls date regular guys, too."

"And what about Tufa guys and . . . ?"

I was teasing, and I thought he was, too, but his look was dead serious. "The truth? I don't know. I mean, I know there have been Tufa like . . . us . . . before, but they don't get stories and songs sung about them. So I don't know."

"Maybe you could be the first."

"Don't joke. When it happens, it's awful. I've seen it. It's like a heroin addict who can't get high no matter how much they shoot up."

Well, things had gotten grim fast. Then again, that accurately described the way Emily seemed to feel about Ray. When I remembered how she'd behaved that day at his apartment, it didn't seem so far-fetched, and after talking to her just now, it occurred to me that perhaps I should watch my own step here. I dipped a chip and said, "I need to ask you something, C.C., and I'll understand if you want to smack me afterwards."

"Not much chance of that after I saw you handle those Durants."

"Do you think we could go back to the chapel and dig up that spot I showed you?"

He looked at me with steady disbelief. "You're kidding, right?"

"No. I know this will sound crazy, but the entire cast of Ray's show is obsessed by this, and if I come back without an answer, they'll lynch me."

"The Durants won't be so easy to surprise next time. They're likely to just shoot you from the woods and be done with it."

"You think they'll stake the place out?"

"Is it really worth it just to see what's buried in a hole?"

"For me, yes. If you don't want to help, I can't blame you. But you're the only person I know who knows where it is. I could never find it again."

Before he could answer, another truck pulled up beside his. A beautiful dark-haired woman was behind the wheel, and she said, "Hey, C.C.," as she parked. After a moment she came around the two vehicles, carrying an equally dark-haired little girl less than a year old.

"Hey, Bronwyn," C.C. said. He held out his hand, and I thought they were going to shake, but instead he made an elaborate gesture, which she returned. I'd never seen anything like that before. "Bronwyn, this is Matt. He was Rayford's friend in New York. Matt, this is Bronwyn Hyatt—"

"Chess," she corrected.

"Sorry, Bronwyn *Chess.* She got married."

I stood for the introduction. Like C.C., the newcomer was backlit by the sun, so it wasn't until she moved and the light fell on her face that I recognized her. I stared. "It's you," I said in a shocked whisper.

"It's me," she said.

"So you saw her on TV, huh?" C.C. said.

"What?"

"She was a war hero. Well, I guess you still are, right?"

"I was never a hero," she said. Her baby pulled at her hair. "Well, not until this one came along. Every day she doesn't go for a ride in the dryer is a day I'm heroic." She smiled. "I'm kidding, you know."

"No, it has nothing to do with the war," I said. "I saw you when you came to visit Ray in New York."

Her easy smile changed to a forced and obviously false one. "Me? I haven't been to New York since before she was born, and then it was just overnight. Now, if you'll excuse me—"

"Then you've got a twin," I said, not about to let this go. "We talked at the press preview the night Ray died, less than a week ago. I was as close to you then as I am now. You asked me if we'd stop the show if Ray told us to."

"What's a 'press preview'?" she asked innocently.

Now I started to get mad. "It's when you do the show for the critics."

"Well, it's a coincidence. It must be. Did this visitor have a baby with her?"

"No."

"Then I promise you, it wasn't me, because she and I go everywhere together." The baby smacked her mother's cheeks and giggled. "Well, it was nice to meet you, but I have to pick up some diapers before this little lady gets tired of sitting in her own pee." She turned and strode into the convenience store, more quickly than her casual air would imply.

"That was strange," C.C. said.

"That was bullshit," I said through my teeth. "I swear it was her."

"Why would she lie about it?"

"I have no fucking clue. But she just did. Unless she *does* have a twin?"

"Folks say all us Tufa look alike. But no, she's only got brothers. Well . . . had brothers. One of them died a while back."

"Then it was her. I mean, I'd swear on a stack of Bibles with a gun to my head." I started toward the store. "I'm going to go talk to her some more."

C.C. grabbed my arm. "Whoa, wait a minute. That might work in New York City, but not here."

"I'm not going to *hit* her, C.C."

"That ain't what I mean. She's important."

"Yeah, I know, she's a war hero, so you said."

"No, she's more than that." He paused, debating whether to continue, then blurted, "She's what we call a First Daughter."

"And what is that?"

"The firstborn daughter of a firstborn daughter. And she's pureblood Tufa."

"Which means . . . ?"

"It means there's etiquette involved."

I looked up into his strong, sincere face and saw he meant every word. He was, in fact, rather scared of this young mother.

She came out of the store, waved at us with the hand carrying the pack of diapers, and got into her truck without another word. I said nothing.

As she drove off, C.C. said, "Thank you."

I muttered insincerely, "You're welcome."

"All right."

"All right, what?"

"All right, we'll go back to the chapel. But not during the day. We'll go at night. That's when the Durants are usually too drunk to be much trouble."

"Usually?"

"Those are the best odds I can give you."

"Tonight?"

"No, tomorrow night. Tonight . . . I have something else I want to show you."

You can imagine my first thought, but there was nothing sexual in the way he said it. Then I wondered if perhaps I should be worried. Had I shown too much disrespect to the so-called First Daughter so that he now believed I needed to be taken out and taught a lesson . . . perhaps permanently? But no, I could be wrong, but not *that* wrong. "I'll look forward to it. Do I need to dress up?"

"Ha! No. It's not formal." He met my eyes, and this time

there was definitely something there, something a good deal more intimate than secrets buried in churches.

"I'll look forward to it," I said again.

Before we could proceed to any interesting innuendo, yet another truck pulled up beside C.C.'s. This one was loud and rusted, and squeaked when it came to a halt.

"Oh, shit," C.C. muttered.

"What?"

"Let me do the talking," he said.

A man got out of this truck. He was about thirty, with Tufa hair and teeth, but a shifty, vaguely dishonest air about him. As he approached, C.C. made a quick, elaborate gesture with his hand, just as he had for Bronwyn Chess earlier. The newcomer responded with a different one.

"What's up, Cyrus?" he said. Then he looked closely at me. I realized he was trying to fake being tough, like a bad actor. "Who's your friend?"

"Matt Johansson," I said, and stood to shake hands.

His grip was faux firm, just like his glare. "Judging from that accent, you ain't from nearby."

"No, I'm from New York."

"He's a friend of Rayford Parrish's," C.C. said quickly, as if I was about to get myself into trouble.

"A friend of Rayford's from the big city," the man said. He sat beside C.C. and rested his arms on the table. I sat back down, too. "Yeah, now that I think about it, I've heard about you. Sure was a shame to hear about his passing. Kind of you to bring his ashes back home."

"He was glad to do it," C.C. said.

"Were you?" the man asked me.

"I was."

"And I hear you been doing a little sightseeing up in the Durants' holler."

"He wanted to see the old chapel," C.C. said.

"Now, why would a Yankee give a shit about an old broke-down church?" He said this in reply to C.C., but looking at me.

"I'm sorry, who are you?" I asked. I was already annoyed by Bronwyn Chess, and this wasn't helping.

"Everybody calls me Junior. I'm what you might call a person of authority. Nothing official, no badge or election or anything, but . . ." He smiled and shrugged, as if his power should be obvious. "So why *did* you want to see that church?"

"My friend Ray wrote a play about the chapel, and it's going to open in New York City in a week. While I was here, I wanted to see the real place that inspired him."

"You know that's on private property, right?"

I was starting to really dislike this guy, and truthfully, felt a little cocky after my trouncing of his friends, the Durants. "Is it yours?"

"Mine? Naw. But the people it belongs to are mine. I'm responsible for them. And if they get hurt, I'm always concerned."

"Did they get hurt?"

"They said you used some kind of kung fu on 'em."

I laughed. "Me? I'm a Broadway dancer, do I look like Jean-Claude Van Damme to you?"

He leaned back and looked at me anew. I sat as limply and non-butch as I could, and it took all my self-control not to bat my eyes at him. At last he said, "Well, then, you tell me what happened."

"They told us to leave, so we left. We didn't want any trouble. Did they?"

Again Junior was silent; then abruptly he got to his feet. "Hope you enjoy the rest of your visit," he said, then went back to his truck. A moment later it started and he rattled off down the highway.

C.C. laughed. I realized I'd never heard him laugh, not like this. He sounded a lot like Burt Reynolds. "That'll rattle around in his head for a while," he said. "I'd love to be a fly on the outhouse wall when he tells the Durocs that they were beat up by a dancer."

"Will it cause you any trouble after I'm gone?"

"I hope so," he said, still laughing. "I purely do hope so."

17

We drove along for several minutes before I realized we weren't headed back to the Parrish farm. I looked over at C.C. sharply. "Uh . . . where are we going?"

"I want to show you something," he said.

"I thought that was tonight."

"Yeah, that's something different. This has to do with Rayford's show."

I'd already seen the chapel, so I couldn't imagine what he meant, but it wasn't like I had any choice, although I did briefly consider leaping from the truck into the trees. The road wound through the woods, until at last we stopped at a spot that, to me, looked like every other place along the road. "We have to walk a bit from here," he said.

The trail was clear, even if it bore no sign of recent passage. Insects buzzed in the air, and shafts of sunlight came through the trees. It was certainly beautiful, but also spooky, as if strange things might lurk in the deep shadows between the pools of illumination.

Then we emerged into a clearing. In the center was a small, fenced-in graveyard with perhaps a dozen headstones. Three enormous crows lifted off as we approached, their caws echoing in the silence.

C.C. opened the gate in the waist-high fence. The hinges squeaked like the sob of a lone mourner. The place's atmosphere was somber, and I said softly, "What's this?"

"A graveyard. Don't they have these in New York?"

"Yes, but I assume there's a reason you brought me to this particular one."

He stopped before one small, weathered headstone. Greenish lichen grew along the curve at the top. "Well . . . this is where they buried one of them people Rayford wrote about."

I got a chill despite the hot sun. "Really?"

He patted the stone. "This is Byrda Fowler."

Fowler. They had no last names in our play. I reverently knelt before it and put my fingers on the stone. I could make out the name, the salutation, HERE LIES just above it, but the dates were worn and indecipherable.

Around the base of the tombstone were several flat, smooth rocks. "What are these?"

"Markers of respect. Visitors leave them."

So Byrda wasn't totally abandoned. I also remembered the box of rocks I'd seen at the bar dance. "Should we leave some?"

He held out two from his pocket. "Got us covered."

I carefully placed mine on the tombstone's cracked, crumbling base.

"I've heard tell some folks have seen her haint around here," C.C. said.

"Not at the chapel?"

"Haint can be in more than one place. Haint can be wherever it wants."

I stood back up and wiped my hands on my jeans. "Have you ever seen a ghost?"

"Oh, yeah. Three. One time when I was a little boy, this old woman walked across our yard one afternoon. Right as she reached the road, she vanished. Just went poof right in front of me and my cousin. We ran inside and hid under the kitchen table. Never saw her again."

"And the others?"

"One other one was just like that. A young man in Confederate gray walking across the field while I was out plowing. Got about ten feet away from me and disappeared, just like that old woman. Never said a word. But the other . . ."

He paused, mustering the story. I wanted to put my hand on his arm, let him know he wasn't alone, but even though we'd kissed that morning, I wasn't sure whether he'd welcome that.

"I was fishing one day, about three years ago," he began. "Off by myself, at this creek I know about. This old man comes out of the woods with a cane pole, says howdy just as nice as you please, and sits down right beside me. I mean, close enough I could see the whiskers in his beard. He drops his line in, and I do remember thinking I'd never seen such a smooth drop, it barely made the water move. Then we sat there, watching our floats, just bullshitting about the day. He told me all about his grandkids, about his farm, just the normal stuff you'd talk about. Only strange thing was the way he looked when I mentioned my truck, like he had no idea what I was talking about."

Again he paused, and when he spoke again, his voice shook in a way I'd never heard before.

"And then I looked over at him, and I could see through him. I mean, right through, like he was superimposed on a picture or something. And he smiled at me, and it was the scariest thing I ever did see, before or since. Then he just faded away." He laughed at his own terror. "And I ain't never been back to that fishing hole, I tell you that."

"Wow," I said. I had no context for that sort of thing.

"I don't know how it is with regular dead people, but the

Tufa dead, they don't always move on. If they got business, they stick around until it's taken care of."

That was the whole point of Ray's play, so it made sense. "Thanks for bringing me here, C.C. You think Byrda would mind if I took some pictures?" I knew Julie would love to have one. She plays Byrda in the show.

"I reckon if she minds, she'll let you know."

I took out my phone and tried to open the camera app, but it wouldn't work. I turned the phone off and back on, and it still wouldn't work. "Huh," I said.

"Camera not working?"

"No."

"Then I reckon she's letting you know."

That sent a fresh chill through me. I looked down at the stone and said, "Okay . . . Byrda . . . message received. I mean no disrespect. I'm just going to take a picture of the graveyard in general, if that's okay."

I went through the gate and moved a few feet away. When I tried again, the app opened with no problem. C.C. stepped out of the way, and I took several pictures in rapid succession. I put away my phone and said, "Thanks, Byrda. Rest well."

I looked back just before we entered the woods and saw that the three crows had returned to their perches.

When we got back to the Parrish farm, it was midafternoon. C.C. excused himself to go check on Gerald's tractor out in whatever field he was plowing. I went to my room and found, to my great discomfort, Thorn seated on the edge of my bed.

"Hi," she said. She had a guitar across her lap. "Close the door, would you?"

"Uh—"

"Look, I'm sorry about yesterday. But please, close the door. I need to tell you something in private."

I hesitated for a moment, then did as she asked.

"Thank you. You want to sit down?"

"I'll stand, if that's okay. What's up?"

She strummed an E chord on the guitar. "I need to clarify what I was asking you yesterday. And what I was really talking about."

"I think I got the idea."

"No, you didn't, because I came at you all wrong, and I apologize."

"No need."

She strummed again, and said, "Yes, there is. I really had no interest in you, sexually. Even if you were straight. But . . ."

She noodled on the instrument, a tune I didn't recognize but that fit perfectly with the kind of music I'd heard at the barn dance. "You see, I want the same thing Ray did: to get out of here for a while. I know the mountains are lovely, the clean air is great, blah blah blah. But I've got nothing to compare it to."

"Okay. . . ." I had no idea where this was going. Or rather, I had a very good idea where this was going.

"I admit it," she continued. "When you first got here, I intended to seduce you and use you to get out of here. I'm not proud of it, but you have to use what you have to work with to accomplish your goals, you know?"

"Yes."

"So now . . . I want you as a friend."

"I am your friend, Thorn."

"Good. Then as my friend, I'm begging you: Help me get out of here."

I lowered my voice. "Are they keeping you here against your will?"

"What? No!"

"Then how can I help you?" I asked guardedly.

"First, listen to this and tell me if you think it's any good."

She strummed again. I felt a great sinking feeling, because if there was one thing I hated, it was being asked for my opinion on a song or a play by a struggling artist. In my experience, there was usually a reason they were struggling, and usually it was that they sucked. Or if they didn't, they brought nothing new to the table, just rehashes of whatever songs or shows that most inspired them. I can't tell you how many friends and acquaintances had brought clones of *Wicked, Evita,* and any other popular show to me to see what I thought. So I prepared my usual answer: *I think it shows a lot of promise.* It always sounded flat and unconvincing to me, but the artists were so desperate for reassurance, they jumped on it like it was a rope and they were in the water beside the *Titanic.*

But as she began to sing, I realized that, in this case, my presumption might have been misplaced.

> *You were there my whole life*
> *Many times I wished you weren't*
> *From the cold mornings at the bus stop*
> *To the summer days when we'd get burnt*
> *You taught me how to fish and swim*
> *You made fun of me for dresses*
> *You beat up the boys who treated me bad*
> *And helped clean up my messes*
> *You flew to the city because you had to*
> *And I understand, and I agree*
> *But the woods and roads are so empty now*
> *When it's no longer you and me. . . .*

When she finished, I had to wipe a tear from my eye before speaking. "Wow, Thorn, that was beautiful."

"I wrote it the night before you got here," she said evenly, arms folded across the top of her guitar. "Took me about an hour. They say the best songs come fast."

"Why didn't you play it at the wake?"

She shook her head. "The wake was a celebration. You don't want to make people sad when they're happy." She paused, then said, "So do you think I could make it in New York?"

"What do you mean by 'make it'?"

"Make a decent living with my music. Playing in a bar or something."

"Well, you're a beautiful girl, and if you've got other songs this good, you'd probably get a gig somewhere. But I don't really know much about the music scene, except as an occasional fan."

She began again, only this time it was a grinding, bluesy number. I hadn't seen her retrieve it, but now she had a slide on her left hand. She sang:

> Down in the holler where the good ones play
> You'll find me waiting there all alone
> A torn dress off my shoulder and a flower in my hair
> If you come to me, you'll never go back on your own.
> I can turn you into dust with a flick of my hip
> I can put you on your back, or your knees
> Because down in the holler where the good ones play
> The bad ones can do as they please.

There were more verses, and then she finished with a blistering solo that, even on an acoustic guitar, made the room seem warmer than it had been. Thorn suddenly seemed sexy even to me; I could just imagine how she'd affect a straight listener.

She looked up at me, and instead of the grin of smug satisfaction I expected to see after this virtuoso performance, she looked small and uncertain. "Am I as good as the people you usually see?"

There was no denying the truth. "You'd blow most of them into the East River."

At last she smiled, with none of her usual mockery and sarcasm, and it was dazzling. "Back during the winter, I played with a band called Tuatha Dea when they came through. They said I was good enough to make it, too."

"There you go, then."

"So . . . can I come back with you? And stay with you for a while until I get on my feet?"

I stood there speechless, not from outrage, but fighting the urge to say, "Sure!" My life was complicated enough without a straight girl roommate, especially a straight girl from the smallest town I'd ever seen, with stars in her eyes and a belief in her own specialness. Yet there I was, already thinking the word "roommate," and envisioning us walking down Canal Street like the couple on the cover of the *Once* soundtrack.

I was saved, if that's the right word, from making a commitment by the sound of a door slamming into a wall and C.C. shouting, "Ladonna! Get help, Gerald's been shot!"

18

Thorn and I rushed into the kitchen in time to see C.C. carry Gerald in through the back door and lower him gently into a chair at the table. There was blood on his left shoulder, and his face was pale and slack-jawed.

C.C. was drenched with sweat from the effort and could barely breathe. Gerald was not a small man, and evidently C.C. had carried him quite a distance. Ladonna pushed her way past us and, with a wail, ran to Gerald. "Oh Lordy, what's happened? C.C., what happened?"

"Shot just . . . came out of . . . the woods," C.C. gasped. "Didn't see . . . anyone. . . ." But he looked right at me, and I knew exactly who'd done it.

Ladonna pulled open Gerald's shirt, revealing a nasty round wound, ragged in his pasty flesh. I had to look away—I had no stomach for that sort of thing. Beside me, Thorn gasped.

Ladonna's momentary panic changed to grim purpose. "Thorn, get on the phone and call Bliss Overbay. Then let Mandalay know what's happened. Matt, start some water boiling. And grab C.C. a beer from the fridge, would you?"

"Yes, ma'am," Thorn and I said together.

I filled the pot from the stove and started it boiling, handed the still-gasping C.C. a beer, and then helped Ladonna ease Gerald up onto the table. He was breathing hard, and his eyes never left his wife as he reclined, his muddy boots dangling off the end.

I heard Thorn in the living room conversing urgently with someone. I said, "Shouldn't we call 911?"

"That's who Bliss is around here," Ladonna said. Blood pooled beneath Gerald and dripped from the table. Its metallic odor overpowered the kitchen's normal homey smell.

"What about the police?" I offered.

"Time for that later. Gerald, can you hear me? Speak to me, honey. Say something." She lightly slapped him. "Say something!"

He coughed and said with great dignity, "What would you have me say, woman?"

"Does it hurt?"

"I reckon so. Did you expect it not to?" Then he coughed again, and a little spray of red stained his lips. I knew from the movies that that meant it was serious.

The front door burst open and Bliss Overbay rushed in carrying a first aid bag. I'd heard no siren or vehicle; how had she gotten here so fast? We all stepped aside as she expertly snapped on blue latex gloves and bent over Gerald's wound. "What the hell happened to you, old man?" she drawled with mock casualness, but her movements were all urgent business.

"Bullet was heading south for the winter, and I got in the way," Gerald said.

"You sure did." He winced as she probed at the hole. "I won't bullshit you, Gerald, this is pretty bad. We got to get the bullet out, and I think it might've knocked the corner off a lung."

"That explains that blood I keep tasting," he rasped. At this news, Ladonna let out a little sob, and he reached out to take her hand. "Now, you just calm down there, old woman, Bliss has got everything under control."

"I've got water boiling," I said helpfully. They ignored me.

Thorn grabbed my hand and pulled me away from the table. She whispered urgently, "Is there a song in your show about Daddy?"

"I . . . what?"

"In that play Rayford wrote! Did he write a song about anyone's daddy?"

"Well, there's one the female lead sings about missing her father on her wedding day."

"Can you sing it?"

I looked at her. There was no mistaking her urgency, or seriousness. "What good would that do?"

"Daddy's a *Tufa*," she said, as if I were an idiot and that explained everything.

"I'm sorry, Thorn, I'm glad to help, but—"

"If you want to help, get your ass over there and sing that song."

She pushed me back toward the table. Gerald moaned and weakly squirmed as Bliss worked over the wound. C.C. sat watching, silent and distraught. Ladonna stroked Gerald's hand.

Thorn said, "Y'all, Matt here is going to sing for Daddy." Then she forcefully jabbed me in the back.

I took a deep breath. I'd never sung this number, and although I heard it almost every day, it hadn't permeated me the way my own songs did. Still, if it would help . . .

I remember how rough your hand felt on mine
When you walked me to that old school bus
That day I was so scared to leave home alone
But you made sure I knew I was loved
Now here I am, in my white dress and veil

Beside the man I love
But the man who first owned my heart
Blows in the winds above. . . .

I sang softly, not wanting to disturb the medical work. Bliss's gloved hands were dark with blood now, and she worked over the wound with metal instruments I couldn't identify. My voice wobbled a little, and I had to look away. I closed my eyes and tried to visualize the stage, Cassandra in her costume wedding dress, hands clasped and singing as the spotlight bathed her face.

My daddy was strong, my daddy was tall
He sang, and danced, and played
And whenever I cried, he was there with his arms
To drive the bad feelings away. . . .

And I felt that *click* in my head, and heart, that said I was in the pocket. It wasn't just about hitting the notes; it meant I'd locked into the emotion of the character singing the song. I didn't even realize it, but I began singing in my full voice, the one that filled the Armpit to the back row, even without the microphones. I forgot the life-or-death drama playing out three feet away from me.

And when I opened my eyes between the end of the chorus and the second verse, for an instant I swear I saw Ray standing beside his mother, one hand on his father's forehead. He glanced up at me with that unmistakable half smile of approval, then vanished in the breath between lines.

I'd had plenty of practice carrying on despite all sorts of distractions, from other performers passing out to audience members jumping drunkenly onstage, so the apparition didn't trip me up. I kept singing, even though I was absolutely certain I had not imagined it.

Bliss rose up with something small and metallic caught between the tips of her long tweezers. Blood dripped from it. C.C. held out an empty coffee cup, and it made a solid *clang* when it hit the bottom.

When I finished the last chorus, a voice said at my elbow, "How is he?"

I jumped. The young girl from the wake, Mandalay, stood beside me. She wore a tank top and cut-off shorts, and her bare feet were dirty. I hadn't heard her come in, and her commanding presence was totally at odds with her age.

As if to emphasize that, Ladonna, C.C., and Bliss all paused in what they were doing to make elaborate little hand signs at her. She quickly made one in response.

"I got the bullet out," Bliss said. "I think he'll be okay. It was a .220."

"What does that mean?" I asked.

"Size cartridge you use to hunt deer."

"And it ain't deer season," Mandalay added.

"He was coughing up blood," I said, trying to be helpful. "Maybe he needs to be—"

"If Bliss says he'll be okay, then he will," Mandalay said. She was a tall girl, so when she looked at me, she didn't have to turn her face upward much. But there was something in her eyes that wasn't childish. Not at all. "I promise."

"Matt sang for us," Thorn said quickly, as if to make sure the girl knew I'd helped. "One of Ray's songs, from his play."

"It helped," Bliss said. "A lot."

Now the girl smiled up at me, and suddenly she *was* a child again. "Thank you. Around here, singing the right song at the right time is a big deal."

"You're welcome," I managed to choke out. I caught C.C.'s eye, and he winked.

What the hell is going on? I thought. First a demand that I sing, then a ghost, and now some girl acting like she had all the authority in the world. And everyone else seemed to agree with her.

Gerald sputtered a little, then said weakly, "In case anybody's interested, I'd like to get off this damn table. Y'all making me feel like a casserole."

"Keep your old ass still while I patch you up," Bliss said.

"Yes'm," Gerald said, immediately cowed.

"Thorn, get some blankets ready on the couch," Bliss ordered. "And go rustle up a fresh shirt for your daddy. A button-up one, not a pullover."

Thorn left to do her assigned jobs, but I was still lost. "So . . . he's not going to the hospital?"

"No need," Ladonna said with visible relief. "Bliss done took care of him. With your help—so thank you, son." She patted me reverently on the shoulder, like I'd done some amazing thing.

"What about the police?" I pressed.

All eyes turned to Mandalay. She asked, "Who did this?"

"The Durants," C.C. said. "Matt and I were up on their land this morning, and Matt . . ." He trailed off and looked away.

"What?" the girl prompted.

"Well . . . he kicked Winslow Durant's ass pretty good."

Everyone but C.C. looked at me with disbelief. Even Gerald raised his head. "I know martial arts," I said, a little defensively.

"Why were you up there?" Mandalay asked sternly.

"We were just—," C.C. started.

"I wanted to see the chapel of ease," I said. "Ray's play is all about it, and I wanted to get some pictures to show the rest of the cast. We didn't start the fight. And it wasn't really a fight: They had guns, I just took them away. Then we left."

Mandalay barked out a giggle, then fought to keep her face straight. "Did you?"

"He did," C.C. confirmed. "Took about three seconds. They

were probably aiming at me when they hit Gerald. Not that I reckon it bothered them much."

"That sounds likely," Mandalay said. "I reckon I'll need to talk to Junior, then."

"He already tried to tree us at the Fast Grab," C.C. said. "So he knows all about it."

"I'm sure he does. Well, I'll take it from here, and I hope it isn't necessary to say this, but leave the Durants alone until you hear back from me." She looked at C.C., then at me for emphasis. "Please?"

"Sure," C.C. said. He made another hand gesture.

She kept looking at me, waiting for my response.

"I don't know your little finger-wiggles," I said. "And not to be rude, miss, but I'm not sure exactly why this is any business of yours."

"You see a little girl, don't you?"

"Well . . . yeah."

"I understand. It's what I see in the mirror, too. But it's not all I am. I don't have time to make you a believer, but I do need you to accept that I have deserved authority. Can you go along with that?"

"Uh . . . sure, I guess."

"Then please, give me your word that you won't go bother the Durants any more until you hear back from me."

"Okay."

"Thank you."

She nodded to the rest of us, then went out the front door. When the screen slammed, I jumped, and the spell was broken. "Okay, *who* was that?" I asked, probably more urgently than I needed to.

"I'll explain later," C.C. said. He stood up and said, "Gerald, you reckon you can walk to the couch, or do you need me to carry you?"

"To the *couch*?" I exclaimed, alarmed at how high my voice went. "We should put him to bed. He needs a doctor. And we need the police. Somebody just tried to *kill* him."

"Calm down, sweetie," Ladonna said in her kind and warm way. "I know this may seem stranger than a bull with an udder, but I promise, we know what we're doing. Them Durants, they got their own ways up there. No police would ever find them. And there's no police in Cloud County, anyway." She said the last bit with a *What can you do?* shrug.

"You don't have cops," I repeated.

"Don't need 'em," Gerald said as C.C. helped him sit up. A white bandage covered his shoulder, and Bliss cut away the rest of his blood-soaked shirt. Then she fastened a sling to hold his arm in place. "Mandalay will handle it. That's her job."

"She's a *kid*!" I exclaimed, astounded that such an obvious thing needed to be pointed out.

Thorn almost giggled. I glared at her. "So this is funny to you?"

"No, not at all," she said, still trying not to laugh. "It's just that when you know about us, it'll—"

The accumulated fear, frustration, and annoyance finally burst out. "Know *what*? What is this great secret that everybody keeps hinting at? I see a man with a bullet hole in his shoulder who bled red just like anyone else, and you're telling me just singing a song at him is as good as taking him to the hospital?"

They all stared at me now, even Gerald. I felt my face burn. Then Thorn slipped my arm through hers. "Matt, there's some things you need to know. Come with me."

"No," C.C. said. "I'll tell him."

"Okay," Thorn said. To me she added, "Just wait until he explains things, honey. It'll all make sense then. Maybe not good sense, but sense."

As Gerald—a man who, minutes before, had been about to die of a gunshot wound—settled onto the couch and demanded the remote control, I remained standing, transfixed by all this apparent insanity. What bizarre parallel universe had I wandered into? And what if C.C.'s "explanation" was the permanent kind that resulted in me keeping company with Ray Parrish, wherever he was these days?

19

I went onto the front porch and pulled out my phone. I needed contact with my world—you know, the normal, rational one where singing didn't immediately heal gunshot wounds and people didn't listen to little girls in life-or-death situations. I've never wanted to see bars on my cell phone more than I did then, but it still resolutely said, NO SERVICE. And there was no way I was having this conversation in the Parrishes' living room.

Frustrated, I looked around. It was late afternoon, and the sun had turned amber. There was no sign of any vehicle Bliss used to get here, no fresh tire marks in the yard or disturbed dust on the drive. The girl Mandalay had vanished into thin air as well. The only living things were the dogs, Ace and Tom, sprawled flat in the shade beneath C.C.'s truck.

A crow cawed in the distance. Did they always sound like they were making fun of you, or was this crow just amused by me in particular?

I sat on the front porch swing, rocking vehemently (yes, it can be done) until C.C. came out and leaned against one of the supports.

"So is Gerald over being shot yet?" I asked, the sarcasm so heavy, it made even me scowl. "I mean, that usually sets you back a whole fifteen or twenty minutes, doesn't it?"

"I know what it looked like," C.C. said. "But you saw it: he *was* shot, and it will take him a while to recover. We're not superhuman or anything."

" 'We'? So if I shot you, you'd be back on the couch watching TV a half hour later, too?"

"I don't know. If Bliss got here in time, and there was someone to sing the right song . . . then, yeah, maybe."

"So it was all about the song?" I said, ratcheting up the sarcasm even more.

He looked at me seriously and said, "Yes."

I stopped pushing against the porch, and my momentum gradually slowed. He *meant it.* C.C. truly believed that if I hadn't been there, to sing that particular song at that particular moment, Gerald might be dead now.

It hit me like a thunderbolt. C.C. was *nuts.*

"You don't believe me, 'cause it don't make sense anywhere else but here," he said.

"On the porch?"

"In Cloud County. Where the Tufa have been for thousands of years."

"Thousands?"

"Thousands."

"And how is that possible, since the country's only a couple of hundred years old? Are you saying you're Indians?"

"No. They got here about seventeen thousand years ago. We were already here."

There was no levity, no sense of teasing in his words, despite their obvious ludicrousness. He looked at me with the steady, even gaze of someone absolutely secure in his delusions. I said, "So . . . you're descended from Vikings?"

He smiled a little. "They got here *after* the Native Americans."

"And you know that because you were here."

"No, I was born later. But . . . you've met people who were here then."

"Who were here thousands of years ago?"

"Yes." He paused. "I'll prove it to you as soon as it gets dark."

I stood up and blurted out, "I think I should go. Can you give me a ride to the airport, or somewhere where I can call a taxi?"

He put his hands on my shoulders. An hour ago, I might've melted right there from his touch, but now I wanted nothing but to be away from all these insane people. It occurred to me that I'd never seen the inside of the barn, and wondered how many bodies might hang there, souvenirs of these (I was sure now) cannibalistic hill-dwellers.

Still, I didn't pull away, and he didn't hold me the way you did someone you were about to kill. In return, I didn't punch him in the throat and run screaming down the road. He said, "I'm going to tell you something, and then I'm going to show you. You won't believe either, but I'm hoping that taken together, you'll see I'm telling the truth. Okay?"

"I seriously doubt that."

"Do you know the term, 'Tylwyth Teg'?"

"No."

"How about 'Yvwi Tsvdi'?"

"That's not even a word. How do you spell that?"

He laughed. "I'm not sure. I've never seen it written down. What about 'Tuatha de Danaan'?"

"Aren't they a Celtic band? Thorn told me about them."

"That's Tuatha Dea."

"Oh. Then no."

"Then how about . . . 'the Good Folk'?"

I was about to say no to this one as well, but something clicked. I'd heard that term in college, in an English class. "That's what they called fairies in folklore, right? I mean, fairies with wings, not fairies . . . like us. So they wouldn't get mad at you."

He nodded, and the indiscreet "us" didn't seem to bother him. "That's right. I have a lot of . . . Good Folk . . . in me. So do the Parrishes. So does Bliss. Mandalay, the girl you met? She's entirely Good Folk."

My brain turned this around, looking for the hole where I could insert the logic key. I didn't find it. "Wait, so you're telling me you—"

"All the Tufa," he corrected. "It's what we are. Some of us have more of it in us, some less. But we all have some."

"You're saying you're *fairies*."

"That's not the word we use."

"But it's what you're saying."

He shrugged and nodded, all one gesture. "And I was right—you don't believe me, do you?"

I gestured around me at the run-down house, the yard with its dogs and old cars, the trees and sky and mountains, all normal, tangible, real. "You have to admit, this isn't exactly Never Never Land."

I shut up as Thorn joined us on the porch. She stood beside C.C. and also looked at me dead seriously. "Y'all done told him?"

"Yes," C.C. said.

"That explains the look on his face."

"You believe this, too?" I asked her.

She snort-laughed. "I better. It's the truth."

"So . . . where are your wings?"

C.C. and Thorn looked at each other. I couldn't tell what passed between them, but then C.C. said, "Take a walk with us?"

"Is it the same 'walk' all the other Yankees who've disappeared took?"

"What other Yankees?" Thorn asked.

"He's being sarcastic," C.C. said. "We won't hurt you. I promise. If you don't trust me . . ."

He let it trail off. I looked into his eyes, the same ones I'd gazed into after that smoldering kiss up at the chapel, and saw—or at least hoped I saw—no guile, no danger. I couldn't read Thorn's expression, but since C.C. trusted her, I decided I had to go along with it, too. So I nodded.

"Mom!" Thorn yelled back into the house. "We're taking Matt out for a walk. Might be back late."

"All right," Ladonna called back.

"Y'all quit yelling, I'm trying to watch the game!" Gerald complained.

This resembled no fairy-tale household I'd ever read about. "Wait, I have to ask: Are you absolutely sure he doesn't need a doctor? He was shot, with a bullet. I saw it come out. He was spitting up blood."

"He'll be fine," C.C. said.

"I'm fine," Gerald said, although it must've been to Ladonna, since there was no way he could have overheard me.

"See?" Thorn said.

There was no convincing them, and for Gerald's sake, I truly hoped they were right. So I gestured for them to lead on.

We crossed the side yard and entered the woods along a narrow trail. C.C. took my hand, and if Thorn, trailing behind us, thought anything of it, she kept quiet. The trees overhead grew taller and thicker as we walked, blocking out the light from the setting sun. Animal noises I didn't recognize filled the air. The trail rose gradually, until at last it was so steep that C.C. released me so that we could all use our hands to climb the slope. Luckily roots and low branches provided convenient holds.

I didn't think we'd been hiking so long, but when we finally emerged onto the flat, treeless top of a hill, it was totally dark. I looked back, and even from this height saw no lights from the town or any of the other farms, no cars traveling on roads or any sign of civilization. There was just mile after mile of treetops in the silvery moonlight.

"Wow," I said. "Where are we?"

"Somewhere special," C.C. said. The wind blew then, not harsh but enough to make its presence known. It felt great on my sweaty face after the climb.

"So . . . what happens now?"

C.C. and Thorn held hands and walked out into the open space. The shadows from the moonlight hid their eyes from me. Then they began to undress.

If they'd jumped up and down shouting dirty limericks, it would not have startled me more. Thorn, wearing only a sundress and a pair of cowboy boots, finished first, and stood unashamed, waiting for C.C. He finally also stood naked beside her, their bodies like ivory in the light. The sight was simultaneously innocent and erotic, and I felt myself caught between those two responses, half turned-on and half delighted.

"Close your eyes, Matt," Thorn said. Her voice was musical, and the wind seemed to follow its cadences. "Don't open them until we tell you."

I did so. The wind continued to sigh around me, and I seemed to hear distant voices singing melodies I couldn't quite catch. Then over them rose a voice I did recognize: Thorn, singing.

> Oh, time makes men grow sad
> And rivers change their ways
> But the night wind and her riders
> Will ever stay the same. . . .

Past the song, past the wind, past the other voices, I also heard something that sounded for all the world like gigantic wings flapping. Not bird wings, and not the leathery snap of bats; instead, these were graceful sweeps, swooshes that I realized might have been generating the very wind that blew around me. But still, mesmerized by Thorn's voice, I kept my eyes shut.

"Open your eyes, Matt," C.C. said.

I did.

Thorn and C.C. were where they'd been moments before. Except . . . they weren't. Where two people had been, now stood two magnificent, magical beings with enormous, diaphanous wings, like those of some gigantic butterfly. The wings sparkled in the moonlight, and through them I saw the hazy silhouettes of the trees on the opposite side of the clearing.

Then my logical brain kicked in. These had to be fakes, appliances of some kind, even though the two were naked and there was no sign of any straps holding them on. I walked toward them slowly, and the wings moved, flexing with their breath.

"You wanted to see our wings," Thorn said with a smile so seductive, it almost worked on me.

"This is who we are, Matt," C.C. said. He looked more handsome than ever, his shoulders broad and his body sculpted like some romance cover model. "This is *what* we are."

"We're real," Thorn added. "We're the Good Folk."

I had no available words, so I reached tentatively for the edge of Thorn's nearest wing. When I touched it, it felt like silk paper, delicate and fragile. Yet I sensed that it wasn't, that any weakness was simply an illusion.

My touch made Thorn gasp in an unmistakably sexual way. She closed her eyes and sighed.

I turned to C.C. and, my fingers shaking, caressed the edge of his wing. He responded with a similar sigh, and put a hand on my cheek. He pulled me into a kiss.

As he held me, I felt Thorn's hands lift my shirt up, and I let her take it off. I looked up into C.C.'s shadowed, enigmatic eyes as Thorn pressed herself against my back and began kissing my shoulders.

My voice shook as much as my hands as I asked C.C., "Can you fly?"

He smiled and pulled me into his arms. And then my feet left the ground.

As we rose into the night, the wind grew stronger, seeming to help lift me and keep my weight from hanging in space. C.C. and I kissed again, and Thorn's hands reached from behind me to unbuckle my jeans. It was all so mind-boggingly arousing that I didn't know or care whose hands caressed me, as long as C.C.'s arms were around me.

"This is just for the two of you," Thorn whispered in my ear. And then she was gone.

C.C. and I kissed some more, turning in the sky, his wings effortlessly holding all our weight. I wondered how I'd ever find my clothes again, and imagined them spiraling out of the sky and landing across some old lady's porch rail. But truthfully, at that moment, I didn't care. I just didn't.

And then I opened my eyes and saw, unbelievably far below and shining in a moonlit clearing, a gray rectangular shape. It was the chapel of ease, glowing like a beacon in the darkness.

And then I didn't care about that anymore, either.

20

Things got . . . fuzzy after that, the way sex does some-times when you totally lose yourself in it and your brain disengages so it doesn't ruin the fun. Eventually we came back down to earth, literally and metaphor-ically, in the same clearing we'd departed from, and our carnal adventure became much more mundane, though no less arousing. Finally, spent and exhausted, we lay looking up at the stars, legs entwined, until Thorn appeared and, amused, tossed me my clothes in a bundle.

"You're lucky I found everything," she said wryly. "Now, get dressed, you two. It's getting late."

I sorted through my clothes so I could put them on. I still couldn't tell you how long this adventure had taken, or how long we'd been gone from the farm.

Then, fully dressed and woozy from sex and magic, we walked out of the forest together, me between C.C. and Thorn, and all of us kissed each other good night with the sad resignation of knowing this would likely never happen again. But it had definitely happened . . . hadn't it?

I watched Thorn sashay across the yard toward the

house, the hem of her sundress swaying against her calves. She hummed a tune I didn't recognize, and her arms swung with weary contentment. C.C. and I remained at the edge of the forest, holding hands, silent until we heard the screen door slam.

I turned to him and said softly, "You don't have to leave."

"I can't stay," he said with a sad smile.

"Then I could go home with you? . . ."

He shook his head. "Not tonight."

"Are you sorry this happened?"

"Not at all," he said, and his kiss convinced me.

"Then why can't I go with you?"

"Because I didn't get anything done workwise today, so I'll be heading out in—" He pulled out his phone and checked the time. "—a few hours. But I'll come by after breakfast, don't worry."

He kissed me again. I watched him climb into his truck and drive away, the noise incredibly loud in the night's silence. His taillights disappeared as he turned onto the road.

I was left outside alone. The wind continued to blow through the trees, and I sat on the porch swing, which luckily didn't squeak when it moved. What had just happened, what I'd just learned and experienced, wouldn't process; my brain had no context for it. I was numb, not just from physical satiation (and there was plenty of that) but from simply being brain-fucked by all this.

Still, the night and the swing began to work, and I grew sleepy. The swing sported a pair of musty old all-weather pillows, so I kicked off my shoes and stretched out as comfortably as I could. My overstimulated body gradually wound down, and I suppose at some point I dozed off. That is, until a familiar voice said, "Hey."

I opened my eyes and half rose on my elbows. He sat at the other end of the swing, my feet in his lap. He wore the same tattered denim jacket, and grinned like he knew the biggest secret in the world.

I said, "Ray?"

He put his finger to his lips.

"Ray?" I repeated as a whisper, and sat all the way up.

"Hey, Matt."

"Am I . . . Is this really happening?"

"Who am I to say, man?"

I looked around. It was still night, yet somehow I could see everything in exquisite detail. I could feel Ray's presence beneath my feet, too, so I discreetly drew up my knees. "Shouldn't you have, like, a blue glow around you or something?"

He laughed. "What, like I'm some Obi-Wan Kenobi? Foolish you are, yes."

"That's Yoda."

"I was never a fan. It didn't have any good songs."

I'd never met anyone who wasn't a *Star Wars* fan, so I doubt my subconscious would have made that up. Okay, then, this was reality, at least for the moment. "What is . . . Why are you here?"

"That's the question I've got for you, actually."

"Why am I here?"

"Yeah."

"Because I brought your ashes home."

"Yeah, I appreciate that. But *now* why are you here? Come on, it's rhetorical, I know why you're here. It's because of the chapel of ease."

I said nothing, but I couldn't deny it.

"And now maybe C.C., too," he continued. "But the chapel is at the heart of it."

"Yeah, I suppose. Maybe."

"So back to my original question: Why?"

"Because you were supposed to tell us the secret."

"What secret?" he said with a laugh. "What's buried there?

Dude, I told you, it *doesn't matter*. It's the mystery that counts, not the solution. Suppose you find the bones of a dead baby—what then? Or a box of Confederate gold? Or a diary with its pages all crumbling, telling old family secrets?"

Those were, in fact, ideas we'd had and pinned on the backstage board, and it made me wonder anew if this wasn't all coming out of my subconscious. I'd heard of lucid dreaming, but never experienced it; was this what it was like? It made sense that I'd conjure up Ray after everything that had happened, but was this what I'd have him say?

"So is anything buried there, or did you make it up?" I asked.

"Oh, no, there's something there. I've seen it. I'm just asking, what will knowing that change?"

"It'll mean you kept your promise, for one thing," I said, a little annoyed.

He looked away with a scowl. "Yeah, I know. But you want to know a secret?"

"Sure."

"I was planning on weaseling out of it."

"So you made a promise you intended to break?"

"No, I made a promise to give you guys something else to focus on. You were bringing my show to life, I would've done or said anything to help with that."

I was fully alert now, and close to being pissed off. "That's pretty fucking manipulative, man. We trusted you."

"That's showbiz."

"So you're not going to tell me, then?"

"What, now? Is that why you think I'm here?"

"I don't have a clue why you're here. Or even *if* you're here."

"Are you planning to help my sister get out of Needsville?"

"Yeah," I said before I even realized I meant it.

"Good. She needs it. She's more talented than I was. But just . . . be gentle with her."

I remembered the way she'd behaved earlier, in the air. My God, that really *had* happened. "She seems pretty . . . sure of herself."

"She is. She's tough and smart and driven. That's why I want you to be gentle with her. If you're not, no one will be. They'll see that toughness and think it goes all the way to the bone. It doesn't."

I nodded. "Okay. I'll watch out for her."

"Thanks." He smiled again, then lightly punched my shoulder. I felt the impact as if he were as real as me. He said, "So you and C.C., huh?"

I grinned. "Yeah."

And suddenly I snapped wide awake. I nearly fell off the porch swing before I caught myself. My heart ping-ponged around in my chest, and I gasped for breath.

One of the dogs—Ace, I think—emerged from beneath the porch and came up to rest his head against my leg. I scratched him behind his ears as I waited for my pulse to calm down. Clearly I'd been dreaming, but did that mean I *hadn't* actually spoken to Ray's ghost? Was there some rule that said ghosts couldn't show up in your dreams?

I looked up at the starry sky visible past the porch overhang. Had all that been a dream, too? I mean, could I really have been up in the air with my literal fairy lover?

I shook my head rapidly to clear the last of the cobwebs, then went inside to my room as quietly as I could. I undressed and eventually fell asleep, half-expecting Ray to return in my next dream. But he didn't, and whatever I did dream didn't stick with me the next morning.

21

At breakfast, Gerald seemed stiff and cranky, but otherwise in pretty good shape for a man who'd been shot less than twenty-four hours earlier. He still wore the sling, and his shirt was awkwardly buttoned so that the bandage beneath it showed. The rest of the family acted as if nothing had happened, including Thorn: she smiled at me with no hidden mischief or knowing glances. It made me doubt my own memories.

As I sat nursing my coffee and ignoring my eggs, I looked around at this family and tried to process what I'd learned. If I was right, if my experiences last night had been genuine, then they *weren't human*. They were unearthly supernatural creatures, hiding behind the images of regular small-town folks.

I thought back to the people I'd seen and met at the barn dance. Were *they* supernatural as well, hiding diaphanous, shimmering wings beneath their old suits and overalls? It seemed impossible, but either I'd hallucinated the previous night, or my whole view of the universe would need to change.

And Ray . . . Ray had been a fairy, too. Big, goofy Ray, with his cowboy boots and sloppy ponytail, could transform into a creature that could fly effortlessly around Manhattan. Or could he? Could they only change here, where they were safe and secure? I remembered that night on the roof after the preview, the last time I spoke to him before he died. He kept looking up; was he expecting his fellow Tufa to swoop down and carry him off?

"Anybody want the last biscuit?" Gerald asked, and when no one spoke, he grabbed it with his good hand. Ladonna bent over him, cut it open and buttered it, then kissed the top of his tangled hair. He said, "I reckon I better call Bliss and ask her how long before I can take a shower, or y'all will make me start sleeping out in the barn."

"I'll call her later this morning," Ladonna said.

I watched her carry her plate to the sink, scrape off the remains of her eggs, then rinse it and set it aside for washing later. When I looked back at the table, Gerald was watching me.

"Son, I hope you'll excuse my language," he said, "but you present the appearance of a man who knows he's about to shit a pumpkin."

"Gerald!" Ladonna scolded.

"Well, look at him. He keeps staring at us."

I looked at Thorn for some guidance, but she just sipped her coffee. At last I said, "I had some pretty strange dreams last night."

"That'll happen," Ladonna said, and patted my shoulder. "But you're awake now, and everything's normal."

That made me stare some more. Thorn smiled behind her coffee cup.

As she refilled Gerald's coffee, Ladonna asked, "Matt, would you mind singing some more of the songs from Rayford's show? Gerald was telling me last night how much he wished he could've paid more attention to what you sang yesterday."

"I was kind of preoccupied with not bleeding to death," Gerald said.

That brought me out of my haze a little. "I have the whole score on my iPod. All the demos. It's Ray singing, too."

"We'd love to hear that, too," Ladonna said. "But not right now. Right now, we'd like to hear you sing it just for us."

"Nothing beats hearing it live," Thorn interjected.

I helped wash the dishes; then we adjourned to the living room. The three of them sat on the couch and I stood in front of the television. I wondered about Ray and his strange appearance on the porch. Was that how a ghost, or rather a "haint," really manifested? Or had I just internalized C.C.'s story of the old man at the fishing hole, overlaid it with my own memories of Ray, and then dreamed the whole thing? And if it hadn't been a dream, was he also here now, waiting to pass judgment on my performance just as he had in New York?

I began with the overture number, the same one I'd performed at the wake, and essentially sang them the whole score. I did better on my own songs, since I'd practiced them more, but I didn't do too badly on the others. It took a little over an hour, some of the songs didn't really translate to a capella, and I had to stop once to rest my voice and rehydrate. But they seemed really pleased with what their son had created.

As I sang, I watched them, wondering anew about their wings. They weren't just folded up under their clothes: Thorn's sundress was far too light to disguise that. So was it some kind of physical transformation, like a werewolf? No, that wasn't right, either, because they didn't look any different in their fairy forms.

And yet they *did*. Naked, their wings flexing in the moonlight, they'd both looked *perfect*. As she sat before me now, Thorn was thin and rather wiry; last night she'd been curved in just the right exquisite places. C.C., as good-looking as he was normally, had been a god. Whatever they did, however they changed, it was almost as if the skin they wore now was the disguise, a way for such perfect beings to move among normal people and not cause riots.

And then I remembered the word: "glamour." It was how the fairies disguised themselves in stories, and made people see what they wanted to see. But had I seen their glamour last night . . . or was I seeing it now?

When I finished the last chorus, Ladonna wiped away tears and said, "That's some beautiful music, Matt. Wasn't it, Gerald?"

"It purely was," he said. He wasn't crying, but the sadness in his voice made up for it. "He must've worked awful hard to get that good."

"He was always revising and tweaking," I said, trying not to cry myself. "That line about, 'the things we most want to stay sharp / turn dull before the others,' he put that in just a couple of days before . . ." A tear escaped and ran down the side of my nose. I wiped it away.

"Thank you, Matt," Thorn said. She hadn't cried, but I could tell she was moved.

"So I reckon when you see the show," Gerald said, "you find out what's buried in the chapel."

"Uh . . . no, actually," I said. "You never do."

"Huh." He turned to Ladonna. "You ever hear of anything being buried in that old chapel?"

"Not a peep," Ladonna said. "Seems like it'd make a lot of people want their money back."

"It kind of works in context," I said.

The screen door opened and C.C. entered. I almost gasped out loud as he filled the room with his presence. I wanted to rush to him, but of course, I couldn't do that in front of all these others.

He saw everyone's expression and said, "Wow, what's the bad news?"

"Matt was singing for us," Ladonna said.

"The way y'all look, he must've been awful."

"No, he sang all the songs Rayford wrote for his play," Thorn said. "They're sad."

I looked at the two of them, remembering what we'd all three done the night before and wondering if it was suddenly as vivid to them as it was to me. But neither betrayed anything out of the ordinary.

"I'm sorry I missed it," C.C. said. "If it's all right, I'm going to take Matt out for lunch down to the Pair-A-Dice."

"You gonna go back and fix that tractor?" Gerald asked C.C.

"Why? You ain't going to be plowing nothing," Ladonna answered. "You're going to sit right there on that couch and surf all them channels you pay for every month and never watch."

"I'll do it this afternoon," C.C. promised. "And I'll even wipe off the blood for you at no extra charge." He turned to Thorn. "You want to come?"

She smiled wistfully. "No, I think you two have more to talk about than I do."

"See you later, then."

I followed C.C. out to his truck, and it wasn't until we were down the road and out of sight of the house that I asked, "Did last night really happen?"

"You think you dreamed it?"

"I dreamed talking to Ray. Did *that* really happen, too?"

"Around here, it might. If he came back as a haint, you might see him almost like he was still alive."

"'Around here' seems to be a weird place."

He laughed. "That's true enough."

We didn't hold hands this time, but there was a comfortable air between us, the kind that develops when two people realize they're compatible in ways other than sex. It struck me that I'd known C.C. for only two days, and might know him for only one more; I was scheduled to fly back tomorrow. But being with him felt old and comfortable. It would never be that way with Joaquim, although I wondered if it was with whomever he was seeing behind my back. Hell, for me it had never been that way with *anyone*.

"So where are we going?" I asked.

"The Pair-A-Dice. It's a local roadhouse, but they serve terrific burgers and fries. It's the one spot in the county that anyone, from either side, can come and not run into any trouble."

If I'd thought about it, I would've realized what he meant by that, but I was still fuzzy from the previous night and the emotional impromptu concert. I watched the pattern as sunlight flickered through the trees, idly wondered if Bigfoot lived in these woods, and almost fell back asleep before C.C. said, "Well, here it is."

It was a long concrete building with two big wooden cutouts of dice perched at the roof's peak. They'd been recently repainted, but the wood itself was warped, cracked, and needed to be replaced. A row of small birds sat along the top edge, and took off as we got out. A half dozen other vehicles parked around the building, all old and worn.

When we went inside, I was a little taken aback. Much like the barn where they'd held the wake, the Pair-A-Dice's inner proportions didn't seem to quite match its outer ones. It wasn't outlandish, like *Doctor Who*'s TARDIS, but it did seem odd. I resolved to pay more attention when I left to see if I was imagining things.

There were mismatched tables at one end of the room, and a small stage at the other. A battered piano rested beneath an enormous old heater that hung from the ceiling. A bar ran along part of one wall, and behind it was a window into the kitchen. A broad-shouldered girl seemed to be the only server working.

We took seats at an empty table, and C.C. motioned for the girl. As she dropped off water and silverware, she said, "Hey, there, C.C. Who's your new friend?"

"This is Matt, from New York. He was a friend of Rayford Parrish's."

"Oh," she said sympathetically, "I'm so sorry for your loss, then. I didn't know Rayford that well, but he always seemed nice. And he sure could sing."

"He was," I said. "And he could. Thank you."

C.C. ordered burgers and beer for us both, and when the server left, he said, "I hope that wasn't too presumptuous. It's just that they're famous for their burgers. And the fries ain't bad either."

Impulsively, I said, "I don't think anything's too presumptuous after last night."

His cheeks actually turned pink, and he looked away. But he smiled.

I indicated the stage. "So, do they have a lot of music here?"

"They do. Like I said, both sides can come here and not fight. So this is where they jam instead. You be surprised how well people who hate each other's guts can get along when they're playing. If we could just take it outside this building—"

Without warning, a man sat in one of the other chairs at our table, directly across from me. He leaned his elbows on the table and asked, "So what are you two queers talking about? Who's gonna suck whose dick?" He smiled, revealing a mouthful of perfect white teeth.

I didn't move. This guy radiated the hateful, entitled air of a full-time bully, and even though he looked to be about thirty years old, he had the swagger of a teenager. He also had a family resemblance to Winslow and Mustache Durant. I looked over at C.C. for confirmation.

"Nobody's talking to you, Billy," C.C. said. "Why don't you just run off and fuck some more pigs?"

"Woo-hoo, must be that time of the month for you, huh?" Then he looked at me. "And this must be the New York faggot who knows fung ku." He mockingly exaggerated the last two words.

"This is Billy Durant," C.C. said. "You met two of his brothers."

"Winslow still ain't walking quite right." Billy's grin widened. "But I reckon you *would* know how to handle a dick."

"What do you want, Billy?" C.C. demanded.

He pointed at me. "This fella's done started a feud. Trespassing, assaulting my brothers . . . probably cocksucking while he was there, too. What're you gonna do about it?"

"He's not going to do anything about it," I said. This Billy was exactly the kind of person my dad made me sign up for martial arts to face, and just as before, I wasn't about to back down. "*I* might, though, if you don't go the fuck away."

Billy snapped his fingers, and three more men, obviously Durants, stood up and surrounded our table. They stood shoulder to shoulder, blocking us from the view of the room, and their musty, animal smell made me want to gag.

"You threatenin' me, you Yankee faggot?" Billy said, still grinning.

"No," I said seriously. The mental image of him spitting out those perfect teeth was growing sharper and more vivid. "I'm not threatening you at all. I'm asking you to go away and leave us alone. We know you shot Gerald Parrish yesterday."

"Me? I wasn't nowhere near the Parrishes. I got witnesses, right?"

He looked at his brothers, and they all nodded.

I glanced at C.C. Although he tried to act tough for my benefit, I could see the fear in his eyes. He was strong and physically intimidating, but he wasn't a fighter and had no idea how to handle this type of conflict. A rush of protectiveness for him came over me.

"Isn't that convenient," I said to Billy. "You may have had nothing to do with that, but anything that happens next . . . well, that's on you."

I should've been nervous, but the emotions of the last twenty-four hours had left me worn out and single-minded. And that smug grin was the final straw.

Billy put a big pocketknife in my face, the tip of the blade right at the end of my nose. "How about I shove this beautiful Case knife right up your ass, you Yankee faggot?"

I met his smile with one of my own. "Dude, I hate to tell you, but if you're into shoving things up other guy's asses, that makes *you* the faggot."

That did what I wanted, which was to break his control. He drew back his arm, a stupid move since he was in the perfect position to slash my face with very little effort, but now he was angry and wanted the satisfaction of a stab.

I used my right hand to turn his arm aside as the knife came at me, and drove the blade into the padded back of the empty chair. Then I stood a little and used that momentum to add to the power of driving my left elbow into the side of his head with all the considerable force I could put behind it. The impact stunned him, and he slid from his chair to the concrete floor. His nearest brother, instead of catching him, stepped aside to let him fall. His head made a loud *bonk*.

I jumped up into a defensive stance. The other Durants were momentarily too startled to make a move. I readied myself to take them on; if I kept them off balance, I might be able to put them out of commission before one of them shanked me. But before I could, a female voice said loudly, "Billy Durant!"

We all turned. The woman I was sure had visited Ray in New York, Bronwyn Chess, stood in the doorway. She had no baby with her now. About half the people in the place scurried past her to get out of the building.

"You know this ain't the place for that kind of nonsense, Billy Durant. What do you think you're doing?"

Billy climbed back to his feet, using the chair and his nearest brother for support. "This faggot sum'bitch just broke my skull!" Billy said woozily.

"Yeah, well, *this* bitch is going to break your neck if I don't see you moving." She made one of those hand gestures, and the sound of chairs scraping on concrete was loud in the silence as the remaining bystanders moved away from us.

Billy Durant shoved one of his other brothers aside and looked hatefully at me. "This ain't over. You think going back to New York'll make you safe, but we can find you anywhere."

"You've already found me twice," I said. "Hasn't worked out too well for you either time."

His face turned red, but his brothers pushed him toward the door. They all had their heads down in either shame or fear, but Billy managed to get in one last glare as the door closed.

Bronwyn sighed and shook her head. She picked up Billy's dropped knife and sat down at our table. Around us, conversation resumed, but a lot more quietly than before. I could guess what they were all talking about.

"You boys seem to cause a ruckus wherever you go," Bronwyn said, and flicked her finger at the cut Billy's knife had made in the chair back.

"They caused the ruckus," I said, and sat down as well. I was secretly tickled that I used that word, which I'd learned from the play, in actual conversation. "We're just the ruck-ees."

"Did you hurt him bad?"

"I rang his bell, that's all."

"Might've been better in the long run if you'd cleaned out his belfry. How long are you in town for?"

"I leave tomorrow."

"Good. Not that I have anything against you, but the world just spins better if the Durants stay up on their mountain."

Emboldened by my victory, I said, "You know, you can deny it all you want, but I know that it *was* you in New York visiting Ray."

Before she could respond, C.C., who'd been absolutely still and silent through the whole altercation, said quietly, "He knows about the Tufa."

Bronwyn looked from him to me. "What does he know?"

"What Thorn and I showed him last night. How to ride the night wind."

She thought it over, then said, "Come with me, then." She stood and waited for me to do the same.

I looked at C.C. He said, "Go on. You don't have to worry about Bronwyn. You can trust her."

The server brought our burgers, sliding them in front of us and then dashing away. More out of obstinacy than hunger, I paused long enough to eat some of the fries. Then I followed Bronwyn toward the door. I tensed as we approached, worried that she was leading me into an ambush, but when we went outside, the Durants were gone.

She led me to the edge of the gravel parking lot, near the forest. Then she turned to me and crossed her arms. "What the *fuck,* man?"

"Ask the ones who started it."

"I'm asking you."

"What do you know about C.C.?"

"What, that he's gay? Everybody knows that. Nobody cares."

"The Durants seemed to care."

"The Durants just like to fight. If you'd been Asian, they'd be telling jokes about slanted eyes and Pearl Harbor. You shouldn't take it personally."

"I don't take that personally. I take guns being pointed at me and knives in my face *very* personally, though."

"I just mean—"

"Did you kill Ray?" The question came out before I could catch it, and it stopped her cold.

She stared at me. "What in the world makes you ask that?"

"Given what you people are, what . . . he was, I assume you were there to tell him if he didn't cancel the show, he'd be in trouble. And he wasn't about to do that. So . . ."

She seemed really hurt by the accusation. "Look, I don't know what C.C.'s told you—"

"I'm not talking about C.C. I *saw* you in New York, remember? We *spoke*. Stop pretending it wasn't you."

"—but Rayford was my cousin. We were family. I used to listen to him sing when we were kids and wish I could sing like that." Her eyes narrowed with genuinely scary anger. "Goddammit, I wasn't there to hurt him. We just didn't want him drawing attention to us. We like being here in the middle of nowhere, with nobody bothering us. If C.C. told you anything about us, I know he told you *that*."

A light went on in my head. "But you *did* have that dreadlocked girl follow him around."

She started to dispute this, but then nodded. "I needed eyes on the ground. It's hard for me to get away with the baby. And she worked cheap. She thought I was some producer looking to get a scoop on the competition."

"So if you didn't kill him, what did he die of?"

"He died of what they said, I suppose. A brain tumor, right?"

"Fairies can get brain tumors?" It was a cheap shot, and I knew it as soon as the words left my lips.

"Most of us are mainly people now!" she snarled through clenched teeth. "We've bred with your kind for centuries, *millennia*. There's few of us left who are pure Tufa. Ray certainly wasn't one. But he was sure Tufa where it counted—in his song." She sucked in a long breath, and when she spoke again, she was calmer. "But that's not why I wanted to talk to you. You leave tomorrow, right? I want your word that you'll stay at the Parrishes' until then. I don't want you going anywhere you might run into the Durants."

"What'll stop them from coming to the farm? They shot Gerald yesterday."

"I know. That's being dealt with. But this is about you."

"You want me to promise I won't go looking for a fight?"

"I want you to promise you won't go *anywhere*."

"Sure, why not?" I said with a shrug.

She wasn't that distracted by her grief. "That's not a yes."

"All right, yes. I promise. I'll stay at the Parrishes'."

"No matter what?"

"Yes."

She looked at me for a long moment, gauging my honesty. At last she nodded, said, "Come on, then, your lunch is getting cold," and led me back to the Pair-A-Dice.

She should've looked more closely, though, because my fingers were crossed behind my back. In a land where fairies greeted each other with fancy hand gestures, I assumed this childish tradition might still count. It didn't really matter, though; like a teenager told not to hang out with disreputable friends, I was more determined than ever to get back to the chapel and see what was buried there.

22

After lunch, C.C. and I rode silently in his truck until he finally said, "How did you do that?"

"Do what?"

"Handle Billy Durant."

"Well, I just knew how to hit him right where—"

"No, I mean, how did you stay so calm? I damn near pissed my pants. I'm not a coward, or at least I don't think I am, but . . . we were surrounded. And in case you didn't know, most of them had guns. I bet Billy even had a gun, he just likes showing off with that knife because he ordered it off a shopping channel."

"It's just . . . how it works," I said, struggling to find the words to describe something I'd internalized to such a degree. "A fight is just a technical problem, like repairing a machine is for you. If you get mad or scared, it just makes it harder. Same thing with acting, or dancing; when you're onstage, you can't freak out. So you just learn to stay calm."

He nodded as if he understood, but I wasn't sure he did. "When did you learn to do all that?"

"When I was a teenager. Right after I came out to my parents."

"How'd they take it?"

"They were a little upset at first, but not for the reasons you think. They just knew how hard it would make things for me. Then my dad told me he wanted me to also learn a martial art. He said that people would try to hurt me for no other reason than being what I was, and he wouldn't always be able to protect me, so I needed to learn to protect myself."

C.C. shook his head. "Wow. You're a lucky guy to have a father like that."

"Do your parents know?"

"I figure everyone knows, but I haven't officially come out. Does that make me a coward, too?"

I so wished we weren't in the truck so I could at least hold him while we talked. "No, man, you're not a coward. First, when and where and how you do that is entirely your own business, nobody else's. And second, being afraid is *normal*. You think I wasn't afraid with that knife in my face? I was scared shitless, too, let me tell you. Deep down, I was just as afraid as you. Maybe more so: except for you, I don't really know anyone here who'd care if the Durants cut me into tiny pieces."

He smiled a little. "Thorn might shed a tear."

We both laughed.

After another bit of silence, I said, "Can I tell you something?"

"Sure."

"It may sound a little loony."

He gave me a sideways, *you've got to be kidding* look. "You really think so? After everything *I've* told *you*?"

"Good point. It's about my conversation with Ray. The dream one I told you about." I related everything about my encounter on the porch, and he listened without comment. When I finished I said, "So, what do you think? Did I really see Ray's ghost?"

"In your dream? You can see anything in a dream."

"Not just there. When I was singing yesterday, while Bliss was working on patching up Gerald, I closed my eyes for a minute and when I opened them, I thought I saw Ray standing over his father. He looked as real as anyone else. Then he just . . . disappeared. Like the old man at your fishing hole."

"Is that all?"

Something else occurred to me. "Don, the reporter, got a picture of something that looked like a person standing behind me. It was too blurry to tell for sure, but . . ." I shrugged.

C.C. thought this over, then said, "I don't know."

"You don't know if it's a ghost?"

"I don't know if it's Ray's ghost."

"It sure looked and sounded like him."

"That ain't always the case. But I know someone who might know."

"Who?"

"She's a local hoodoo woman. Do you know what that is?"

"No, but it sounds flamboyant."

That made him smile. "Yeah, she can be. Her name's Azure. She knows about this sort of thing. Haints, and curses, and spells and such. She can tell the future."

"She sounds like a witch."

"Some might call her that. Nobody around here would, though."

"Is she friendly?"

"She's . . . prickly. But she does help people."

"Even Yankees?"

He laughed. "Yeah, even Yankees."

"Then let's go."

If I thought the road to the chapel of ease had been rough and untraveled, it was nothing compared to this. We left black-top, then gravel, then dirt, then what appeared to be two ruts with a grass strip between them, until at last we drove through a small field right up to the edge of thick woods. When we parked, it was next to a huge rock, almost as high as my shoulder, that had symbols carved all over it. There was no sign of a house, or any other human being, and once again I thought about how unlikely it would be for anyone to find my corpse out here.

We got out of the truck. I had no idea where we were in relation to anyplace else. I asked, "Sure there are no Durants around here?"

"The Durants wouldn't come near Miss Azure."

I indicated the markings on the stone and asked, "What are these?"

"Beats me. Not too many people can read that language."

The symbols were, in fact, divided as words would be, and some did look like sentences. But they overlapped and went in all directions, making it hard to follow particular lines. Some of the carving was ancient, if the wear on them was any indication, while some looked as sharp and clean as if they had been made last week. "What's the point of it, then?" I asked.

"I didn't say *nobody* could read it."

And that was all the information I was going to get. I followed him around the boulder, up a rise, and along the ridge at the top. The trees were thick, and if there was a trail, I couldn't see it. I thought of the smug parkour runners who made such a big deal of traversing things like railings and park benches. I wondered how long they'd last in these woods.

The air was still and muggy, and I was so busy avoiding obstacles that at first I didn't realize it was dead quiet. But it was: no birds, no insects, no wind. Just our footsteps.

Suddenly C.C. put his hand on my chest and hissed, "Shh!" Ahead something moved, but the dense trunks blocked my view of it. I tensed, imagining one of the Durants, or some other redneck thug. Then it stepped into the open.

It was something like a deer. I'd never seen one except at

the zoo, and those weren't nearly the size of this one. Its head rose at least as high as mine, and it sported gigantic antlers that branched into over a dozen thick points. It was backlit by the sun, and seemed to be posing in profile for our benefit. Then it turned and stared at us with the haughty superiority I'd seen in some choreographers.

"What is that?" I whispered.

"That," C.C. said equally as softly, "is the king of the forest."

Well, he definitely had the crown for it. With one hoof he scraped the ground in front of him. Was he about to charge?

Other movement caught my eye. Two skinny, doglike creatures walked through the trees, appearing and disappearing as they stalked and circled the deer.

"Are those wolves?" I asked softly.

"Coyotes."

"Are they going to hurt him?"

"No, they're his bodyguards."

"Something that big needs bodyguards?"

"Something that important does."

The stag stopped his pawing and studied us for another few moments. Even at this distance, the look in his eye reminded me of the way certain producers looked at you in auditions, fully aware of their power and hoping you were, too, for your own sake. Then he turned and walked away into the forest. His coyote attendants followed.

In that moment, I glimpsed him between the trees and he seemed to be a man, not a deer, still sporting the enormous antlers. The coyotes were slender young women with dreadlocks and feral grins. Then they were gone.

"Did you see that?" I asked C.C. very quietly.

"See what?"

I let it drop. I was already starting to doubt my own perceptions, since I was seeing (and apparently chatting with) ghosts. Deer men and coyote girls might be the last straw.

When he was certain the path was clear, C.C. led us farther along the ridge. I looked around for any sign of the deer, but there was nothing. We found an actual trail, marked with bicycle reflectors nailed to tree trunks, that led down the slope into a small hollow between the hills. The trail turned into a kind of rustic sidewalk, paved with smooth, flat stones. It led us to a small cottage.

At first it reminded me of a Thomas Kinkade painting. Logs formed the walls, and wide wooden shingles covered the peaked roof. Smoke rose from the stone chimney. If seven dwarves had emerged to do the yard work, I'm not sure I would've been that surprised.

Then the non-storybook details announced themselves. Three solar panels gleamed among the wooden roof slats, and a satellite dish was clamped to one corner. I heard music through the small, open windows: Pharrell Williams's "Happy."

C.C. stopped several feet from the door and hollered, "Miss Azure? You home?"

The music stopped. The door opened and a woman peered out from the dark interior. She had the inevitable black Tufa hair, streaked with silver and tied in a long braid that fell over her shoulder. She was tall and slender, and it was hard to tell her age. She peered over her glasses at us and said, "That must be Cyrus Crow hollering my name."

"Yes, ma'am," C.C. said.

"Who's that with you?"

"Ah, this is my friend Matt. He's from New York."

"How in the world did you meet somebody from New York? You using one of them online dating sites?"

Well, clearly *she* knew about him. He laughed and said, "No, ma'am, he was a friend of Rayford Parrish's."

She pondered this for a moment. People around here did that a lot. I suppose most of us could probably stand to think a moment or two before speaking, but I'd never seen it as a cultural norm before. At last she said, "Well, then, y'all come in."

As we approached, something poked out beside her feet. It was small, white, and seemed to be grinning. Its mouth was filled with long, sharp teeth.

I stopped dead. "What is that?" I asked, not caring that I sounded like a wuss.

She looked down. "Oh, that's Ketchum."

"*What* is that?"

"That's a possum," C.C. said.

"Ketchum, you go on, you're making people nervous." She nudged the animal with her foot, and it waddled out and across the yard. It wasn't very big, but it was strange-looking, and its ratlike tail sent a familiar shudder of revulsion through me. I hoped those things never crossed the Brooklyn Bridge and set up in Central Park.

Her cabin, or cottage, or tiny house, or whatever the hell you want to call it, was dimly lit by natural light through the windows. It smelled of potpourri and cooking vegetables. It was rustic in the extreme, and cluttered with items I couldn't identify. Many of them appeared to be musical instruments, and from the way they were scattered around the room, they weren't just there for show. Still, I saw the Spotify screen before she closed her laptop, so she wasn't any sort of anti-tech Luddite.

Three cats draped like accent pieces over the old furniture, but thankfully I saw no more possums. A door led to what I assumed was a bedroom, but otherwise the living room, dining room, and kitchen took up one big open space. The table was laden with various drying plants, and something simmered on the stove.

"Excuse the mess," Azure said. "I wasn't expecting company."

Aren't you supposed to be a fortune-teller? I wanted to ask, but all the Southern politeness had rubbed off on me.

She moved some papers from the kitchen table, stirred

whatever she was cooking, and said, "Now—what can I do for you gentlemen?"

C.C. looked at me. "Matt here thinks he has a haint."

"Is that a fact?"

Stated so baldly, it sounded goofier than I'd expected. "Well . . ."

"Have you seen the dead?"

"Kind of."

"Was it someone known to you in life?"

"Yes."

"And has it spoken to you?"

"I guess. I mean, it—"

"Sit down," she said, and gestured at one of the chairs. I sat, and she washed her hands at the sink. "Any other signs?"

"Uh . . . not that I know of."

"How about omens?"

"What's the difference?"

"A sign is something that's supposed to be there but still gets your attention. An omen is something that ain't."

"Ah. Good to know." I looked over at C.C., who stood patiently by the front door. With his rugged, rustic solidity, he looked like part of the decor.

"Cyrus, sit down, you're making me nervous," Azure snapped. To me, she said, "A haint ain't always a bad thing. Sometimes they have something important to say, and that's why they stick around. Did this one tell you anything important?"

"No, we just . . . discussed work."

"And what kind of work do you do?"

"I'm an actor."

She cocked her head and looked at me oddly. "Well. I ain't never met a real actor before. You been in anything I might know?"

"No, I'm mainly a stage actor. In New York."

"Broadway?"

"Sometimes."

"Ah, so that's how you know Rayford Parrish."

"Yeah. Yes, ma'am," I corrected quickly.

"May I see your left hand?"

I let her take it. "You read palms?"

"I read signs," she said without looking up. "Sometimes it's in a palm, sometimes in tea leaves, sometimes in the way the clouds move."

"Must be tiring." I winced at my own sarcasm.

She looked up. "You're trying not to be a smart-ass, son, and I appreciate that, but your snark is still coming out. Why do you believe in medicine?"

"I beg your pardon?"

"Why do you believe that when a doctor tells you something, it's right?"

"Well, I guess . . . because it works."

"Do you understand how or why it works?"

"Not really."

She tapped my palm with one long finger. "This is the same way. It works. You may not know why or how, *I* may not know, but it gets results."

"It does," C.C. said.

That made me smile. "I apologize. I'm a little disoriented by a lot of what I've seen the last couple of days, and I tend to fall back on sarcasm when that happens. I'll try to watch it."

She nodded maternally, and I half expected her to muss my hair. "That's the right thing to say, son. Now, let me see what I can figure out here."

She got close to my palm, and I had the absurd idea she might lick it. But she just studied it in light I would've thought too dim for such close-up work.

One of the cats stretched, then hopped down from its perch. I noticed that the many knickknacks hanging from the wall appeared to be mostly small animal skulls, some painted with designs and symbols that, to my untrained eye at least, resembled those on the boulder.

At last Azure sat up and said matter-of-factly, "You've got yourself a haint, young man. And let me guess: it's young Mr. Rayford."

"Yeah. So what do I do?"

"Listen to it. Find out what it wants and give it to it."

"I would, but I'm leaving tomorrow."

"You think a haint can't follow you to the big city?"

"I spoke with it last night. Well, early this morning. We had an actual conversation. It didn't mention anything about needing something from me."

"Then it ain't ready to tell you, or you ain't ready to hear."

This was all needlessly cryptic. "Okay, suppose I don't want to have a haint. Is there a way to get rid of it? Besides giving it what it wants?"

"Become a haint yourself."

"I'd rather not."

She laughed. "C.C., take your friend home, or wherever he's staying. I suspect tonight's going to be pretty eventful for him, so he might want a nap."

"That's all?" I said.

"Hey, it's your haint, not mine. But if you're leaving tomorrow, and what the haint wants from you is here, then a lot's going to happen real soon. Or . . ." She trailed off with a shrug.

"Or what?" I pressed.

"Or you ain't gonna be leaving anytime soon."

I stood up. "Thank you," I said uncertainly.

Azure nodded. C.C. made a hand gesture at her, which she returned. As we stepped out the door, I said, "We saw a great big deer on our way in. C.C. said it was the king of the forest. Is that a sign or an omen?"

She cocked her head, suddenly a lot more interested. "Did you, now. Cyrus, were you planning to mention that?"

"I didn't think it—"

"Do you know nothing about reading signs, even after all this time?" To me she said, "That was an *omen*, young man."

"Does that change things?"

"It doesn't change it, son, but it ratchets it up. The king don't come out for just anyone rambling through the woods. He must think one of you is a big deal."

"It can't be me," C.C. said.

"No, it don't seem likely, given everything else swirling around this boy." She looked at my face so closely, I expected her to squeeze a blackhead off my nose. "I reckon the message this haint has for you ain't just for you, son. It's bigger than that if the king is concerned. You best try to find out what it is before something bad happens."

"To me?"

"Or someone close to you."

"I don't think Ray would—"

"Haints ain't always what they look like. Might not be your friend. Might be a palimpsest of your friend—you know what that is?"

"No."

"It's like a sketch of your friend, drawn over your memories. It can fool you into thinking you're talking to him, but all you're talking to is a determination strong enough to come out of the grave to get something done."

"I don't understand."

"Most of the time I don't, either," she said with a laugh. "Y'all be careful, now. Bless your hearts."

We drove—or rather, bounced—in silence until we got back onto the actual paved highway. Azure's bizarre warnings rattled in my head in the same way I did in the truck's cab.

"Should we have paid her?" I asked. "Or at least offered?"

"She don't do this for money," C.C. said. "She's a professor at East Tennessee State."

"She's a college professor?"

"World-renowned folklore expert, if you can believe it. Wrote three books so far."

"I guess you never can tell about people."

"That's the pure-D truth."

At last, when the ride was finally smooth again, I turned to C.C. and said, "I have to go back to the chapel tonight. I have to find out what's buried there. You can call me crazy if you want, but I know I'll hate myself if I go back to New York without at least trying."

"Do you think that's what the haint wants?"

It was the exact opposite of what Ray wanted, but I wasn't going to let a ghost dictate to me. But then again, Azure had hinted at the possibility that this ghost might not really be Ray after all. If it wasn't, then perhaps finding the secret was what the real Ray, the dead one, actually *did* want. Still, I was sure of one thing. "It's what I want."

"Are you asking for my help?"

"I am. I have to know. It's a secret that Ray never got to tell, and if that dream ghost was real, it's one he never meant to tell. He was going to weasel out of his promise to tell us."

"So it's revenge?"

"It's . . . balance. We're bringing his world to life. He was wrong not to tell us. Even if no one else ever finds out, we deserve to know."

C.C. frowned as he mulled that. "So can a bunch of actors keep a secret?"

I thought of the great skein of gossip woven by actors in a company. "That's a separate issue. So . . . will you help? Will you take me back?"

"After being threatened with a knife, and Gerald being shot, and a haint telling you not to, you want to sneak back onto the Durants' land?"

"I do."

"And dig up something that may not actually be there."

"You saw the spot. Something's there."

"I saw a bare patch of ground inside a ruined building. It could just be because the sun never quite hits that spot, so nothing grows."

"Could be. Only one way to find out." I took his right hand and kissed the back of it. "Come on. After all this, you know you want to know, too."

He drove some more, then said, "All right. But we're not going in there all haphazard like we did before. We need a plan."

"Okay."

"And I'm in charge. If I say we're done before we get what you want, then we're done."

"Agreed."

He turned to me and smiled at last. "And when it's over, you *better* make it worth my while."

"*That* I can promise," I said.

23

The afternoon took forever to go by. With nothing to do, I was aware of every . . . creeping . . . moment, and it was maddening. I tried to nap, but between anticipation of the night raid on the chapel, and the worry (okay, fear) that Ray might show up in my dreams again, that wasn't going to happen. C.C. went off to fix the tractor, abandoned in the field yesterday when Gerald was shot. So I was truly at loose ends.

I kept checking my phone for any signal. Occasionally I got one bar, but no texts from Joaquim or Emily came through. Then it dinged, and I saw I had a voice mail from Emily.

"Hey," she said. She sounded like an old woman, weak and worn out. "It's not there. I've been looking through his files, I haven't slept, I haven't eaten . . . it's just not there. It was the last gift he might've had for me, Matt, and now I'll never get it. He really is gone."

The message ended. I tried to call her back, but there wasn't enough signal for it to go through. I texted her, *Hang on. Going to find out tonight.* But it wouldn't go through.

Frustrated, I went to the kitchen for a drink of either

the tooth-rotting sweet tea or something harder, which I couldn't find. As I stood at the kitchen window, Gerald came out of the barn, toting a bag of feed on his shoulder. It wasn't his injured shoulder, but his sling was gone, and he moved as if it no longer bothered him. In a world of haints and little-girl mayors, this didn't seem quite so disconcerting, but it was still weird as fuck. I mean, I'd seen the bullet hole, the blood, the way his face had gone pasty white like old faded linen. And that had been *yesterday.*

I watched him carry the feed, knowing what I did about the Tufa, and tried to imagine him naked, with huge wings. He spat on the ground beside the pigs and looked so comfortable in his overalls that for a moment I doubted what I'd seen and experienced. But then, Thorn was their daughter and Ray was their son, so if I believed it about them, I had to believe they got it from their parents. Which meant that, at that particular moment, I was watching an actual fairy scrape manure from his boots on a fence.

I wanted to laugh out loud, but I didn't. Instead I went outside and said, "Can I give you a hand with that?"

"Naw, it ain't nothing," he said. He continued on to the pen, where three small pigs scurried to the ancient trough. The wind changed, and the smell made me scrunch up my face and breathe through my mouth.

Then Gerald put his head down on his arms atop the nearest fence post. I quickly went to him and said, "Are you all right?"

He looked up, and I saw tears in his eyes. "This used to be Rayford's job. Growing up, he was the one who always fed the pigs. He'd slop 'em with table scraps every night after dinner. He wasn't no shirker, but he purely hated them pigs."

I was taken aback by this sudden emotion from a man who'd been so solid and taciturn. All I could think to say was, "I'm sorry."

He wiped his eyes, leaving dirty smears on his face. Then he held up his big, meaty hand. "He was my first little baby. I remember when he was born, he was so tiny and red, I was afraid he'd slip right through my fingers. My daddy told me, 'Ain't nothing like seeing your own flesh and blood there before you,' and he was right." He gestured at the yard. "He used to run around here in his damn diaper, chasing the dogs and the chickens; you couldn't keep pants on him." He laughed, then began to sob.

I put my hand on his shoulder.

"I loved that boy," he continued. "I didn't understand him, but I sure did love him."

"He knew you did," I said.

"But I didn't get him. His whole thing with musicals, with wanting to go to New York. Tufa don't leave, or at least they don't stay gone. I warned him."

I looked everywhere but directly at him.

He gazed out across the rolling mountains. "I hope he was a good man to y'all Yankees. I hope he didn't forget what I tried to teach him. Be good to your friends. Listen to their songs. Try to leave things better than you found 'em."

Now I was crying, too. "He sure did that, Mr. Parrish. Everyone who knew him loved him because he made us all feel special."

He hugged me then, probably the most enveloping, all-encompassing hug I'd ever experienced. His big, solid body shuddered as he cried. I hugged him back as best I could, but felt spindly and spare compared to his masculine strength. I realized this was probably the first time his grief had come out, and he could only show it to me, a stranger whose presence wouldn't be around to remind him of it later.

He withdrew, wiped his eyes with one big forearm, and without looking at me said, "Thank you, son. I apologize for that."

"No need to," I said, and dried my own eyes with my shirttail.

He turned away and started back toward the barn. "Got some stuff to attend to. Tell Ladonna not to hold dinner for me, okay?"

"Yes, sir."

He walked with heavy, defeated steps down the hill to the barn. The scale of what had happened hit me then. I'd never lost a parent, and my brother was still alive; some friends had passed away over the years, but I'd avoided any loss that was so deep, so devastating.

Then I heard him sing. His voice was eerily similar to Ray's, but deeper, and raspier.

> *Oh, the deacon went down*
> *To the cellar to pray*
> *He found a jug*
> *And he stayed all day. . . .*

I stayed there by the pen, no jug in hand, listening to the pigs happily chow down and gazing out over the mountains.

How could a race of fairies exist like this? I mean, every single one of them I'd heard sing or play was an extraordinary musician. Certainly Ray was, and Thorn seemed to have inherited the same talent. Ray had made it big in New York, and if he hadn't died, he'd have been the toast of the theater scene; so why didn't any of the others try? Why did they live in poverty, isolated from the world? Why had Gerald said, "Tufa don't leave"?

I found Thorn noodling on her guitar on the front porch, a laptop open next to her. I stayed back and watched her for a while. She would try out a chord, change it, and then write it down when it was right. Finally I cleared my throat; she looked up and said, "Hi. Out of sorts without C.C. to drool over?"

"No, I'm fine."

"Have you been crying?"

"What? No. Just some hay fever, I think. I'm just curious about something. Can I talk to you?"

"After last night, it'd seem rude to give you the cold shoulder."

I ignored the comment. "I wanted to ask you something about the Tufa."

"Yes, we like monster truck shows. Nothing like the rumble from an alcohol-burning 575 engine, I tell you what." She shivered happily, and I wondered whether or not she was kidding.

"No, not that," I said, and gestured around me. "It's . . . why do you live like this?"

"In a house?"

"In a . . ." I lowered my voice. "In a run-down shack in the middle of nowhere. Like you're . . ."

"Poor white trash?" she finished in an exaggerated Southern accent.

"Your words, not mine. But yeah."

She rested her chin on the edge of the guitar's body. "How do you think we ended up here? We didn't start here. We come from a place called Tír na nÓg. Ever heard of it?"

"No."

"No reason you would have. We all lived in a forest, and were watched over and protected by the woodsman. Well, one day he made a bad bet, and somehow our queen found out and wanted to see the outcome. Normally it would have been no problem, but with the queen watching, the woodsman got nervous. He lost the bet, and as a result, the queen banished him. She flung him across the sea, and since he was our leader, we all got flung with him. We traveled west until we ended up here." She smiled, a kind of sad and tender look I'd never seen on her face before. "You believe that story?"

"I believe you believe it."

She chuckled. "You charmer, you. So yeah, here we were. And then people started showing up. The Native Americans were no trouble, they left us alone and we left them alone, except for friendly relations. But then the Europeans came in, and they fucked up everything. They killed anyone who didn't look like them, took all the land because they didn't believe the Indians were actual people, and essentially acted like assholes to a whole continent. Then when they started bringing Africans here as slaves, they noticed that we—the Tufa—looked like we might have some African in us, too. So they tried to include us in their view of the world. Well, we weren't too happy about that, so we just pulled back into our little hills and hollers. That made us both dangerous and scary to them. And that's pretty much how they still see us today."

"Are you?"

"What, dangerous and scary? We can be." She strummed a chord and added, "Does that answer your question?"

It did, at least for the moment. "What are you working on?"

"A new song about love."

"A love song."

"No, that's different. Want to hear what I've got so far?"

"Sure."

She strummed her guitar a couple of times, finding the right chord, then began.

> He was a black-haired boy with a smile like the sun,
> And he knew there was someone for him.
> He was a singer and dancer from a faraway land,
> With no idea how this song would end.
> They looked at each other and the meaning was clear
> Two men with one heart between them
> And when they first touched, all the questions were
>   answered
> Each could see that the other perceived him. . . .

When she was done, she looked at me for a reaction. I said, "I bet I know where you got the idea."

"I bet you do, too. That last line of the chorus needs work, though. Maybe 'believed him'?" She strummed and sang it softly, trying out the new words.

"If you play that around here, won't it make things a little awkward for C.C.?"

"Do you think nobody knows? Here's a secret: *Everyone* knows. And nobody cares. It's not like he's the only gay Tufa. He's not even the only gay Tufa on this farm."

That took a minute to sink in. "Wait . . . you?"

She grinned. "Surprised? Imagine the look on my parents' face when they find out."

"They don't know?"

"I haven't made it official. But they know I don't date, and I have a couple of girlfriends I'm *very* close to."

"But when you first asked to come with me to New York, you offered . . ."

"And I would've paid up. That's how bad I want to get out of here. But that doesn't change who I am. We don't buy into your attitudes about sex."

"Mine?"

"Non-Tufa in general. If we like somebody, or something looks like it might be fun, we do it. We don't worry about labels. And we don't feel guilty later."

"That must be a great way to live."

She half shrugged. "It's not bad."

"The outside world isn't that way. I'm not sure you'll like it."

"You mean you're not sure I'll fit in."

"That, too," I admitted.

"I'm willing to take that chance. I can't be who I really am here, and it's got nothing to do with who I like to fuck. I need to see what the world is like."

Just then C.C. came around the house, wiping his hands on a rag. He had one smear of grease on his cheek. "So what are you two talking about so seriously?"

"Music and love, what else is there?" Thorn said.

"I'm going home to clean up," C.C. said to me. "I have some calls to make. I'll be back about sundown. You be ready?"

I was a little disappointed that he didn't ask me to come with him. I'd love to help him shower. "Yeah, I'll be waiting."

"Good." He started to turn away, then stopped. "Remember: if this looks too dangerous, we'll walk away."

"Whoa, what are you two up to?" Thorn asked.

"We're going back to the chapel," C.C. said. "Matt's bound and determined to find out what's buried there."

"Are you sure that's a good idea?" she asked seriously.

"Not really," I said.

"I think it's stupid as hell," C.C. said. "But damn it, now I'm curious, too."

"Even if someone gets hurt?" She looked from C.C. to me.

"No one's going to get hurt," I said.

"Except a few Durants," Thorn said with a sly smile. "Right?"

"No, not even them," C.C. said. "They're already mad at us; we don't need a real feud after all this time." He looked at me. "We have to live here after you're gone, you know."

"I'm not arguing with you," I said.

"Okay. See you soon."

I watched him walk away. Thorn leaned over and kissed me on the cheek, then took her computer and guitar inside. I took out my phone and looked at it, expecting the NO SERVICE notification. Yet to my surprise, I saw that I actually got a solid signal.

I didn't hesitate. I dialed Emily first, but got her voice mail. Then I called Neil.

"Hello, Matt," he said seriously when he answered. "How are you?"

"Okay."

"Still coming back tomorrow?"

"Yes. I'm going out tonight to resolve our little mystery once and for all. I have some locals helping me."

"That's good." He paused a long moment, and I got a sinking feeling, the way you do when your subconscious knows that bad news is coming. My first thought was that the show had been canceled for some reason, possibly some legal snag since the writer/composer was dead. But I turned out to be totally wrong.

"I'm guessing you don't know this," he said. "Remember Ray's girlfriend, Emily? Well, she's dead. She killed herself yesterday."

My legs grew weak, just like the cliché. I sat down on the porch steps. "What happened?"

"She jumped out her window. Note said she couldn't live without Ray. I had no idea they were so serious, they'd only been dating a little while."

I recalled the way she'd behaved that day in his apartment. "Oh my God."

"The cast took this hard. They really need you to come through for them, Matt. They need to know this secret."

"You said it wasn't important."

"It wasn't before. It is now. They'll see it as a sign from Ray that he's watching over them."

"If he's doing any watching, it hasn't been very much help so far."

"That is true enough. Any more tragedy, and we'll be the new Scottish play."

He meant the superstition that all productions of *Macbeth* were cursed, especially if you said the play's title anywhere but onstage. Although we were all professionals, I knew how the cast felt, and how it could affect the show. Even after the ecstatic reviews, bad word of mouth from the first paying audiences could end our run as easily as bad press, and a sad, depressed cast couldn't help but be disappointing.

"Like I said, I'm going tonight," I told him. "By tomorrow morning, I'll know. I'll send you pictures."

"Thanks. And I'm very sorry, Matt. I know she was your friend even before she started dating Ray."

"I appreciate it, Neil."

I hung up and sat there, staring at the ground. First Ray, then Emily . . .

"I'm sorry I wasn't there," I whispered, hoping Emily's spirit could hear me.

Ray had said, "Women who fall in love with Tufa men have a very hard time if we go away." Was this what he meant?

I was too cried out to muster fresh tears, but I sat for a long time, letting the emotions roll through me. C.C. wasn't sure if our budding relationship would send me into such despair, but did I dare take the chance? Or hell, was this how it manifested, with this almost unbearable compulsion to find out what was buried in the chapel? Deep down, was it all just to stay near C.C.?

I still had my phone in my hand, and I opened the photography app, intending to call up pictures I had of Emily. Yet the first one that came up was one I'd taken at the cemetery, near Byrda Fowler's grave.

I stared at it. Something was there, but I couldn't quite see it. I turned the camera around, tilted it, squinted at it.

And then I saw it.

It was made from the patterns of light hitting the ground through the trees. A woman's shape, in a long dress that appeared white because it was made of sunlight. There was her arm, and her shoulders, and her head with long shadowy Tufa hair. Her high forehead was one bright patch, and pits of darkness made her eyes. There was only one person it could be.

Byrda.

She hadn't let me take a picture of her headstone, because she wanted me to see *her*.

That, of course, made no sense in the real world. But here in Cloud County, it seemed entirely possible.

I put my camera away. Then I went inside and helped Ladonna get dinner ready.

24

As good as his word, C.C. showed up just as the sun slid behind the mountains. Only he wasn't alone. Another truck followed his, and from it emerged a big man with sandy hair, the first Tufa I'd seen without the jet-black locks. I realized he might not be a Tufa at all.

I sat on the porch swing with Ladonna, sipping iced tea and swatting away mosquitoes that braved the creosote fumes from the candles. The tea was so sweet, I worried that I'd either be diabetic or running around like a wired toddler before I finished it. Thorn sat on the steps, noodling on her guitar.

Fireflies sparkled in the yard; I'd seen them very seldom growing up, and not in the numbers they seemed to be here. Ladonna had just sung a song about a little girl in her nightgown chasing after fireflies, and when I asked about it told me it was by someone named Caroline Herring.

C.C. came up onto the porch and said, "I bet I missed a good dinner, didn't I?"

"Pork chops and homemade applesauce," Ladonna said. "There's leftovers if you're still hungry."

"No, I grabbed a sandwich at home."

"Bologna and cheese ain't no substitute for good home cooking, young man."

"Why, Miz Parrish, you been spying on me?"

Ladonna laughed, then looked at the other man, who stayed in the yard, hands in his jeans pockets. "Doyle, how are you doing?"

"Fine, Miz Parrish," he said. "Sorry to hear about Rayford."

"I appreciate that, Doyle. And how's Berklee and that new little baby?"

"Fat and happy. Both of 'em," he added with a grin.

To me, C.C. said, "Matt Johansson, this is Doyle Collins. He's been a friend since high school. He's gonna help us out tonight."

We shook hands. "Pleasure to meet you, Matt."

"Likewise."

"I hear you're an actor."

"That's right."

"Do you know Keanu Reeves?"

"Uh . . . no. I work in New York, mainly onstage."

"So do you know Liam Neeson?"

"I've met him."

"What's he like?"

"He's tall. Really tall."

Doyle nodded sagely, as if I'd confirmed his deepest suspicion.

C.C. looked up at the sky. "Reckon we should get going. Matt, you ready?"

"I am," I said. "What's the plan?"

He cut his eyes at the Parrishes. "I'll tell you on the way."

"Plausible deniability," Thorn said.

"I better not get a call from nobody official telling me to come pick you boys up," Ladonna said.

"No, ma'am," Doyle said. "I wouldn't want my wife to get that call, either."

I followed C.C. to his truck. Doyle got into his own vehicle and left before we did. I said, "So what's he going to do?"

"He's the Bandit."

"I beg your pardon?"

"You ever see *Smokey and the Bandit*?"

I had a vague mental image of Burt Reynolds in a black car. "No."

"Doyle's going to run interference for us, and try to get the Durants to chase him. That way they won't be expecting us."

"You hope."

"I do. But just in case, look in that box."

He indicated the shoe box between us on the bench seat. I opened it, and saw two handguns: one a revolver, the other an automatic. He added, "There's also a shovel so we don't have to dig with our bare hands, and a heavy gear bag in the back, in case we find anything."

I was still staring at the weapons.

"You ever shot a gun before?" he asked.

"Just onstage. And it was loaded with blanks."

"Well, these ain't."

"I don't know, C.C."

"Do you remember what happened to Gerald? The Durants will shoot us if they can. They've got rifles and shotguns. And if we get a hole blown in us on top of their mountain, there's no song strong enough to save us."

I still shook my head. "Not for me, man. Take one for yourself."

"You think your muay buay stuff will help you?" he almost shouted.

I realized he was scared to death of what we were doing; he was doing it only because I wanted him to. I felt a fresh rush of affection and tenderness for him. Calmly, I said, "I think we'll be in and out before they even know we're there, right?"

"That's the plan," he agreed through clenched teeth.

I stroked his cheek with the back of my hand. "Thank you, C.C. This means a lot."

"I hope it's worth it."

"So do I."

The wind blew more intensely than I'd yet seen it, bending the pine treetops. I wondered if a storm might be coming, but the stars and moon shone unobstructed above us. I felt the presence of the guns even more than I did the wind, their cold metal weight absorbing the night's fear and uncertainty. I began to really understand their appeal; certainly one in my hand right now would go a long way toward making me feel more secure. But it would be a false security. In a land where fairies flew and ghosts stopped by to chat, I couldn't imagine a gun would be a real defense.

We took a different route to the Durants' land this time. The road seemed rougher and more convoluted. C.C. drove in silence, the light from the dashboard casting his grim face in a greenish-blue pallor. Since I could see only what the headlight beams showed, there was no scenery to absorb, just the bit of road constantly ahead of us.

Finally we reached a crossroads. The moonlight lit it up, and we slowed as we approached, even though there was no stop sign. C.C. stopped in the middle, and we sat in silence.

At last he said, "Right on the other side of this crossroads, that's where the Durant land starts."

The headlights illuminated a sign nailed to a tree that read, PRIVATE PROPERTY. KEEP OUT UNDER PAIN OF ASS-KICKING. It was painted in red ink on a ragged piece of board, and whoever did it misspelled "pain" as "pane."

I thought again about the guns in the box between us, and said nothing.

"I hope you won't think less of me for this," he said, and reached under the seat. He pulled out a bundle of cloth and unraveled it to reveal a small jar wrapped in a towel. The fluid inside was clear like water. He asked, "A little liquid courage. You ever had moonshine?"

"People still make that?" I said. It seemed impossibly quaint, something from *The Beverly Hillbillies*.

"Oh yes, indeedy," he said, and unscrewed the lid. He took a small sip and closed his eyes. Then he said, "Want a snort?"

"A 'snort'?"

"That's what we call it. Or a slug. Or a swallow." The last word came out *swaller*.

I took the jar and sniffed. It didn't really smell like anything, so I took an experimental sip. It burned all the way down.

"Wow," I sputtered as I handed back the jar. "And you enjoy that feeling, huh?"

"I enjoy the feeling that comes *after* that."

I coughed a couple of times. We had alcohol and firearms; now all we needed was tobacco. I wondered if I should ask for a cigar. "What doesn't kill you makes you stronger, right?"

"So they say."

"Another sip of that, and I'll be Superman. So you know the people who made that?"

"Oh yeah. My cousins. They inherited the business from their parents, and their grandparents before that." He took a bigger swallow, and fought to keep it down. He choked out, "That's why it's so smooth."

"I thought it was illegal."

"It is."

"Oh, that's right—you don't have law in this county."

"Sometimes the Feds come in, snooping around. But it usually doesn't work out too well. Back in the '60s or '70s, a revenue man came up in here, and stopped at my cousin's house. His daddy, my uncle, was just a little boy then, and he was the only one home. Revenue man asked my uncle where his daddy was, and he said, 'Up in the holler, makin'.' Revenue man said, 'I'll give you ten dollars to take me up there.' My uncle held out his hand, and the revenue man said, 'Naw, you get it when I come back.' My uncle said, 'I'll take it up front, 'cause if I take you up there, you ain't comin' back.'"

I laughed, but declined a second swallow. I was too fond of a working esophagus.

C.C. took one more drink, then put the lid back on, carefully rewrapped the jar, and put it back under his seat. His phone dinged with a text. "Looks like Doyle's where he needs to be."

I checked my own phone: no bars. "Why do you get a signal out here and I don't?"

"I'm holding my mouth just right. You ready?"

My eyes were still watering as he put the truck in gear. "Not going to get any readier."

"Then here we go. *Faugh a Ballagh.*"

"What does that mean?"

He laughed. " 'Get outta the way.' "

We met no traffic, nor saw any other sign of civilization. The road followed the terrain, which isn't always the best thing for a road to do. I'd never gotten motion sickness in my life, but after the third or fourth hill that we topped, only to drop over the other side, that little swallow of moonshine threatened to come back up with projectile urgency.

Then C.C. switched off the headlights. The moonlight was bright and strong, but it was still a little unnerving to drive this way.

We reached the top of a hill and pulled off the road into the woods, along a little path that led to a small, straggly cornfield. The plants were barely up to my waist. We got out, and C.C. said softly, "Quiet closing the door."

He took the shovel from the bed and tossed the bag to me. I wondered if he also had one of the guns. "Be as quiet as you can," he whispered. "There's a lot of Durants, and they have a lot of dogs."

"Wait, I thought they were supposed to be busy chasing Doyle."

C.C. looked at the time on his phone. "Not yet. And if they know we're here, they'll know exactly what Doyle's up to. And we'll be screwed."

So he'd white-lied to me about how safe this was. Great. Oh, who was I kidding? I wouldn't have changed my mind. The desire to dig into that ground and see what was there was stronger than anything I'd ever experienced. If he'd said Freddy, Jason, and the guy from *Halloween* were all on the prowl, I would've still insisted.

"Where's the chapel from here?" I asked.

He pointed across the field, into the dark forest. "About a mile that way. You up to it?"

"I am. And thank you."

He kissed me. "You can do that later. Come on."

We moved through the corn as quietly as we could, which truthfully wasn't all that quiet. The leaves brushed against me, their sharp edges nicking my bare hands. When we reached the forest, C.C. signaled for us to stop. He listened for a long time, but all I heard were insects and a distant owl.

He turned to me. "I'm going to do something that'll seem stupid." Then he peeled off his T-shirt and handed it to me. "Turn that inside out for me."

I looked from the shirt to his bare, sweaty torso. "I'm sorry . . . what?"

"Turn my shirt inside out. It's good luck to wear it that way, but only if somebody else turns it for you."

"Seriously?"

"Does that sound like something I'd make up on the spur of the moment?"

I did as he asked, handed the shirt back, and he pulled it back on. The white tag on the collar seemed to glow. He said, "Do you want yours turned out?"

"Do you want me to?"

"Well, I always want to get your shirt off you. But this time, it's for a whole different reason."

I smiled back at him, took off my shirt, and handed it to him. He flicked it inside out and passed it back. I pulled it on, and when I finished, I felt his hands at my waist and his lips on mine. We kissed in the moonlight until the wind suddenly picked up, at which point he broke away and said, "We better get going. Another couple of minutes, and I'm liable to forget what we came here for."

We moved on into the woods, which didn't have the courtesy to grow in neat rows like the cornfield. The terrain rose, and grew rockier, and before long I was sweating and breathing hard. We stopped at the top of a ridge, and C.C. looked over at me. I could see his grin in the moonlight.

"I thought you dancers were in great shape," he teased.

"Yeah, for dancing," I wheezed back. It hadn't occurred to me to stretch out, but now I wished I had. My thighs and calves were killing me.

I followed him down the ridge and back into the woods. We passed by a small clearing with a strange stone tower in it. I whispered, "What's that?"

"That? It's the old Geesey place."

"What's the tower for?"

"That's a chimney. It's the only part made out of stone, so it's all that's left."

Once he said it, I saw the outline, and spotted the grate, and hearth.

"He's one of the reasons the chapel is there," C.C. continued.

"Did he build it?"

"Not exactly. See, old Samuel Geesey and his two brothers murdered Locksley Durant, but were never brought to trial for it. Had something to do with a swindle over a mule ol' Locksley sold 'em. Even back then, everybody figured one less Durant was a good thing. But it ate away at Samuel's soul, the idea that he'd murdered someone. So he wrote to the nearest Catholic priest, over in Knoxville, I think. Said he'd pay for it if someone built a church he could go to. So the priest happily took his money, and then actually spent some of it building a chapel of ease, instead of a regular church. Old Samuel went there all the time until he died, but he never managed to see a priest or confess his crime."

That didn't quite mesh with the other stories I'd heard, but I guess details could get lost, changed, or just made up over time. I looked at the old chimney and said, "How long ago was that?"

"I'm not sure. Quite a while."

We continued on through the woods, up and down, around and through, until I was so thoroughly disoriented, it felt for all the world like we were headed back to the truck. I got my second wind, though, so I had no trouble following C.C., and even overtook him in a couple of places as the hike wore on him.

Finally he stopped again, took a moment to catch his breath, and said, "See that hill just ahead? The chapel is right over that. We're coming to it from the same direction the Durants did the other day."

I looked behind us nervously. "So this is how they'd always come?"

"Oh, hell no. This was the longest way possible. But I figure if they *did* come, they'd take the short route. This way we'd most likely miss 'em."

That made sense. C.C. opened the bag I carried and handed me a bottle of water. I gratefully drank, then passed it to him.

He said, "Remember the plan. When we get there, we dig as fast as we can, and whatever we find goes into the bag. We'll have plenty of time to look at it once we get back to the Parrishes'."

"Okay."

He took out his cell phone and dialed. After a moment he said, "We're ready. Where are you? Okay. See you later. Have fun."

I pulled out my own phone but, as usual, had no signal. "Who's your carrier?"

Before he could answer, we heard the faint, distant sound of a loud, powerful engine. "That's Doyle, getting the Durants to chase him," C.C. said. "Come on."

We moved fast now, and apparently without worrying about any noise we made. At the bottom of the gully, we splashed through a small stream, then climbed up the hill. At the top, we emerged into the chapel clearing.

The stone edifice stood out just as it had before, almost glowing in the moonlight now that my eyes were fully adjusted. I remembered how it had looked from the air, like a beacon for lost souls. We stopped again and listened for movement, but heard nothing beyond the usual night sounds and the distant, faint roar of Doyle's engine, now accompanied by a second one. It appeared that the Durants had taken the bait.

"You have a flashlight?" I asked C.C.

"In the bag."

I felt inside and found it.

As we reached the break in the wall where the door used to be, we heard a distant, loud *whump*. It was hard to tell direction with all the hills and mountains, so we looked around for the source. Then C.C. said, "Look."

I followed his gaze. A faint spot of bright yellow and orange could be seen coming from a distant gully, barely visible through the trees.

"Is that Doyle?" I asked.

"Or the Durants," C.C. said. His voice was hollow; I knew he was thinking about how Doyle had been involved because he, C.C., had asked him.

I'd never heard a vehicle—or really, *anything*—explode in real life, so I had no real idea what I'd heard. But it had to be serious to carry all this way, and it sure wasn't difficult to imagine a truck skidding off one of these roads and down the side of a mountain, and bursting into flame when it hit bottom.

In the moonlight, C.C.'s face was tight with worry.

"It might be somebody else entirely," I said.

"Not up here." He dialed a number on his phone, but I could tell from his response that no one answered.

We watched as the glow continued. Whatever was burning was in no hurry to stop. I said, "What do you want to do?"

"Dig up what we're here to dig up," he said.

"If we need to leave—"

"If it was him, we can't help him now. If it wasn't, it's none of our business."

So that was that. We went inside the chapel walls. Something scurried away in the loose leaves piled up by the wind. I shone the flashlight circle on the ground where the secret was buried.

I said, "C.C., do you think this is wrong?"

"What? You're worrying about that *now*?"

"Well—"

He grabbed me by my shirt. "I don't give a fuck if this is right or wrong, Matt. We're here now, and we're going to fucking settle this. The time for second thoughts was back on the porch, not now."

I'd never seen him angry, and it brought me up short a little. I said, "Okay. Sorry."

He released my shirt. Then he grabbed it again, and kissed

me. "Me, too. I'm a little tense." He released me a second time and said, "You hold the light. I'll dig."

"No, it's my place."

"How many holes have you dug in your life?"

He had me there. "Okay."

I kept the light shining on the ground, although the urge to watch C.C.'s muscles as he worked was pretty strong. I also tried to listen past the *shuck-shuck* sound of the shovel, for any sign of someone approaching.

Then the metal blade loudly clanked against something solid.

I held my breath as C.C. reached into the hole and pulled out a rock. He tossed it aside and resumed work.

He removed five more stones before he stopped and said, out of breath, "Man, I'm three feet down and there's nothing but rocks. I don't think there's anything in here."

I had been so preoccupied over what might be there that I hadn't seriously considered that possibility. Burying something any deeper in this soil would be a real challenge. Yet how could I leave without being sure? "Here, let me dig for a while," I said, and offered him the light.

He scowled at me. "No, that's all right, I'll go a little deeper. Hold the light steady."

I did so, kneeling so close that dirt from each spadeful sprayed on me. I realized C.C. was humming to himself, pacing each move. After a moment, I recognized the melody: it was "I Know a Secret," from Ray's show. Julie, as ghost-Byrda, sang it bent over the facsimile of the very spot we were digging.

> *What's buried here, only I can tell*
> *What lies below, is known only to me*
> *No one even knows about this place*
> *Except the wind, the sky, and the trees*
> *Yet what I have hidden is more precious than gold,*

More valuable than the blood in my veins
And someday, oh, someday, I may be able to share it
With the man who gives me his name. . . .

Part of me, the rational part, wondered how the hell he knew this song. He hadn't been there when I sang the score for the Parrishes. But most of me was just wrapped up in the magic of this moment, of this song in this place at this time.

I began to sing along, softly at first. C.C. expertly harmonized. I'd never heard him sing, and his voice was a rich, full baritone. *Of course he sings like an angel,* I thought. *He's got wings, after all.*

Then the shovel hit something that wasn't stone.

25

The flat sound of metal against wood told me that, whatever it was, it was no rock. C.C. abruptly stopped singing, put the shovel aside, and knelt over the hole. "Hand me the light," he said.

He shone it on a piece of wood at the center of the exposed dirt. I knew nothing about how wood aged, but this certainly looked ancient. Only a tiny portion was uncovered; the whole thing could've been as small as a shoe box, or as big as a coffin.

He gave the light back to me and dug with his fingers, searching for the edges. It didn't take long.

"Can you tell what it is?" I whispered.

"Just a minute," he said. "I think I've got it."

With a grunt, he pulled a small wooden box from the ground.

The circle of light on it shook, because my hands trembled with excitement. Dirt covered most of the surface, and C.C. spent a moment brushing it off. There were no external markings of any kind, nothing helpful like a label that read, CONTENTS: ONE (I) SECRET DIARY, or CAUTION: PROOF OF ILLICIT MARRIAGE, SHAKE WELL BEFORE USING.

He turned it. A small, old padlock held it closed. It looked like it would come off with one good hammer blow.

Something moved in the darkness. I jumped and stared, but saw nothing.

"What?" C.C. asked.

I continued to peer into the shadows. "Probably just the wind. Right?"

He said nothing.

And yet . . . did the shadowy forms of the trees make the outline of the king of the forest in human form that I thought I'd glimpsed that afternoon? Were branches his antlers, a broken stump his muscular torso? Or was I just projecting?

I tore my eyes away. My heart threatened to jump up through my throat. "C-can you open it?"

"Just put it in the bag," C.C. said. "We can look at it later."

I took it from him. It was heavy, and solid, and nothing seemed to move inside it. I turned it this way and that, looking for anything that would tell me what it was beyond a box. Whatever it contained would solve a mystery that I, and all of us involved in *Chapel of Ease,* had obsessed about for weeks. I'd promised Neil pictures, so still holding the box and flashlight, I tried to get out my phone.

"Stop that!" C.C. whispered as he climbed out of the hole. "Just put it in the goddamn bag, we have time for all that shit later."

I knew he was right, but having it here, in my hands, inches from my eyes, was almost too much to resist. Surely the old lock would break loose with very little effort, and then—

C.C. snatched it from me and stuffed it into the bag. "Don't get hypnotized, we're not out of the woods yet. And I mean that literally. Now, come on."

We had to use the light to get out of the ruins because our eyes were no longer adjusted to the dark. We were just about to reach the trees when a loud *kerrack!* rang out, and something struck the tree nearest my head, spraying wood splinters into my face. Luckily nothing hit my eyes as I ducked and then threw myself on the ground. Belatedly I thought to turn off the light.

This time there were no taunts, just silence as the Durants waited. I imagined smug, grinning Billy, just itching for his chance. It scared me, but it also pissed me off.

"They've got night-vision scopes," C.C. whispered. "They're just waiting for us to stand up."

"They can wait," I whispered back. "I don't suppose you brought one of those guns?"

"You said you didn't want to."

"And you listened to me? I'm a Yankee!"

He whisper-laughed at that, then said seriously, "We have to split up. They won't know who to shoot at. Can you find your way back to the truck?"

"Uh . . . maybe. That way?"

"Yes. We'll meet there."

He rose into a crouch and scurried into the trees. There was another loud gunshot, almost simultaneous with the thump of something solid into wood. C.C.'s movements continued afterwards, so I knew he wasn't hit.

But he'd been right about the night-vision scopes. I'd seen them used on TV and in the movies, but that gave me no practical idea about how to evade them long enough to get into the woods. And I couldn't just stay here and wait for them to find me.

I thought of something else I'd seen in the movies and felt around for a stick or rock. I found a fist-size stone, then rose up enough to throw it. It crashed loudly in the night silence.

They shot again, right at me. The bullet struck the ground six inches from my head, sending an arc of dirt into my hair.

That was incentive enough. I got up and ran, hoping the trees would make it hard for them to follow. Two shots rang out; they sounded completely different, which I assumed meant they were from two different guns.

A voice, much closer than I expected, said, "Go git 'em!" And then I heard something *growl*.

C.C. had mentioned that the Durants had dogs. I'd seen a pair of them when we barreled past their house two days before. I knew people with dogs, and our family had even owned one when I was a kid. But I *never* heard any dog make a noise like this. Whatever breed it was, it was big, and strong, and way too close.

And that brings us up to where this whole story started.

26

It took maybe ten steps for me to get thoroughly disoriented, so that I had no idea if I was running toward C.C.'s truck. I kept my arms up in front of my face, and despite everything flashed on the ludicrous line from *Phantom of the Opera:* "Keep your hand at the level of your eyes!" It made no sense when I saw the show, and because of that, it stuck with me. Now it was a literal instruction, because I needed it to block the branches and vines.

And no matter how fast I ran, or how many times I zigged and zagged, I heard the dog getting closer. First his paws, then his growling, then his *breathing.*

Finally, I gave up. I stopped, groped around until I found a fallen branch, and backed up against the biggest tree I could find. I held the stick like a baseball bat and waited to see my pursuer.

He—I assumed it was a he—padded out of the shadows into a thin patch of moonlight. In my terrified state, he looked as big as a horse, and the first thing I thought of was *The Hound of the Baskervilles.* Reading that story as a child, I always wondered how anyone could be so scared of a mere *dog.* Now I knew.

He had short hair that shone where the light hit it and rippled over his muscles. I couldn't see any teeth when he growled, but I was pretty sure they'd be huge, too. The stick in my hand could not have felt more inadequate. I remembered Rick Moranis in *Ghostbusters,* facing down a hellhound, and thought, *Who ya gonna call?* Nobody came to mind.

He was less than ten feet away now, and his masters drew close as well, although with far less speed and grace. Apparently they trusted the dog to do most of the dirty work of catching me. Which, of course, he had.

And now he was about to finish the job.

Then, for no obvious reason, he took a step backwards and growled in a completely new way. Suddenly he was *frightened.*

Something moved in the corner of my eye. Had the Durants flanked me, or had I just run straight into their clutches? I turned.

A man emerged from the forest and stood beside the same tree I cowered against.

Although I couldn't see his face, his body shape told me it wasn't C.C., or his friend Doyle. All the Durants I'd seen had been larger as well. He was shorter, and slighter, than any of them. He had an unruly shock of dark hair silhouetted by the moonlight, and wore overalls. He carried no weapon, yet the dog continued to back away, his growl now becoming a low, keening whine.

I glanced from the dog to the man, not sure what exactly was happening. Why did this guy frighten the dog so much?

And then I saw the obvious. I mean that literally: faintly but distinctly, I saw the moonlit trees *through* the man's form. He was a ghost.

A *haint.*

But this wasn't Ray; that was certain. Everything was different.

He turned to me, and at last I saw his face. He was young,

barely out of his teens, and his clean-shaven face was sad and forlorn. He looked right at me, right *into* me, and with a fresh jolt of recognition I realized who he had to be.

Not Shad.

The nameless ghost.

I still clutched my stick, although it was as useless against a ghost as it was the Hound of the Durants.

He made no effort to speak, just continued to look at me sadly, as if I'd somehow done something awful that he'd known I was going to do, but hoped I wouldn't. Or perhaps I was projecting. Then he raised his arm and pointed.

I looked the way he indicated, and saw only more forest. Then I realized he was pointing at the way I'd just come, back toward the chapel of ease. I shook my head.

He pointed again, more vehemently. Then he grabbed my upper arm.

I felt him, just as I'd felt Ray's presence under my feet on the porch. His fingers were thin, small, and no stronger than a man's, certainly no spectral death grip. Was this really a ghost? I was about to pull away when I heard the dog yelp in pain.

Billy Durant, carrying a flashlight and shotgun, stood over the cowering dog and drew back for another kick. "You god-danged fucking waste of fucking dog skin!" he said. The dog cried out again and huddled as close to the ground as he could, eyes looking up pitifully.

"Don't kick the damn dog, Billy," Winslow said as he appeared, carrying a large rifle with a huge night-vision scope.

"I'd cut his damn balls off, if he still had any," Billy snarled.

Now I was puzzled. I was, at most, ten feet away from them. I wasn't in shadow, and I wasn't hiding. How could they not see me? I stayed very still, and the ghost at my elbow did not move, either.

"So what do we do now?"

"We keep after him. He's a Yankee city-boy faggot, he ain't gonna get away."

"I dunno. . . ."

Billy looked at his brother. "What's wrong with you now?"

"There's something weird about this spot. Don't you feel it?"

"Yeah, but so what? We ain't stayin' here. Now, get moving before I kick your ass, too."

"You got a lot to learn about motivatin' people, bro," Winslow said. He shuffled past me, within inches, and so did Billy. The dog scurried off in another direction, presumably back toward home.

I looked down at the ghost's hand on my arm. Was *that* why they couldn't see me?

When the sound of their footsteps faded away, the ghost released me. Again he pointed back toward the chapel. This time I nodded, turned in that direction, and when I looked back, he was gone.

I listened for any movement. I heard a scuffling in the leaves, but that was probably some harmless animal . . . right? And the wind above, making the tops of the trees creak . . . that was harmless, too. Oh boy. Despite the summer heat, I felt a real chill crawl up the backs of my arms, jump to my spine, and make its way to my neck. I'd just been touched by a *real fucking ghost.*

I climbed slowly, my hands numb and my heart pounding. What the hell had just happened? Had the ghost of a character from the play really made me invisible? Was that even possible? Yet how else to explain the way the Durants walked past me, close enough to hear me breathing, and didn't notice me?

Then I had a terrifying thought: What if *I* was a ghost now, too? I stopped and took several deep breaths; ghosts didn't breathe, so that was a good sign. I touched the nearest tree, and my hand didn't pass through it. Another plus. Just to be sure, I pinched myself on the arm. Yep, it hurt.

I reached the chapel clearing. Everything was the same, but there was a clarity in the moonlight that hadn't been there before. I made out every detail in the stone, every leaf on the ground. I held up my hand, and could see every crease, every hair, every bit of newly accumulated dirt. It was exactly like the night on the porch, when I'd had my talk with Ray. And that had been a dream. Hadn't it? Still, it was undeniably magical, and I stood very still, taking it all in.

Then a girl emerged from the other side of the forest.

She was young, barely a teenager, and had the black Tufa hair. Her dress was long and old-fashioned. I couldn't hear her feet on the leaves, although I should've been able to. She carried what looked like a copy of the box we'd dug up, its wood new and shiny. And she was crying, her face contorted with emotion she could barely get out. If I concentrated, I could just pick up the sound, as if it were coming from a great distance instead of mere yards away.

I knew exactly who, and what, she was. The high forehead and dark eyes from the graveyard image made of shadows and sunlight were unmistakable. I so wished Julie could be here to see this.

"Hello?" I called tentatively. She ignored me.

She went into the chapel, and I followed. She put the box on a window ledge, then produced a shovel from the shadows. Still sobbing, she dug in the very spot we'd excavated before. But now the dirt was undisturbed, all evidence of our excavation gone. Was this *ghost dirt,* then?

"Uh . . . excuse me?" I said, louder than before. She still didn't acknowledge me. I risked her name. "Byrda?"

Behind me, a tall young man with rolled-up sleeves and suspenders stepped into the chapel. He, too, had the Tufa hair, only his was wavy and hung down past his ears. He had a slightly weak chin and a huge Adam's apple. Was this Shad?

He said something, and despite our proximity, I made out only "honey," and "angry."

I focused intently to try to catch the words as Byrda responded. "Don't tell me not to be angry! I have every right to be angry! How am I supposed to face people after what you did to me?"

"It wasn't that big a deal," the boy said.

"Maybe not to you! Maybe you do it to girls all the time! But it was a big deal to me!"

"Honey," he said, and started toward her.

She raised the shovel like a weapon. "I'll cut your damn head off with this if you try to touch me, I swear."

So the maybe-Shad had done something to Byrda, perhaps of a sexual nature. Is that what she meant about facing people? I felt conspicuous and awkward, but they paid me no mind. I eased closer, but their voices grew no louder.

"You can't just bury things, honey," the boy said.

"The hell I can't! There won't be nothing for anybody to find now! You won't catch anybody else up here in this church, so this will stay hidden for good and forever. The only people who know about it are me, and you, and him. I ain't gonna tell nobody, and if you do, my daddy and brothers will change your voice for you, sure enough."

"Honey, please," he said, and from the back waistband of his pants, he pulled a gun. It was a big revolver, and it looked like a cannon. "I don't wanna have to do this. Please don't make me."

She froze, shovel in hand. She glared at him and said, "Ain't nobody but *you* makin' you do this."

"Let's just go back home and talk about it, okay?"

"Home? *Home?* What home? That house you share?"

"Honey—"

"Either shoot me or go to hell, Shad, I don't care which," she said flatly. "I really don't."

They looked nothing like the actors about to play them in New York, and nothing like I expected. They were so *young*; Byrda had the beginnings of that hard-edged look of Ladonna Parrish and Bliss Overbay, undernourished and overworked, while Shad was all gawky knees and elbows, having not quite grown into his adult self. And, if our story was correct, he never would.

Sure enough, the nameless ghost appeared at the door, dressed just as he had been at our earlier encounter. This time, though, he spoke. "Shad, what're you doing?"

Shad turned, and the gun swung with him. The nameless ghost ducked away. "Man, put that thing down!"

Shad did, holding it against his leg. "Sorry, Dobber," he said.

Dobber? I repeated to myself. His name was Dobber? I wondered how super-serious actor Stanley, who played him in the show, would take that.

"You and me need to talk," Dobber said.

"Oh, I think he's done enough talking to both of us," Byrda said bitterly.

"I didn't mean no harm," Shad said.

"Oh, really? You and Dobber were supposed to be in love, and then you come courtin' me, all, 'I ain't sure,' and, 'I ain't never been with a girl,' and all that other bullshit."

My eyes opened wide. What was I hearing? In the play, Dobber declared his unrequited love for Shad. But here it seemed they were already a couple, and everyone knew it. Just like everyone knew about C.C.

Then Shad raised the gun and pointed it at Dobber. He had tears in his ghostly eyes when he said, "I'm sorry, Dob. I do love you." And he fired.

Unlike the distant words, the gunshot was loud and immediate. I jumped, and in that same instant the ghosts disappeared, along with my extreme night vision. Yet I still smelled cordite.

"Holy shit," a voice said behind me.

I spun around. A teenage boy stood holding a rifle, which he'd evidently fired at the exact same instant as Shad. He turned toward me, pointing the gun at my midsection. Already keyed up, I reacted instinctively, and in moments held the gun while he lay moaning on the ground, hands clamped between his thighs.

"Who are you? One of the Durants?" I demanded.

"Ow! Yes . . . What the hell did you do that for?"

"You shot at me!"

"I wasn't shooting at you. Didn't you see them?"

"See who?"

"The chapel ghosts. I mean, I'd heard of 'em, but nobody I knew ever saw 'em. I thought they were just a story to keep people away."

"And so your first instinct was to shoot them? Shoot at ghosts?"

"Yeah, reckon that wasn't too smart."

He moved so that the moonlight struck his face. Although the Durant genes were plain, he really was a kid, and lacked the malevolence I'd seen in his older brothers. Perhaps it would develop later, along with facial hair and a deeper voice. I offered him a hand and helped him to his feet.

"Thanks," he said. "Do you know where Billy and Winslow are?"

"They went thataway."

"Can I have my gun back?"

"How do I know you won't shoot me?"

"Because I didn't when I had the chance."

"Your brothers want to."

"Yeah, well, they're assholes. They want to shoot me sometimes, too. I was out here to tell 'em Junior wants 'em to come home. We got a fire to put out." He extended his hand. "I'm Logan."

"Matt."

"You must be the Yankee fa . . . I mean, the Yankee who beat up my brothers."

"Yeah. It was self-defense."

"I ain't doubtin' you. That's why Junior sent me to fetch 'em, so they won't get beat up again."

I wondered if this was the same Junior who'd tried to interrogate me outside the convenience store. I imagined there were a lot of "Junior's" around here.

I gave him back his gun. "You better go find them, then, before they hurt themselves or someone else."

He looked out at the woods. "Sure wish I'd brought a flashlight."

"Sure wish I hadn't dropped mine."

"And . . . I'd appreciate it if you didn't say nothing about seeing me. I'm the youngest, so I already get picked on a lot."

"They'll never hear it from me."

He smiled. "Thanks."

He went off in the direction I'd indicated. Truthfully, I had no idea if that was the right way. I took a moment and oriented myself, then headed into the woods toward what I sure hoped was C.C.'s truck. I concentrated on movement, avoiding low branches and tangling vines. I tried not to dwell on what I'd seen or learned. After all, the real secret was waiting for me in that bag, right? What the ghosts had shown me was mere context, mere *prelude*.

After what seemed like hours, I reached the truck. None of its lights were on, and I didn't hear the engine running. I hid behind a tree, watching. Someone sat behind the wheel, but I wasn't sure if it was C.C. It could've been a Durant, with his brothers crouched down in the bed.

I threw a small stick. It struck the front near a headlight and bounced harmlessly off. The door opened, and by the dome light I saw that it was, in fact, C.C. "Matt?" he whisper-called, one of the guns held ready. "Is that you?"

"It's me," I said as I rushed over to the vehicle.

As I climbed in, he said, "I was starting to get worried."

"I got worried twenty minutes ago," I said truthfully.

"I heard a shot."

"It wasn't at me."

When we were out on the road and headed home, I said, "Have you heard from your friend Doyle?"

"No," he said tightly. "I haven't."

"Should we try to find him?"

"We'd be driving right into a herd of Durants with a bon-fire handy. I'd just as soon not."

I touched my face and realized my cheek was numb where splinters from that first shot had sprayed into it. I felt the tiny ends protruding from my skin. The visor had a mirror with lights on either side, and I saw that a half-dozen shards stuck into me.

"You all right?" C.C. asked.

"I've got some splinters."

"I'll pick 'em out when we get back to the Parrishes'." He squeezed my hand, all it was safe to do as he drove.

The bag with the box sat on the seat between us. I wanted to pick it up, to feel the weight of whatever we'd found, the tangible proof that there was an answer to *What is buried in the chapel of ease?* But instead I flashed back to the spectral trio's near-pantomime I'd witnessed, and wondered if this act of desecration had been the reason for their appearance this night.

27

When we got to the Parrish farm, the porch light was on and Thorn waited on the swing. As we came into the light, she saw my face and said, "Good God, what happened to you?"

"Oh yeah. It's nothing."

"It looks like you ran across a herd of little bitty Van Helsings who thought your cheek was Dracula."

The absurdity of that image made me laugh. I leaned against the nearest porch post and felt my legs begin to wobble with exhaustion.

"Shh, Mom and Dad are sleeping," Thorn said.

"Has Doyle Collins come by here?" C.C. asked.

"No." As C.C. turned to look back toward the road, she saw the bag over his shoulder. "What's in there?"

C.C. took the box from the bag. In the light from the porch, it looked even older and more worn, the wood faded to gray and the lock a sculpture made of pure rust.

"Is that it?" she asked softly.

"That's what we found, yeah," C.C. said. "We don't know what it is yet."

The two of them exchanged a look; then she said, "Let's go inside and find out, then."

"I can't," C.C. said. "I have to go look for Doyle."

"I'll go with you," I said.

"No," he said sharply. Then his expression softened, and he touched my cheek. "You stay here, so I know you're safe."

I started to protest, but the simple affection and worry in the statement cut me off.

"Find out what's in here," he added, and handed me the box. The weight of the thing surprised me, but at that moment, I was more concerned with C.C. I looked up into his eyes and said, "Be careful."

"I will. Take pictures for me, okay?"

"Okay." He got back in his truck and roared off, leaving Thorn and me on the porch.

"I hope Doyle's okay," I said.

"Me, too," Thorn said. "He's been C.C.'s only real friend for a while. He used to fight bullies with him in school, so C.C. never had to stand alone." Then her attention went back to the box. "So that's what all the fuss is about."

I looked at the box again. Its antiquity made it seem sad, somehow. "It's what we found."

"You really have no idea what's in it?"

"Nope. We didn't open it."

"Why not?"

"There were . . . complications."

"Durants?"

"Yeah. And . . ."

"What?"

"Haints."

She put her hands to her mouth to stifle a giggle.

"What?" I said, tired and annoyed.

"It's your accent."

"Oh, *I* have the accent?"

"You do here." She looked closely at the box. "I reckon we won't learn much more by staring at this, will we?"

"Reckon not."

She giggled. "You're doing it again."

"Oh, shut up. Wait until you hear how people pick on you in New York. Where can we look at this?"

"If you can be quiet, come on into the kitchen."

We went inside, and Thorn spread newspaper on the table before we set down the dirty box. She turned on the light over the table, and I finally saw it clearly.

The box's corners dovetailed together, and the rusted heads of tiny nails were flush with the wooden surface. The top had two big hinges, and a latch closed with the small, ancient, rusted padlock.

I flicked the padlock with my fingertip. "How do we get that off?" I asked,

"Rub its G-spot," Thorn deadpanned.

"Ha."

"Step aside."

She took the lock in her hand and twisted it slowly. When it wedged against the latch, she turned it harder, and one end of the shank popped free. She removed the lock and placed it beside the box on the paper. "That might've been worth something," she said sadly.

"The lock?"

"Yeah. People love anything that might be from the Civil War. Reenactors come all over themselves for stuff like this."

"Maybe you can fix it and sell it."

"Are you kidding? I can't stand reenactors. They think if the war had gone the other way, the world would be perfect."

Now nothing stopped us from opening it. We stood silently, the crickets outside providing the background chorus. Ladonna or Gerald snored softly behind their bedroom door in counterpoint. At last I said, "Well . . ."

"It's what you came for."

"Yeah, but . . ."

"You're kidding me. Second thoughts?"

I saw the sad face of Byrda's ghost in my mind's eye. "I'm just not sure, all of a sudden."

Thorn snickered. "Yeah, that figures. All men are afraid of commitment, even the gay ones. Well, I'll leave you and your box to talk it over. I'll be on the porch if you want me."

"Wait, you're not curious?"

"Oh, sure, I'm curious. But I'll find out later. I'll leave the moment of discovery for you."

She closed the screen door softly behind her, leaving me speechless. I quietly pulled out a chair and sat down, then rested my chin on my folded arms and stared at the box. There was a slight gap under the lid; it would take nothing to reach over and lift it, exposing the secret that Ray had wanted so badly to keep.

As if cued by my thoughts, Ray said, "Well? What's stopping you?"

It says a lot that in four days, the presence of the ghost of a friend no longer made me want to run screaming from the room. I didn't look at him as I replied, "I'm not sure, man. Maybe it's you."

"Me? All I am is dust in the wind. Isn't that what ol' Miss Azure said?"

"She said you were just pretending to be Ray."

"Well, there you go. If she's right, what you do makes no difference to me now."

I touched the side of the box reverently, with just my fingertips. "Is this really what you were talking about? The secret of the chapel?"

"You mean, is that what I was writing about?"

"Yeah."

"It is."

"And you know what's inside it?"

"I said I did."

"Yeah, but do you? Like you also said, all that mattered was getting the show onstage. You would've said anything to make that happen."

"Touché, man. You got me there. But in this case, I really do know what's in there."

"How? The ground didn't look like anyone had dug it up recently."

"Maybe I did it years ago."

"Why are you being so fucking enigmatic?"

"I'm a haint, it's what we do."

This made me turn and look at him. He was as solid as Thorn had been, still dressed in his denim jacket, his black hair tied back in that disarrayed ponytail. His skin was paler than I remembered, but hey, he *was* a ghost. He crossed his arms and smiled, thoroughly delighted by my discomfort.

"You're enjoying this," I said.

"I'm having a little fun, yeah. But like I said, it's not about me. It's about you."

I lifted the lid an inch. It resisted a little, and when I pulled my hand away, it stayed in place. Through the gap, I saw what looked like the frayed edge of a piece of fabric.

"So close," Ray taunted.

"Stop it!" I snapped. "If you'd just told us about it when we asked you, none of this would've happened. You do realize that if C.C.'s friend Doyle is dead, it's basically your fault."

"He's not dead."

"How do you know?"

He looked at me like I was stupid, then pointed at himself. "Haint?"

He had me there. "Well, if you just tell me what's in the box now—"

"Why should I tell you? It's right there. Lift the damn lid and see for yourself."

Annoyed, I stood up and lifted the lid. "Fine!"

Whatever was inside the box was wrapped in old, faded cloth. It filled the space and gave no hint of the shape beneath it. One frayed edge ran the length of the bundle, begging me to lift it just as the lid had done.

"So close," he said again.

I whirled on him. "Look, tell me what you want me to do here! Do you want me to open it or not?"

He leaned toward me. I wondered if I'd feel anything if I tried to push him away. He said, "I want you to do what you want. That's what you've done all along, isn't it? You went against my wishes, against the advice of C.C. and Miss Azure, against the hopes of the girl who buried this in the first place. You think it was meant for you? In what fucking world could *that* be right? You're just muscling in on history because you can't stand to not know something."

He tried to poke me in the chest on the last few words, but his finger simply went through me. I felt nothing. He looked down at his hand partly inside me, pulled it out, and burst out laughing. So did I.

"Shh, you'll wake Mom and Dad," he said, still giggling.

"The ghost in the woods was solid," I pointed out.

"Yeah, well, he's had a lot more practice than I have."

I calmed down and looked back at the box. I recalled all the guesses we'd posted on that board backstage at the Armitage. Did the box contain gold from the Civil War? A Bible that gave away family secrets? A diary that named illicit lovers? Letters that revealed once-world-shattering secrets? Maybe the remains of a dead, possibly illegitimate, baby? Or just keepsakes from a romance that could never end happily, things that mattered only to the person who buried them?

And did I have the right to know?

The answer was suddenly, totally, obvious.

"Fuck me," I whispered.

"I might've, if you'd gotten me drunk," Ray said. I looked up sharply, and he winked. "Just kidding. Gotcha."

I carefully, reverently, closed the box and pushed the latch back into place. The lock itself was useless now, but I placed it on top. "I guess the secret—"

Ray was gone. I was alone with the box and its secrets, which I now knew I'd never know. I was never *meant* to know.

Something scraped at the glass on the back door. I jumped. In the light, I saw a ragged hand, small and feminine, raking its filthy nails along the outside of the pane.

I got up and opened the door. In the darkness just beyond the shaft of light huddled a small human form. She cocked her head, and the thick strands of her dreadlocks swayed with the movement.

My first thought was the girl from New York, Bronwyn Chess's spy. Then I remembered the attendants of the forest king.

I looked farther into the darkness. Was that an enormous deer standing immobile down by the fence, or just a trick of the shadows and darkness?

I looked back at the girl. Her murky silhouette now resembled something canine.

I should've been afraid, but I was totally calm. Whatever these creatures, these *beings*, were, they had clearly followed me here, and expected something. And I knew what.

"Wait," I said, and retreated inside. I picked up the box, making sure the lid was closed, and carried it out the door. I placed it on the ground at the very edge of the light. The girl/dog didn't move.

"I'm sorry," I said sincerely. "I meant no disrespect."

I turned to step back into the house. Before the door closed,

I glanced back out. The box, the girl, and the deer were all gone.

I sat down at the table again and began to laugh. I was still laughing when Ladonna came out, wrapped in a bathrobe, to see what was so funny. Without knowing the cause, she joined in.

Then our laughter was abruptly cut off by the sound of gunshots from the front yard.

28

I'd heard gunshots in the city before, and had learned to tell them from the noise of old cars backfiring. Here in the mountains, the noise was more plain, without the artificial buildings to bounce off. There was an echo, but it was a classical one, long and distant as the hills passed the sound around.

Ladonna and I ran to the front door. Multiple sets of headlights blazed through the window, and when we went out onto the porch, they blinded us. C.C. stood in the yard between us and the vehicles, Thorn beside him. Someone behind the lights let out a self-satisfied whoop.

Ace and Tom ran from the darkness, barking and growling. They stopped beside C.C.

"You best get them dogs under control if you don't want 'em full of holes," a voice said from behind the lights. I recognized it: Billy Durant.

"Ace, Tom, get up here," Ladonna said. The dogs obeyed, and she held the door for them to go inside.

"What do you want, Billy?" C.C. demanded. There were three sets of headlights, and the rattle of old engines filled the air.

"We want that city faggot," Billy said. "He blew up our shed."

So that wasn't Doyle's truck. C.C. said, "Billy, if that shed blew up, it's because all you dumb-asses know about cooking meth is what you saw on *Breaking Bad*."

"Well, either way, me and him got stuff to settle."

"He'll kick your ass in a fair fight, Billy," Thorn said. "Go home and sober up."

"Oh, I ain't drunk, C.C. And I ain't interested in a fair fight."

"There's a shock," Thorn muttered.

Suddenly a new shot rang out, from behind us instead of in front. We all jumped, and one of the headlights exploded in a shower of glass and momentary flame. I turned, and a rifle barrel poked out through the open living room window.

Gerald had the weapon's barrel resting on the windowsill. He said, "I owe you sons-a-bitches. The first Duroc I get a clear shot at takes one for the team."

"We got your whole family in our sights, Gerald," Billy said.

"Then stick out that cabbage blossom you call a head, and we'll see which one of us is bluffing," Gerald snapped back.

"Everyone," a new voice said, "put down your guns. Now."

The girl Mandalay walked out of the night. She had on cutoffs and a *My Little Pony* T-shirt, and her black hair was braided down her back. She stopped between C.C. and the Durants, facing the lights.

"You heard me," she said when no one moved. "I don't want to hear another shot fired. Turn off those engines and headlights." When they didn't, she barked, *"Now!"*

The engines stopped, and the lights went out. It took a minute for my eyes to adjust.

"Billy, get down here," Mandalay said. "The rest of you Durants, stay there. And put those guns away!"

"Whoa, whoa," another new voice said, and this time the

self-important man who'd called himself Junior came out of the darkness on the other side of the yard. He wore plaid pajama pants and a ratty old Bob Dylan T-shirt, and his hair was mussed from sleep. "The Durants answer to me, Mandalay. You got a problem with them, talk to me."

The girl looked at him. "Junior, know your place," she said, and made a decisive hand gesture. Junior started to speak, then apparently thought better of it, and said, "Yes, ma'am."

"Now—Billy, get down here. And you." She turned and pointed at me. "You, too."

I looked at Thorn, then at C.C. Both looked afraid, and neither spoke up to defend me. So I came down from the porch and crossed the yard to join the girl and Billy Durant, who'd emerged from the darkness, still carrying a gun.

"Put that down," Mandalay ordered through clenched teeth, and he handed it back to one of his brothers. I could now make out three old pickups, each one with at least four people standing in the bed, plus the drivers. Good God, how many Durants were there?

Then Mandalay turned to me, and the anger in her face had absolutely nothing to do with a child. "You lied to Bronwyn. You promised her you'd stay put."

"I had my fingers crossed," I said, and it sounded as weak to my own ears as it must have to hers.

"Yeah, well, you're a jackass *and* a liar." Then she turned to Billy. "And you—you're a coward. Shooting people from the woods."

"Hey, nobody died," Billy said, and started to grin, then thought better of it.

"You got no proof he did it," Junior said.

Mandalay silenced him with a gesture. "I will not have a blood feud break out because of a liar and a coward. So you two, settle this. Now."

Billy put up his hands. "Hey, he knows all kinds of kara-te-mahty. I ain't fighting him."

"Why am I not surprised?" Mandalay said. "Then how *can* we settle this?"

"How 'bout a dance-off, Billy?" one of the other Durants said.

"Yeah!" Billy said, snapping his fingers. "That's it. Let's have a dance-off. One board right here in the yard, him and me taking turns." He grinned at me. "What do you say to that, you big-city faggot?"

Mandalay tapped his chest with her forefinger. "Say that again, Billy, and everyone here will know your dying dirge."

I had no idea why this particular threat worked, but Billy turned white and said, "Beg your pardon, Mandalay," with genuine deference.

She turned to me. "Now . . . what do you say to that, Matt? Do you accept?"

"A dance-off?"

"Flatfoot dancing," Billy said smugly. "They don't teach you that in your fancy New York dance school, do they?"

He had no idea what Ray's show was about, I realized. "No," I agreed. "I never learned that in dance school. But I've seen it a little."

"Do you accept?" Mandalay said again, more urgently.

I sighed, and let my shoulders slump like I had no choice. "Yes."

"What are the terms, then?" Billy said. "I mean, he blew up our shed."

"I had nothing to do with your shed blowing up," I said.

"Shame we can't trust your word on that," Mandalay said dryly. "So what do you want, Billy?"

He grinned at me. Dear God, did I hate that grin. "We get to hunt this boy."

"Hunt?" I repeated. "Like with guns?"

"Oh, we'll use paintball guns," he said, but I doubted anyone present believed him; I sure didn't. "We'll give him a ten-minute head start. And he has to be buck naked, too." The Durants in the trucks laughed at this.

I cocked my head at him and said, "Are you *sure* you're not gay?"

His smile vanished, and he started toward me, but Mandalay stopped him with another of those gestures. Every muscle taut, fists clenched, he glared at me.

To me, Mandalay said, "If you win, what do you want?"

"Their word that they'll never bother the Parrishes again."

She nodded. "You heard that, Billy. If he wins, you are not to ever, *ever* bother the Parrishes again. Not you, not your family, not your friends. Are we clear?"

Billy, his smile tight like a dead body's rictus, said, "Sure thing, Miss Mandalay. Whatever you say."

"Seal it, then."

He stepped back, made an elaborate hand gesture, then bowed. "Sealed."

She turned to me. "I'd ask for your word, but I know what that's worth. Are you still leaving tomorrow?"

"I am."

"Then you just make sure you get on that plane and don't come back, whoever wins. Is that clear?"

"If they win, I don't think you'll have to worry about that."

"If you do come back, I can't protect you. No—if you come back, I *won't* protect you. I can't abide liars."

I admit it, I was a little scared. Angry, too, both with myself and this self-important tween. But I was angrier with the smug hillbilly now laughing with his brothers across the yard.

"Where will we get music?" I asked.

"Right here," Thorn said. I turned and saw her with her guitar. Bliss Overbay, also with a guitar, stood beside her. An old man with a fiddle, a younger man with a banjo, and an old woman with an autoharp were in the process of arranging themselves. I wanted to ask where they'd come from, but by now, I knew better.

Billy carried a flatfooting board from one of the trucks and threw it on the ground between us. "Who goes first?" he asked Mandalay.

"We flip for it."

We did, and Billy won. His insufferable grin grew, if possible, even larger. I understood now why the Joker aggravated Batman so much. "Y'all just stay back," he said smugly, "and I'll show you how a real man spanks the plank."

I bit the inside of my cheek so hard to keep from laughing, I tasted blood.

To the musicians, he called out, "Give me a little 'Flop-Eared Mule,' why don't you?"

The musicians looked at each other, nodded and whispered for a moment, and then the old fiddler sawed out a sprightly melody that the others picked up and filled out. Billy nodded along, getting the time, then stepped onto the board.

I admit, I was feeling cocky about this contest, and that lasted for another five seconds. Then I saw just how good Billy Durant was at this. Apparently, even professional Broadway experience didn't automatically mean you'd be the best dancer in the room. Or the yard.

Not to sound like one of my hosts, but Billy fucking tore that wood *up*. His feet were a blur, the sound they made a steady tattoo that kept thoroughly on beat. In the light from the porch he made faces, he struck poses, and totally made the moment his own. When he finished with a flourish, I had the same thought I'd had earlier in the night, in the woods near the chapel.

I was screwed.

Face gleaming with sweat, he hopped off the board—a real stage hop, with his knees drawn up and his feet behind him—and landed right in front of me. Grinning, always grinning, he said, "Follow that, killer."

Oh boy.

I looked back at C.C., who had that same frozen expression he'd had at the Pair-A-Dice. He saw me and gave a helpless little shrug. I was on my own.

I continued to scan the yard, hoping against hope I'd see Ray there, or that he'd whisper in my ear and give me some sort of hint. But evidently he was gone, his task as a haint completed once I decided not to look in the box.

Billy was out of breath, and between gasps taunted, "Well, Mr. Homo-sex-you-all, what you got for us?"

"Billy!" Mandalay snapped.

"I didn't say 'faggot,'" he said, mock offended, continuing to sweat and breathe hard.

To me, Mandalay said, "It's your turn now. What music do you want?"

I thought about the dances we'd learned for the show. I'd practiced only one, from the wedding scene, because that's the only time my character danced. I'd seen the others, but never really committed them to memory. And they were all done to original music by Ray, which these musicians wouldn't know. Well, given everything I'd learned, that might not be true. But the dance from the show was nothing compared to what I'd just seen.

And then I remembered Ray's performance at Stella's studio the first day of dance rehearsal. The day he'd shown us, not only how to dance, but that you could dance that style to anything. A light went on in my head.

I motioned C.C. over. Softly I asked him if the band knew the song I had in mind.

"I'm sure they do," he said.

"Then tell them that's the music I want. Tell them to watch for my cue." And I winked at him.

I turned back to the Durants and Mandalay. I should have

been exhausted after all the climbing, running, and terror I'd experienced, but I felt great: loose, cocky, and ready. It was the same way I felt doing shows after we had the first weekend behind us. I was trusting the musicians to be ready, and to jump in at the right moment, but given what I knew about them, I really had no doubts. Magic could do anything, right? "My turn, huh? Stand back."

I stepped up to the board and gingerly touched it with my foot, as if I expected it to bite. I played the uncertain city slicker to the hilt, stepping onto the board, testing it experimentally to see if it wobbled, then took a deep breath and let it out in a long, mock-defeated sigh.

I looked up at Billy. "Well, Billy, I guess there's only one thing to say."

And then I bellowed, letting my voice go raw and ragged, *"A-wop-bom-a-loo-mop-a-lomp-bam-boom!"*

The band slammed into the song with a ferocity I wouldn't have expected from a roots-music quartet. But they gave me exactly what I needed.

I don't know that I outdanced Billy Durant, but I know I fucking out*performed* him. I was used to both singing and dancing every night of the week and twice on Sunday. He'd done a great job, but it had exhausted him.

I sang the nonsense verses about different girls and danced my fucking ass off. I used the moves I'd learned for *Chapel of Ease* as well as anything else I could think of, staying on that little yard-square piece of wood the whole time. On the final *"A-wop-bom-a-loo-mop-a-lomp-bam-boom!"* I leaped—yep, a goddam *leap*—from the board to the grass, and into a pseudo-hip-hop crossed-arm pose. The music snapped to an end right as I landed.

There was a moment of total silence. Nothing, not even the bugs, made a sound. And then someone let out a huge, long, "Yee-*haw*!"

I turned toward it. The yard was now ringed by dozens of people, most in their pajamas, all of them Tufa, and they applauded. I gestured at the band and joined in the applause. Then I turned back to face the Durants.

Two of the biggest Durants I'd seen so far stood right in front of me, and before I could react, each grabbed one of my arms in hands as big as Wreck-It Ralph's. They twisted my arms behind me, which pushed me forward, just as Billy Durant strode out of the darkness, carrying a baseball bat.

"Billy!" Mandalay shouted.

My adrenaline really kicked in then, shifting everything into slow motion. As I watched, Billy Durant *changed.* In the same way I'd seen C.C. and Thorn bearing those lovely butterfly wings, Billy suddenly sported immense, leathery appendages, with tattered edges and ragged tips. More, his face transformed into something with enormous insectlike eyes and an open mouth that foamed at the corners and revealed long, pointed teeth.

I had no time to plot a strategy, so I used the strength of the men holding me as a pivot and did a backflip. I turned at the waist so that my shins took the blow from the bat early in its swing; if nothing else, years of muay Thai gave me shinbones of fucking iron. It stung, but not so much as a fractured skull would have, and the impact knocked the weapon from Billy's hands. The flip caught the men holding me off guard as well, and I slipped my arms free. When I landed, I immediately grabbed the bat and raised it, ready to fight.

The two big men scurried back to the safety of the trucks. But Billy reached back and yanked a gun from his belt. He leveled it right at me.

We were at most six feet apart. Even in the darkness I could see his face was red with rage. The gun shook in his hand.

I held the bat ready and looked him right in the eye. "Put the gun down, Billy."

He didn't move, except his hand shook more.

"Put it down!" I roared.

He dropped it from his hand. I jumped forward and faked a swing, and he tripped over his own feet, trying to scurry away. He lay there on the grass beside the flatfooting board and looked up at me, small and terrified.

I dropped the bat and picked up the gun. He whimpered and covered his head. "Y'all come help me!" he called to his brothers, his voice high and desperate.

I held the revolver up and said, loud enough for everyone else to hear, "Next time, Billy, it might be easier if you just *mail* me your gun."

There was a moment of silence. Then a sound like a long, sustained wheeze rose up, and finally broke into a guttural belly laugh. And it came from the direction of the rest of the Durants.

Soon they all joined in, and the laughter spread around the circle. As Billy got to his feet and realized they were laughing at him, his face grew tight and dark.

"Shut up!" he yelled as he got to his feet. *"Shut the fuck up!"*

He glared at me, but it had none of his original malice, just the petulant anger of a humiliated child. He ran back into the dark toward his family, and in a moment, their truck engines started. They drove away, pursued by the mocking laughter of everyone else.

Mandalay, with Bliss Overbay behind her, came up beside me. "You planning to keep that?" the girl asked, indicating the pistol.

I extended it butt-first, the way I'd seen on TV. "Would you believe I've never fired a real one in my life?"

"It didn't look like you needed to," Bliss observed.

"Well, you won, fair and square," Mandalay said. "How do you feel?"

"Like I could use a drink," I said honestly.

"I can fix you up," C.C. said, with a hand on my shoulder.

"You're still leaving tomorrow, right?" Mandalay asked.

"I am," I assured her yet again.

"Good. I think the sooner you're gone, the better for everyone."

The observers were slipping back into the darkness. I thought, but couldn't swear, that I saw shadowy human shapes lifting up into the sky, momentarily blotting out the stars. But it was all over in an instant, and even though I knew exactly what I was seeing, I let the reality of it float away as well.

Another truck came roaring down the driveway and slammed to a halt. Doyle Collins hopped out and said, "Did I just pass a Durant convoy coming outta here?"

"You did," C.C. said.

"Is anybody dead?"

"Nope."

It took him a moment to calm down. "Wow. I guess I didn't do too good a job as the Bandit, huh?"

"You did fine. Everything's taken care of."

He looked at me now. "Did you find it?"

"No," I said quickly. "Nothing was there."

I felt C.C.'s eyes burning holes in the side of my head. Doyle said, "No shit. All for nothing, huh?"

"All for nothing," I agreed.

29

I followed the Parrishes inside after the crowd left, including C.C. and Doyle. C.C. kissed me in front of everyone, so if he wasn't out before, he sure was now. And just as he'd said, no one seemed either surprised or bothered by it.

"I'll see you tomorrow," he whispered. "I'll drive you to the airport."

Ladonna and Gerald excused themselves and went back to bed. They took the whole thing in stride, as if life-or-death dance contests happened around here all the time. Considering what I'd seen in just four days, maybe Needsville wasn't as boring as I'd originally thought.

I, however, was way too keyed up to sleep. First, I picked the splinters from my face, which stung as much as you'd think. C.C. had left his jar of moonshine, so I sat at the table and sipped it against the pain. I kept glancing at the back door, but there was no sign that the king of the forest or his retinue had returned. I had no idea why they would, but it was just that kind of night.

"So," Thorn said. "You didn't look in the box, huh?"

"No." I told her about Ray's ghost, and the coyote girl.

"Dang," she said when I was done. "But that still doesn't tell me why you didn't look when you had the chance. Ain't that what this whole trip was about?"

I started to protest, to repeat my standard line that it had been about bringing Ray home, but I was too tired. "Yeah, a big part of it," I admitted.

"So? Why didn't you look?"

"Because I saw the ghosts reenact what happened in the chapel back in the day." Although as I thought about it, I realized I knew nothing, really, about what had happened, or what had really motivated them. But I was sure of at least one thing. "They were just kids, Thorn. If they lived today, they'd be sending selfies and playing *Minecraft*."

"It was a different time. Kids had to grow up early."

"Two of them were gay."

"It happened back then, too," she said with all the compassion in the world.

I nodded. I realized that the thought of Thorn in my life in New York might not be so bad, at least for a while. Then my thoughts turned to C.C. I looked at the front door wistfully and sipped from the moonshine jar.

"He really likes you," Thorn said.

"It's mutual," I assured her.

"It's gonna tear him up to see you leave tomorrow."

"We've only known each other three days."

She gave me her sly little one-sided smile. "Romeo and Juliet knew at first sight."

"That was a play."

"You're an actor."

I rubbed my weary eyes. "I think I'm too tired for sparkling wordplay. Good night, Thorn."

"Good night, Matt. Sleep well."

And I did. I slept with no dreams, no visits from haints, and no sense of unfinished business. I slept the sleep of the justified dead.

I woke late the next morning, and had to rush to get my shower, pack, and be ready on time. When I came into the living room carrying my backpack, C.C. was already there. He looked so handsome, so beautiful, that it was all I could do not to run to him.

"Good grief, kiss that boy," Ladonna said, as if it were the most common thing in the world. So I did.

"Shame you have to go," Gerald said. "Would've loved to hear more stories about Rayford."

"I imagine you'll be hearing plenty, once the show opens," I said. "Reporters will probably be calling at all hours. They might even just show up unannounced."

"Yeah, that won't happen," Gerald said with certainty. "Ain't nobody can find us if we don't want 'em to."

After all I'd seen, I wasn't about to doubt him on this.

Gerald firmly shook my hand and said, "Safe travels to you, young man. I appreciate everything you did for Ray, and for us. You'll be watching out for Thorn, right?"

"I will." I winked at Thorn, who rolled her eyes.

Ladonna took my face in her hands and gave me a kiss on the cheek. "Thank you for bringing Rayford back to us," she said, her voice trembling slightly. "He's where he always wanted to be, I suspect. He's part of the chapel's song now."

"I'm glad I was able to do it, Mrs. Parrish."

"Are you ready?" C.C. asked. "I wanted to show you one last thing before you leave town."

"Sure."

I dispensed hugs, Thorn made sure she had my address, and I let Tom and Ace slobber on me one last time. Then I followed C.C. out to his truck. It was a glorious summer morning, still and clear, except for the tissue-thin mist that clung to the tops of the trees.

We stopped at the closed motel right at the edge of Needsville. The sign called it the CATAMOUNT CORNER. I was surprised to see that none of the windows had been broken. We walked up onto the porch and I cupped my hands around my eyes to peer inside.

"Looks like there *is* a café in there," I said.

"I told you. It only seats about twenty." He paused. "I think I'm going to buy it, if I can track down Miss Peggy and talk her into selling it to me."

I looked around. "Why?"

"I need something solid, something that's mine. I'm too old to just keep working for everybody else around here."

I looked back at the dying little town. "No offense meant to Needsville, but is there enough business to justify opening this place? I mean . . . who comes here?"

"You did. You would've stayed here if it had been open."

"Yeah, but I'm guessing that the niche market of 'people who are bringing a friend's ashes back home' is pretty small."

He smiled. I could watch him smile forever. "There's lots of people all over the country, maybe all over the world, who have a little Tufa in them. And a lot of them get the call to come here and visit. They check out the graveyards, wander up into the mountains and look for old abandoned family homes, and so forth."

" 'Next year in Jerusalem,' " I said.

"What's that?"

"What some of my Jewish neighbors always say at the end of their seder."

"What's a 'seder'?"

"It's a special dinner they have on Passover. You do know what *that* is, right?"

"They show *The Ten Commandments* every year," he said wryly. "Anyway, Miss Peggy always did just fine with the place. I'm sure I can do at least as well."

"Is this what you wanted to show me?"

"Not exactly." He produced a key and unlocked the door. He gestured for me to precede him inside.

The little lobby was decorated in *heavy* country-home decor. The café, its chairs stacked neatly on the tables, was in pretty good shape.

I indicated the key. "And how did you get that?"

"Miss Peggy asked me to keep an eye on the place for her. Make sure nothing got torn up. Place sits empty through too many winters, it falls apart if you don't fix things as they break." Then he locked the door behind us and said, "Come with me."

I followed him into the stairwell and up one flight. He went straight to a particular room and opened the unlocked door. Inside, candles burned and soft music played.

I was still smiling when he closed the door and pulled me into a kiss.

After our lips parted, I said, "Do we have time for this?"

"We have all the time in the world," he said. "You're in Cloud County. Time doesn't work the same for everybody here. And," he added with a delightfully knowing grin, "you *did* promise to make it worth my while to help you."

"Yeah, I did, didn't I?"

No wings appeared this time, no supernatural transformations into magical beings. But that didn't mean there was no magic. Later, as we lay in bed while the few still-burning candles sputtered around us, I thought back on the last few minutes . . . or had it been hours? I was pretty sure that in the heat of the moment, I had blurted out the dreaded L-word. I was also pretty sure I meant it. C.C. had said it back to me, and I decided not to pick the moment apart and look for hidden meanings. Sometimes things just were what they were.

Eventually we got up and took a long shower together. As he was soaping my back, he said, "Where did you get that? Is that a birthmark?"

I looked. On my upper arm was the print of a hand encircling my biceps. It didn't hurt, but when I rubbed at it, it didn't come off.

I remembered the ghost holding me, turning me invisible up on the Durant mountain. "I think it's a keepsake," I said, and told him about it.

We finished, eventually, then dressed and prepared to go. He gave me a gift: a coffee cup with the words, TAKEN BY MISTAKE FROM THE CATAMOUNT CORNER printed on the side. "So you won't forget me," he said.

"Not much chance of that. 'Taken by mistake'? Doesn't it usually say, 'Stolen from'?"

"Well, Miss Peggy didn't want to imply anyone was a thief. That'd be bad manners."

We left the motel and locked it behind us. C.C. paused at the bottom of the porch steps, looked up at the building, and said, "Will you come back and stay here sometime if I'm running it?"

"I'll surely try. You can come to New York, too."

"Yeah," he said sadly.

"I'm serious. You'd love New York, especially Manhattan. There's so many things I'd want to show you. You might even like it enough to stay . . . for a while, anyway."

What the hell had I just offered? First a Tufa roommate, and now this.

"I could make the same offer about here," C.C. said. "What you've seen so far is only the slightest tip of what the Tufa are like. The songs here are—" He paused to look for the right word. "—unimaginable."

I thought of his arms around me as we soared into the night sky. "I have to get back and do the show, at least. People are counting on me. *Ray* is counting on me, and I can't let him down."

"Yeah," he said, even more sadly.

"Look, don't make this the end. We have lives and responsibilities, and neither of us would want to be with someone who abandons that sort of thing. Would we? I wouldn't."

"I guess you've got a point."

"I do. And we'll stay in touch, right? We can e-mail, Skype, talk on the phone . . . and seriously, I want you to come up and see the play."

"We'll see."

Then we stood there awkwardly. I wanted to kiss him, but we were out in the open, and I had no idea what repercussions there might be for him if I did so.

He solved that dilemma by sweeping me into his arms and kissing me the way I'd always wanted to be kissed. We got back in the truck and headed to the airport, arriving in plenty of time for my flight. He kissed me good-bye again, in full view of everyone. A few people applauded.

30

And so the opening night of *Chapel of Ease,* delayed but not forsaken, finally arrived.

Our last rehearsals went like a dream. Everyone loved the pictures of the chapel, and took it fairly well when I said I'd found nothing buried there. I suspect many of them thought Ray had made the whole thing up anyway, so it just confirmed their suspicions. You could feel the relief in the air afterwards, as if a great shroud had been lifted and bright sun now poured in on us.

"I knew it," Mark said. "I knew it all along."

One morning a couple of days after I got back, I went by Emily's building and stared up at her apartment window. I could see an *X* of yellow tape across it on the inside. The fall would've definitely done the job, and I suddenly realized I might be standing exactly where she landed. There were no blood splatters on the concrete beneath my feet, but I still moved aside just in case.

I wondered if Ray, in his capacity as a Tufa haint,

had been waiting for her when she crossed over, or if her entirely human and mundane spirit had to make its own way into the light. I hoped that, whatever waited for her on the other side, it had eased the pain that drove her to jump.

And what would happen to all of Ray's work she had so diligently salvaged? Would her family even recognize it for what it was? Given all I'd learned about the Tufa, though, I couldn't help thinking that it was somehow protected, watched over perhaps by its own sub-haint that would alert Ray if it was about to be used in some way he wouldn't like.

There was a small impromptu shrine on the steps, with a picture of a smiling Emily surrounded by little folded notes from her friends. I put down the rose that I'd brought, and said aloud, "I'm sorry I couldn't do more, Em."

When I turned, the dreadlocked spy stood on the sidewalk, a single white lily in her hand. She was frozen in her tracks, evidently not expecting to see me.

For just an instant, I remembered the dreadlocked courtesans of the king of the forest. But this girl was clearly from, and of, the city. I scowled at her. "And what are you doing here?"

"I was going to pay my respects," she said in a small voice. "I'll leave if you want."

"Did you know her?"

She shook her head. "Just that she was Ray Parrish's girlfriend."

I wondered if she felt responsible, not just for Ray's death, but for Emily's as well. I wasn't about to ask her, though, because deep down, I really didn't want to know. I said, "Are you coming to the show?"

"Are you kidding? I can't afford that. Besides, the tickets are sold out for the whole run."

"What's your name?"

"Jamie. Jamie Byford."

"I'll leave a ticket for you at on-call for opening night. You deserve to see it as much as anybody."

She looked like she might cry. "Are you serious?"

I smiled with irony she would never understand. "As serious as a ghost in church."

Neil made some changes in the show to streamline things and clarify some plot points. He tried very hard to do this in the spirit of what Ray had written, and none of us felt the changes jarred too much. Only Stanley, who played the nameless ghost, put up a fight when his character received the name Arliss. I wondered how he'd take it if he knew the real name he'd avoided.

But, like everything else, I told the cast nothing. The chapel mystery, as far as they were concerned, was closed. The official press release would now say that the story was totally fictional. The ghosts of Byrda, Shad, and Dobber would be safe from prying eyes, as would their treasure.

I broke up with Joaquim right after I returned from Tennessee. It hadn't been terribly traumatic for either of us, which I suppose said something about the relationship right there. He wished me well, I did the same for him, and we went our separate ways.

So now I had no one in the audience who was there specifically for me on opening night. (I didn't count dreadlocked Jamie.) That made me a little sad, but not so much that it affected my mood. I'd spoken to C.C. just before I left for the theater, and he'd said just the right thing to make sure I was at my best for the show: "Whatever happens, wherever he is, Rayford will be proud of y'all."

And "we all," of course, were equally as proud of him and what he'd given us.

The bulletin board that formerly held our speculations about the mystery practically sagged with the weight of the rave reviews pinned to it. A major newspaper said, "The conservative word for *Chapel of Ease* might be 'astounding,' or 'amazing.' You can feel the mountains around you, and even though you know they're merely actors, the ghosts leave you with the chills that real spirits would."

Someone had circled "merely actors" in red, and then added multiple exclamation points on top of it.

"I can't think of a way it could have been done better," another newspaper critic wrote. "Every role is perfectly cast, and every song is magnificently sung."

A blog printout said, "It moved me to tears, both from its heartbreaking modern story, and the ancient tragedy behind it."

Many of the notices mentioned Ray's tragic demise. It was still a terrible thing, but if there was any bright side to it, it was that Ray's death made *Chapel of Ease* the hottest ticket in town.

A sharp pain shot up from my butt. I turned around to see Jason standing smugly behind me. "What was that for?" I snapped, rubbing the spot where he'd pinched me.

"I knew what you were thinking," he said with an insufferable grin.

"Yeah? What's that?"

"'Am I dreaming?' Now you know you're not."

He was exactly right. We both laughed.

"Hey, you hyenas," Ellie said. "Get your stuff on. You have a call in fifteen minutes."

We adjourned to the dressing room. The men all shared one big area, which in the good old days would've housed the diva of the week and all her entourage. We each had our own makeup tables, and were responsible for our own looks. Luckily none of us had anything really complicated, certainly not me. Some basic Pan-Cake, eyeliner, and lipstick were all I needed to transform into Crawford. I did have to add a little extra to cover the scabs from those splinters.

There was an envelope on my dressing table. There was no address, just my name. The card inside had a black-and-white photograph of a barn on it. Across the roof, in huge letters, were the words, SEE ROCK CITY. I opened it and read the message:

You're a great Crawford. You make me wish the story didn't have to turn out the way it does. We should hand out cups to catch the audience's tears. It was signed, *Love, Ray.*

He must've written these up before he died. I tucked the card into the edge of the mirror, the way actors have done since time immemorial. I checked, and the other two actors had similar cards.

I found Neil standing backstage, peeking out at the audience. The crowd was fairly low-key. They'd seen the reviews, knew Ray's tragic story, and understood that there was a lot riding on this. This would be, in a sense, even more make-or-break than a usual opening night: many were no doubt here out of that misplaced communal sympathy that drove people into the streets after tragedies that didn't touch them at all. We had their goodwill for the moment, but only if we convinced them that the show at the heart of all this was solid and magical.

"Thanks for handing out Ray's cards," I said to Neil.

"He wrote them up right before he passed away. I found them and knew he'd want you guys to have them, no matter what."

"I appreciate it, and I'm sure everyone else does, too."

"Look at 'em," he said, nodding at the crowd. "None of them really cares about what they're about to see. Well, maybe a few."

"That's kind of harsh, isn't it?"

He chuckled at his own sarcasm. "Ah, you're probably right. I've been at this so long, I forget sometimes, people's motives are really pure. And speaking of, whatever you did while you were gone, it worked. Your accent is great."

"Thanks."

"Glad you got that squared away before we hit Broadway."

It took a moment for that to register. "Wait . . . what?"

He gave me a sly *gotcha* smile. "We're moving to the Longacre Theatre at the end of this run. You know, on West Forty-eighth?"

I looked around. No one stood near us. I asked softly, "Does anyone else know?"

"Not yet. I'll tell them tonight at the party. But you—" He put a hand on my shoulder. "—you went above and beyond, Matt. I can't tell you how much I appreciate it. So I thought you should be the first to know. Oh—and we'll be recording the cast album in two weeks at the end of this run, so protect your voice." He patted my cheek, then faded back into the wings. I heard him trip over something in the dark, then curse. It almost made me laugh.

An *original cast album*. Since I was a kid and first saw the term on old CDs, I'd wanted to be on an original cast album. And now that dream would come true, all thanks to Ray. I sure hoped he knew it, wherever he was.

The houselights dimmed, and conversation dropped off. The orchestra—well, the band—began the overture, and the energy from the rustic tunes soon had the audience clapping along, something I'd never encountered before. The applause as the music ended was not merely polite, either.

The rest of those in the opening act were now in position around me. I closed my eyes for a moment. "This is for you, Ray," I said softly, then strode onstage as the curtain rose.

The show went great. I could describe it in more detail, but that's the important part. We had no flubs, no one forgot his or her lines, and everyone was *on*. We nailed the motherfucker.

We could feel that the audience was with us all the way, but it still didn't prepare us for the ovation they gave us. Everyone was on their feet, and stayed there. Eventually we all clapped along with them, delighted not only to be in the show, but also to be part of this moment.

If I thought the madness after the press preview was intense, it was nothing compared to this. I swear some people were still clapping as I took off my makeup and changed to street clothes. Ryan, our Shad, kept his character's distinctive hat on as he went outside to meet-and-greet, making sure everyone would recognize him. I hoped he kept track of it; if he lost it, Ellie the stage manager would have his soul for breakfast.

Cassandra, who played Jennifer, caught me as I came out. She tossed her hair, threw her arms around me, and kissed me. "I loved your last number!"

"And I didn't want to strangle you when you tossed your hair!" I said back, in the exact same tone. We both laughed like maniacs.

"Can you *believe* that?" she said, gesturing toward the stage.

"I know," I said.

"We broke their fucking hearts, and they *loved* it!" Tears and sweat left tracks of eyeliner down her cheeks. "I've never been in a show like this."

"Me, neither," I assured her.

"They'll have to extend the run. They can't just close after two weeks! Can they?"

"I don't see how," I agreed, keeping the news about the show's relocation to myself. I wondered how many of the actors would burst into tears when Neil told them. I was pretty sure *I* would.

I found a water bottle in the back of the green room's little fridge, drank it in one swallow and went out front to meet the fans. Unlike the preview, I knew very few of these. But they were just as excited, just as enthusiastic, just as seriously pumped up as that earlier audience. Many of them took selfies with me, and I shuddered at the thought of all those bad photos ending up online. I looked around for Jamie, but if she came, I didn't see her.

The best response came from a friend who was a musician in another Off-Broadway show that had just closed. He exclaimed, "That was amazing! You made me want to line dance with straight people!"

We were having the after-show party in a back room at Stack's, but I was pretty sure we'd end up taking over the entire bar, particularly their karaoke machine. I knew Julie and Mark would probably get falling-down drunk, as they tended to do when they celebrated; luckily we didn't have a matinee tomorrow.

Neil and one of our producers, Monty Madison, started urging people toward the theater's doors. "The party's not here, people. The booze is down the street." Gradually the crowds of both audience and performers thinned out. I was about to follow, when I remembered I'd left my cell phone on my dressing table. I went back to retrieve it.

"Where are you going?" Ellie asked. She had a big ring of keys in her hand.

"To get my phone. I'll be right back."

"I'm locking the doors, so be sure you've got everything when you leave, and make sure it closes behind you."

"Will do."

In the dressing room, which still reeked of our sweat and excitement, I found a text from C.C.: *How did it go?*

I texted back, *Spectacular. Off to the cast party. I'll call you in the morning.*

Glad to hear it, he texted back, along with a picture of himself, shirtless, giving me a thumbs-up sign.

I got a rush of real happiness from that. He wasn't clinging, he wasn't demanding my time or trying to make this in any way about him. He was just there.

Someday soon, I'd have to get him *here.*

I stopped as I was about to open the backstage door onto the alley, and strode alone onto the stage. I looked out at all the empty seats, remembering the packed faces that watched, laughed, clapped, and cheered. The air still seemed to vibrate with the show's energy, the way I knew it would for the next two weeks, and possibly longer.

"So . . . how do you feel?"

I almost shrieked. Ray stood beside me, as solid as if he'd been alive. He had his hands in his denim jacket pockets, and grinned with delight.

"Do you *ever* plan to just *die*?" I snapped.

"Yeah, don't worry, this is the last time you'll see me. I just had to check in after the show, you know?"

"Did you see it?"

"Of course I saw it."

"So what did you think?"

"Pretty good."

" 'Pretty good'?"

"Hey, what do you want? The perfect version is in my head. But you guys got awful close."

"We're moving to Broadway after this," I said proudly. "Did you know that?"

"Yes."

"Well, if you know everything, smart-ass, why are you here?"

"Two reasons. One is to tell you that Thorn is a handful,

and you need to make sure you set up some very clear rules before she moves in. Give her an inch, she'll take I-40."

"Yeah, I can see that."

"Second . . . thank you."

"For what?"

"For keeping the secret. About what was buried in the chapel of ease. I know it wasn't easy for you."

"Can I ask you something?"

"Sure."

"Why did you even *write* that story? What about it spoke to you?"

He paused for a moment, and evidently the effort of thinking made him less substantial, because he began to fade. Then he grew solid again and said, "It was universal. It was a love story."

"But it didn't happen the way your play tells it."

He shrugged. "I'm not a historian, dude. The play was inspired by it, not based on it. Hell, I couldn't really name a character 'Dobber,' could I?"

That actually made sense. "So this is good-bye for real, then?"

"Yeah. Except I got one more thing to tell you."

"What?"

"A gift. Just for you. I know I can trust you to keep it."

He leaned close and whispered in my ear. I felt no breath, and no warmth of a presence, but I heard him quite clearly. When he finished, I knew he was gone for good, forever. I stood all alone on the Armpit's stage.

But he'd told me what was buried in the chapel of ease.

And he was right: it didn't matter at all.

All song lyrics are original, except for those listed below.

CHAPTER 12
"The Unclouded Day"
composed by Joseph K. Atwood in 1885
http://library.timelesstruths.org/music/The_Unclouded_Day/

CHAPTER 15
"The Wife of Usher's Well"
#79 in a collection of 305 ballads collected in the nineteenth
    century by Francis James Child and originally published in
    ten volumes between 1882 and 1898
http://en.wikipedia.org/wiki/List_of_the_Child_Ballads

CHAPTER 23
"Ain't Gonna Grieve My Lord No More"
1865, according to the Public Domain Info Project
http://www.pdinfo.com/pd-song-list/search-pd-songs.php